DEVIANTS

THE DUST CHRONICLES
BOOK ONE

BY **MAUREEN MCGOWAN**

AMAZON CHILDREN'S PUBLISHING

Amazon Publishing
Att: Amazon Children's Publishing
P.O. Box 400818
Las Vegas, NV 89149
www.amazon.com/amazonchildrenspublishing

ISBN: 978-1612-183671

Book design by Alex Ferrari

Printed in the United States of America (R)
First edition
10 9 8 7 6 5 4 3 2 1

THE DUST CHRONICLES
BOOK ONE

This book is for Tracy Caryl McGowan, taken way too soon.

acknowledgments

I am so lucky to have many fabulous writer friends whom I've met online, in writers' groups, and at conferences. Your support and guidance have been immeasurable. The full list of everyone who's impacted my publishing journey would require ten pages, but know that I love and appreciate you all. It really does take a village to keep my chin up and my fingers on the keyboard some weeks.

There is no chance that I would have been able to write this novel without the undying support, tough love, and inspirational pushing delivered daily by my awesome critique partners and best buddies: Molly O'Keefe and Sinead Murphy. Ladies, you make every word I write better, and make every day I have you as part of my life a whole lot more fun. You two are my rocks. Thank you to all my critique partners and beta readers who read drafts of the manuscript in whole or in part, especially: Michele Young, Mary Sullivan, Stephanie Doyle, Joanne Levy, Danielle Younge-Ullman, and Bev Katz Rosenbaum. And a special thanks to Kelley Armstrong for agreeing to read a not-yet-polished manuscript.

I will be forever grateful for my fabulous agent Charlie

Olsen at InkWell Management. He was enthusiastic about the project right from the query stage—and wasn't afraid to tell me. He's become a better cheerleader/supporter/partner than I ever could have hoped for. Thanks go as well to everyone at InkWell, especially Kristan Palmer, Nat Jacks, and Alexis Hurley. I can't describe how wonderful it feels to know you're all in my corner.

A huge thank you to everyone at Amazon Publishing: first and foremost to Terry Goodman, for his unending enthusiasm for this series, and for so graciously giving me up for adoption to the east coast. And to Lindsay Guzzardo for her fabulous help in shaping the book and making it stronger. Thanks also to everyone at Marshall Cavendish Children's Books, especially Margery Cuyler, for her enthusiasm, patience and hand holding through this process. And finally to Jon Fine for offering support and indulging me with 1970's song lyrics.

While we writers are focused on the words, it's often a fabulous cover and the design that drives readers to pick up or download the book. To that end, many thanks to Anahid Hamparian and Alex Ferrari for their work on the cover and internal design.

And finally, many thanks to my family and friends for their support and for putting up with me when I'm so buried in my made-up worlds that I disappear into them for weeks on end.

CHAPTER ONE

THE AIR AT THE UPPERMOST REACHES OF HAVEN IS HOT AND thick with the stench of rat droppings. Small price to pay for free food. Normal girls run screaming when this close to rats, but I can't afford luxuries like fear.

The sky looms close to our building's rooftop, and I duck to avoid cracking my head on a beam. If this section of the dome was ever painted blue, the pigment wore off long ago, leaving barely reflective metal panels.

Bent at the waist, I creep forward and scan the less-than-five-foot gap between the roof and the sky. Heat and darkness press in from all sides and sweat trails down my spine. I wish I could carry some form of light, but a lantern would make the rats run. Behind me, something moves.

I crouch deeper and spin.

"Who's there?" My voice comes out higher than I'd like, and the rats echo with screeches.

rge shadow slides across the roof near an air vent,
ress myself down, gravel digging into my knees and palms. The shadow's too huge to be cast by a person, but my pulse engulfs my senses, blurring my eyes, filling my ears, clouding my judgment.

I blink and the shadow's gone; all that's left is the undulating wave of rats over rats.

Shielding my nose to block the smell, I draw in long breaths. *You're okay. You're safe. No one knows.*

If the shadow was a Comp, he'd arrest me, not stalk from the shadows. And by living inside Haven, we're safe from the Shredders that roam outside the dome.

I'm crazy to imagine danger around every corner, but this sense of being watched has haunted me for the three years since my brother Drake and I became orphans. Growing taller and nearing puberty, my brother's become thin and needs more meat, so I return to my task.

Focusing on the scritch-scratch of rat claws, I home in on individual rodents—sense each body, each breath.

One skitters into a sliver of light and lifts its head to make eye contact.

Big mistake, Mr. Rat.

Held in my gaze, the rodent can't look away. Emotions heighten my senses, and soon I can feel the rat's rapidly beating heart, hear its blood coursing as adrenaline floods its veins. It's as if my fingers are pressed to its pulse, my ear to its chest. But they're not. The sensations build until the rat's completely under my control.

Crushing my instinct to release the poor creature, I dig

for more useful emotions than pity, emotions I'm certain can kill. I think of the person who hurt me most, who shattered my childhood, who betrayed my trust—who murdered my mother.

I think of my father. I think of the blank look on his face three years ago when the Compliance Officers, in their black masks and body armor, took him away.

Hate and anger crash through an inner door and sizzle like water hitting hot oil. Just the fuel I need. Locked on the rat's glare, my eyes tingle and sting. My emotions build, and my curse sparks to life at the back of my eyes.

Focusing my power, I picture the rat's heart, sense it compressing, and will my emotions to squeeze.

The rodent's eyes widen, its whiskers glisten with humidity, and it opens its mouth to reveal needle-sharp teeth. A shudder traces through me but I can't back down. I will do this. I must. Drake needs to eat.

The rodent seizes, every muscle stiffening at once. Its heart rate slows, then it gasps and falls on its side, legs twitching in death throes. Sympathy creeps up my throat, but I push it back down; one rat won't fill Drake's belly for long. When I'm sure it's dead, I pull our dinner forward by the tail and find another victim—then another.

I sway forward, nearly losing my balance. To regain control, I close my eyes and rub my thumb along my mother's wedding band, worn low on my index finger since the day she died. My curse passes, and I slump down to sit. At least this time I didn't pass out.

As useful as it's proved for rat hunting, I hate that I'm a

Deviant. Hate it because it makes me dangerous yet puts me in danger. Hate it because it make me different and lets me do things I can't understand or control. Hate it because it links my DNA to Shredders. But most of all, I hate it because it connects me to my father.

But I'm luckier than most. At least my curse is easy to hide. When my brother's hits, his skin changes, and I once saw a woman, cornered by the Comps, whose hair turned into barbed spikes. Management believes Deviants threaten the safety of Haven, that we're one step away from being Shredders. They want us all dead.

I reach for my knife to skin the animals but hear scuffling behind me.

I am being watched.

Spinning, I back farther into the shadows under the sloped girders of the sky. My ponytail brushes the back of my neck—or was it a rat?—then the light from a portable lantern rises above the roof's edge, followed by a small body climbing over the side from the rope.

"Glory, you up here?" my friend Jayma whispers.

"Over here." Relaxing, I creep forward, dropping my dinner, hoping it'll go unnoticed. Not that I'm afraid she'd report me for contraband rat meat. She'd never do that. She doesn't like seeing dead rats.

"Wow, nice haul." Scout steps into her lantern light. Raising my eyebrows, I shoot Jayma a questioning look, and she smiles softly. Scout pulls his hands from his hoodie pockets and rests them on lean thighs as he crouches to examine my catch.

"I got lucky with my net today." I shift to put the rats in my shadow. "Want one?"

"No thanks." Scout straightens as far as he can. "I can catch rats on my own. Bigger rats. Those don't have much meat."

"Scout has very good aim." Jayma looks at him like he's the god of all rat catching, and he puffs out his chest as much as is possible in his hunched-over position.

"Happy hunting then." I gesture toward the fugitive rats that must have escaped from a farm factory, where rats are raised and slaughtered for food. Or they may have breached the dome from Outside. Out there rats are the only animals that can survive the dust. Rats and Shredders.

Scout pulls out his slingshot, turns, and shoots a small stone into the darkness. Based on the squeaks and skitters, he's hit something, but it's not clear whether his strike was lethal. After pulling a crank torch from his pocket, he winds its handle until a faint light glows, then moves forward to investigate. The rats scatter.

"Isn't he great?" Jayma tucks hair behind her ear, and then turns her lantern's handle a few times before setting it down on the rooftop between us. She's got a smudge on her pale, freckled cheek, and I reach over to wipe it with my thumb. It smears.

"What's on my face?" Her eyes cry distress, then she brings up her sleeve to rub her cheek. "Do you think Scout noticed?"

"It's gone now." I smile to cover my white lie. There's no way to get clean up here in this filth, and Scout's not exactly a master in the hygiene department. I doubt he noticed or cared.

She leans in close. "Do you think he'll ask me?" Red spots flare on her cheeks.

"If he doesn't, he's crazy." I grin, happy she's happy, but an uncomfortable squirming grabs hold of my belly. I can't believe we're sixteen and old enough for official dating license bracelets. Next step is a marriage contract.

But it's not like *I* could date. The risk is too high. If I apply for a license, someone in HR is bound to review my employment records and ask questions about my brother. He can't be discovered. No one except Jayma knows he's alive.

"I need a favor." Jayma's hands slip down to mine. "Scout's going to the Hub, and—"

"Today? On day one?" The Hub's always swarming on the first of the three days designated for employees in our pay-grade to pick up monthly rations. Some people can't plan. But as much as I don't want to go today, Jayma can't go to the Hub alone with a boy without a dating license. If I agree to go, she'll get more time with Scout, even if I'm the third wheel.

"Of course I'll go to the Hub with you." I squeeze her hands.

"You're the best. " She leans in closer. "Plus Management is holding a lottery to celebrate the quarter-end holiday."

"What's the prize?"

"An entry-level Management position. Can you believe it?" Jayma bends and cranks her lantern.

Hope drifts up with the news, filling my head with dreams

of the future. Even employees born into Management families have to work really hard and pass qualifying exams to be eligible to apply for those jobs. "Do you think they'll really promote the winner?"

Jayma nods. "And what great timing—just before we graduate and get our work placements." She smiles and, even though her lantern's fading, I swear the rooftop grows brighter.

My mood certainly does. Imagine having a Management job. And straight out of GT? A job like that might give me the power to protect Drake. There must be Deviants born into Management families, but I'm not sure I've seen one expunged. The possibility of winning tingles, even if the promised prize is a long shot.

Clang. A rock slams into steel at the edge of the roof, and I cringe. The surveillance cameras up here haven't been repaired since before I was born, but too much noise is a sure way to get caught.

"Rat dung," Scout curses, and we look over to where he's been shooting rocks and, based on what I've heard, hitting more roof than rat.

"Are we going to the Hub, or not?" A deep male voice comes from the darkness, and my shoulders shoot up. Cal, Scout's older brother, steps out of the shadows and my heart takes off at full sprint.

Cal grins. "Did I scare you?"

"No." I stand taller and brush my hand over my hair. "When did you get up here?" Has he been there since Jayma and Scout arrived, standing in the shadows listening to Jayma and me? I hope I didn't say anything embarrassing. Anything to reveal how I feel.

Cal's arrival, not to mention the way his blond hair drapes down over his blue eyes, makes it hard to keep calm. While my curse isn't powerful enough to hurt anything as large or smart as a human, it wouldn't do for anyone—even my friends—to associate me with a cramp in the stomach, a shot of pain to the kidneys, a squeeze in the heart. As much as I trust my friends, they can't know I'm a Deviant.

Cal's work boots crunch across the fine gravel; his back and knees bend to fit his tall body into the tight space. "Where's your net?"

"My net?" I can't keep my eyes off Cal's handsome face.

"You said you got lucky with your net. Where is it?"

He *was* listening. I gesture idly behind me.

He tips his head to the side, clearly knowing I'm lying, but he doesn't take it any further. Now eighteen, Cal was top of his General Training class, aced the M-Ap exams, yet got a work placement in Construction & Maintenance. That waste of brains is all the proof I need: Management only promotes from within. My dreams of the lottery deflate.

Cal brushes hair from his eyes, and the light from Jayma's fading lantern sharpens his chiseled features. Always tall and lean, his body's grown harder from physical labor—his neck, his arms, and legs transformed by hard work into strong ropes covered by skin. My eyes focus on his wrist, still without a dating bracelet, but I can't afford dreams.

"Don't you girls look pretty today." His compliment makes my heart stutter.

Cheeks burning I meet his gaze, and my insides squeeze with a sharp stab I only feel around Cal. Buzzing I rub my mother's ring to invite in her calmness, her strength, to push down emotions that make me dangerous to my friends.

"Jayma," Scout calls from the shadows. "Did you bring any stones? I ran out."

"I did." She lifts a hand to shield her eyes from the lantern light bouncing off the sky. "Where are you?"

Scout's hunched silhouette waves a slingshot about fifteen feet away, and Jayma picks up her fading lantern and cranks the handle. "Okay if I take this?" She must really like Scout if she's willing to head into those rats. When she leaves, I'm alone with Cal and the dark.

I didn't think the temperature could increase up here, but Cal's muscular form exudes heat and a strong spicy smell that tempers the rat droppings and makes me feel safe and in danger all at once. My skin prickles with tension that I need to defuse before emotions trigger my curse.

I pick up a rat by the tail. "Want a bite?"

"Very funny." He widens his stance and puts his hands on his hips, copying the way the Comps stand when they want to look particularly intimidating. "Young lady"—there's a sly grin under his stern expression—"did you use ration points to purchase that meat at the Hub?"

Cal is treating me like an equal, not a little girl, and my insides warm. "Of course I did, Officer. Obtaining rat meat any other way is strictly prohibited in the Policies & Procedures Manual. Black-market goods damage the Haven economy and threaten our very way of life."

"Haven Equals Safety." We say the Haven slogan in unison, then laugh. My chest heats.

"Glad to hear you're still drinking the coolade, little lady."

"It's so, so refreshing."

Such a strange expression—none of us knows what coolade is—but it's one of those things that everyone in the Pents grows up saying to describe employees who act and talk as if they're reading straight from the P&P.

Cal's hand lands on my shoulder, and a thrill traces through me as he draws in close. "I've got a secret, but you have to promise you won't tell anyone—ever."

He leans forward, moving his lips close to my ear, and he's all I can smell, all I can feel. His heart beats so strong and steady I feel it inside and melt as his breath burns my neck. *Please don't let my Deviance trigger.*

"I was recruited into the Jecs."

I jump back, alarm causing my heart to race more than Cal's touch. Emotions spark the back of my eyes—anger, disbelief, betrayal. I don't dare look at his eyes and instead stare at his feet. "Why would you do that?"

"Isn't it obvious?"

I straighten and my head bangs the sky.

"Careful." Cal reaches forward and his hand grazes my cheek. "I joined for a chance at a better future, a way out of the Pents."

My breaths come more quickly, but I fight to hold myself together as emotions inflate and threaten to explode like a bomb. "The Junior Ethics Committee?"

His eyebrows draw closer together. "I know some of them are slimy and turn in their friends for petty crimes, but it doesn't need to be like that. The committee's a stepping-stone to a better life. If I work hard, I have a shot at Compliance Officer Training." He grins. "Besides, I'll just go after Deviants."

I'll just go after Deviants.

My stomach caves, my chest tightens. "But—" Words won't come. My tongue's dry. If he discovers my secret, I'm as good as exed.

Cal reaches for me, but lets his hand drop. "I thought you'd be happy. You took the M-Ap exams; I know you're ambitious." His jaw twitches and hurt builds in his eyes, before understanding flashes. "Is this about your father?" He takes my hand. "You must hate him."

My gaze shoots straight for Cal's eyes. "Hate him?" Cal's right, mostly, but the man was my father, and it's more complicated than that.

"Glory, your dad was a Deviant." Cal's voice is hard and deep. "He had to be exed."

Nausea builds and pain crushes my chest as Cal's revelation exposes then incinerates my dream of a normal life, my dream of being with him. My hand, slick with sweat, slides from his grip.

"Say something." He looks worried.

"You'll only turn in the dangerous Deviants, right?"

His head jerks. "They're *all* dangerous. Part Shredder."

"No one knows that for certain." And the idea that I'm related to Shredders, might turn into one, is something

I can't let myself think. My nightmares are bad enough.

"Glory." Cal's voice takes on a patronizing tone. "You can't deny history or science. The Deviants and Shredders both arrived when the earth died."

I bite down on my lip. The earth didn't die—not really—but over three generations ago it was buried in coarse dust from the asteroids and volcanic eruptions. In GT we learned that much of the world was burned, the rest of it buried. We learned how the dust kills normal humans. But some of the things we're taught about life Before The Dust—like air travel and long-distance telephones—seem like science fiction, not history. And since discovering my Deviance, I no longer believe every word we were taught in GT.

No one knows why the dust killed most life on earth. No one knows why Shredders can feed off the dust, or why some people became Deviant, neither Normals nor Shredders. If someone does know, Management's not telling. Everyone knows that neither Deviants nor Shredders existed BTD, and I shudder to think I might have DNA in common with Shredders.

"You won't tell anyone I joined the Jecs, will you?" Cal's forehead wrinkles. He's clearly uncomfortable with my silence, and I wonder what he might do without reassurance.

"I won't tell."

"Good." His shoulders relax. "Because if you told anyone, I'd have to kill you." He laughs and lightly punches my arm.

I force a smile.

Cal leans forward and places his hands on his thighs.

"The first thing they told us at Jecs orientation was, 'Don't tell anyone you're in,' but I had to tell you."

Scout and Jayma approach and save me from asking why. I'm not sure I want to know. Scout's got two rats by the tail, dripping blood, and Jayma's face is even paler than normal. My mind spins. Cal, one of the Jecs? I wonder how far he'll go with his role. Scout's violating policy right now, and it's reassuring that Cal doesn't comment.

"Let's head back down," Scout says. "I've got to stash these at home before we go to the Hub."

I break away from Cal to pick up my catch, but as I'm wrapping them in a scrap of cloth, he steps close.

"Do you know why I trust you? Only you?"

I flick my gaze to his eyes, then down, and draw a ragged breath. *Only me.*

My tongue feels thick. Conflicting emotions wage war inside me.

His head drops, his lips inches from my ear. "You won't tell, right?"

I nod, my neck tense.

He exhales, his breath warm on my neck. "I knew you could keep a secret," he whispers, "because you've got secrets, too."

CHAPTER TWO

BLOOD RUSHES IN MY EARS, AND I PULL BACK, TRYING TO
control the rising terror. What does Cal know? My skin's like
ice, threatening to crack from too much pressure. If he knows
I'm a Deviant, I'm as good as exed.

He touches my arm. "Don't worry. I won't report him."

"Who?"

"Your brother."

My throat closes; my ears fill. It's not me, but Drake who's
in danger. *So much worse.*

Tucking my wrapped rats against my body and zipping
my jacket to hold them down, I head for the edge of the roof
as calmly as I can, but it's all I can do not to run, to get far
away from Cal. As I climb down the rope that provides roof
access, emotion-weighted questions buzz through my mind
like the static on the Hub's TV screens when dust infiltrates
the cameras Outside.

We climb down the rope, one by one, then swing off and into a corridor in the top-level penthouse, where we live. I can't look anyone in the eyes. I don't dare.

"You boys go on ahead. Save us a place in line?" Jayma says. "I need to talk to Glory." She turns to me, concern in her eyes, but I can't look at her long—not while I'm feeling so much—though I'm touched that she's sacrificing her plan to spend time with Scout for me.

"We can wait." Cal's concerned, too.

I shake my head, and flash a grin of reassurance. I can't be around him yet. I need to calm down.

"We'll follow after you boys." Jayma's voice is more force-ful than I've ever heard it, and the boys shrug and leave.

"What's wrong?" she asks once they're gone.

I raise a finger to my lips, and she nods with understand-ing. Too many ears out here in the halls. My throat tightens. I thought Jayma was the only person who knew Drake survived and can't believe she'd tell Cal. But if not her, then who? And what else does Cal know?

I can't overreact. All I'm certain of is that Cal knows Drake's alive. Perhaps nothing more. That's bad enough, but when you've got an emotion-triggered curse, it doesn't pay to imagine worst-case scenarios.

Jayma follows me down the narrow passageway leading to the small apartment I share with my brother. Because of his injury—not to mention his Deviance—he hasn't reported for GT since our parents died, making him unemployed—a Parasite. Cal must know the Parasite part, and as a Jecs he's supposed to report him. But if that's his intent, then why tell me his secret? That would be cruel, and while I can't fully trust him—or anyone—I know Cal's not cruel.

Arms bent, I trail the palms of both hands along the corridor's walls. One advantage of this location is that the Comps' body armor barely fits through. They have to walk sideways.

Reaching our door, I banish my fear and all thoughts of Cal. "Do you mind waiting out here?" I ask Jayma, resting my hand on the bundle of rats under my jacket.

She shivers. "Sure. You know I hate blood."

I push the door until it bumps up against the bracket I molded from scrap metal to prevent the door from swinging wide enough to reveal my brother's presence. Not that passersby are frequent in this narrow hall, but I can't be too careful.

Slipping inside, I quickly shut the door. People claim that Before The Dust, the entire penthouse floor of this building was a single family's dwelling and, supposedly, our apartment was used for clothing storage, but I find that hard to believe. Yes, there is a metal rung along the left side of the five-by-twelve-foot space and holes in the wall where a similar rung might have hung on the right, but even if those rungs were used for clothes, at least one person must have slept in here, too. It's not possible that a sixty-square-foot space was wasted on storage.

Currently, 211 official residents—plus Drake—live on the thirty-second floor pent at the top of our building. Impossible to believe that one family lived alone in the nearly 5,000-square-foot space. Must have been one monstrous-sized family.

I lean against the wall behind the door, one of the only places not covered by nail-scratched drawings of faces and street scenes. My brother looks up from his book and says, "Hi."

His appearance has changed these past months. Stronger lines have cut into his boyish looks, and his face is shifting and hardening like ice crystals on a water bucket. Overwhelmed by thoughts I might lose him, I dive down and pull him into a tight hug.

He pushes me back. "Stop with the mush." He frowns but I can tell he's not really mad, so I don't scold him for using the electric light instead of the crank lantern. Our power rations will drain months before I'm scheduled to get more, but he's stuck in this windowless room, so when our power dies I'll get more points, even if I need to scrounge or steal.

I don't mind being the one who has to do everything. I really don't. But some days I do wish my brother could take care of me. Just for a short while. Just a few minutes. Just so I get a small break.

But there's no sense in wishing for things that won't happen, and right now I need to focus on hiding the fact that I'm scared for his life. I can't share the danger until I develop a plan.

"Look," I whisper and hold up the rats. "I'm going to the Hub for rations, but later we'll have a feast."

"I'll skin them while you're gone." Drake uses his strong upper body to shift himself over on the mattress and then pulls his atrophied legs to follow. "I'm starved."

Me, too, and I wonder how much longer we'll be able to

live on half rations supplemented by contraband rat. By some miraculous error, my brother's employee number disappeared from the HR database right after our father was expunged. Drake's relief when he realized the Comps wouldn't come for him right away was replaced by fear that he wouldn't get food, so I lied and told him that Resources & Allocations still had him recorded in their rations database. They don't.

"Maybe they've upped your rations." I try to sound hopeful as I shift to sit beside him and bump our shoulders. "You're almost a man—nearly fourteen."

"Not for seven months."

"Can't have you getting scrawny." I poke him in the ribs, and he retaliates, poking me under the arm. I squirm away, swatting his hand and laughing. "You need more food. They must be crazy in R&A not to give you more. I'll lodge a complaint."

His laughter vanishes. "Stop pretending. I know."

"Know what?" I reach over to smooth the blanket on his lumpy mattress.

"I know I don't get any rations."

My stomach tightens. "Of course you do." I stand and check our water supply to make sure I don't need to go down two floors to the tap before I go out. Then I peek into our tin waste bucket. Thank Haven it's empty, because lugging that thing down two floors is my least favorite chore. We're luckier than some to have a human waste–collection center and water so close, but waiting in line to empty the bucket can take hours.

"I'm not a baby," Drake says. "I know how things work.

I'm a Parasite. I don't work. I'm not in training. I don't get rations. We split yours."

The back of my throat pinches, and I wait for it to pass before looking into his eyes. Every week I've given him a larger share of my rations without hesitation or comment, and I'm surprised to learn that he's known all along. Who knew Drake could keep secrets?

His fingers brush my hand. "Thank you."

"For what?"

"For taking care of me, like Mom used to."

The word *Mom* takes the strength from my legs. I drop down to sit, and he slings an arm over my shoulders.

"Remember how she used to tell us stories in the dark? I miss that."

"Me, too."

"Tell me one?"

I shake my head. As hard as I try, I can't replace our mom. I can't make up stories—not like she could—and I realize how lucky I am to have had a mother for nearly three years longer than Drake. I was thirteen when she died.

"Come on." He squeezes my shoulders. "You tell great stories."

I jump up. "I need to go. Jayma's waiting."

His upper body straightens and his chin lifts. "She's here?" His voice is so filled with hope that I consider letting her in. Other than me, Drake never talks to anyone, and I can't remember the last time I let Jayma visit.

"She's in the hall."

His expression collapses. "She didn't want to come in?"

It's more than I can bear, so I open the door a crack and invite her inside. As she enters, a huge smile spreads on Drake's face, and he checks his gloves and the cuffs of his long-sleeved shirt to make sure his skin will be covered should his nerves attack and reveal his Deviance.

"Hi, Jayma." His whisper is scratchy, and he pushes dark hair from his forehead. I must remember to cut it.

"Hi, Drake." She returns his smile, and his face brightens as if he's made of electric lights—the bright kind like they have at the Hub.

Oh, no. Clearly my brother is smitten, and I realize I've never told him how Jayma likes Scout. How will I tell him and not crush his heart?

Jayma and Drake make small talk, and when she praises his latest drawings on the lower parts of our walls, he beams then pushes down to lift himself, shifting closer to Jayma.

"Have you spent time on your belly today?" I ask.

He darts his eyes toward my friend.

"Okay," I say. "As soon as we leave, then. You don't want another—" I stop myself from saying bedsore. Being embarrassed in front of Jayma is one more side effect of his getting older.

"Still no feeling in your legs?" Jayma bites her lower lip and looks down.

Drake uses his upper body to move again, as if hoping to impress her with his relative mobility. "My legs are as useless as the day it happened." His cheeks flush.

Jayma slides her shoe along the floor. "It's so horrible to think that your dad—"

"He didn't do it." Drake's voice is too loud, and I turn toward the closed door, hoping beyond all hope that no one beyond it heard him.

"Then who did?" Jayma crouches to meet him eye to eye. "Was there someone besides your family in the room?" The excitement in her voice sounds as if she thinks she's cracked the case, and I want to tell her to give it up. There's no mystery.

Drake looks away. It must have been horrible to witness Mom's murder—our father knocked me unconscious, so at least I didn't have to see it happen—but I'm losing patience with my brother. His outburst, claiming our father's innocence, rakes my nerves.

Drake's in denial. Too young then to face the fact that our father turned against our family. Too optimistic now to believe his own Deviance might someday hurt someone he loves. He's old enough to discuss what he saw, but I don't push it, not with Jayma in the room.

She's still waiting for Drake to answer, and his obvious tension fuels mine. I rub my ring. "We should go."

"I wish you could come with us." Jayma reaches out to touch Drake's arm, but he pulls back. Clearly he doesn't trust his nerves around her. I get that. I've got the same problem with Cal.

Jayma has no idea why Drake can't let her touch him. At least I can trust her to protect his other secret. Jayma knows better than anyone what would happen if Drake's disability were discovered. Failing to report an injury or illness is almost as bad as being Deviant.

"You should visit more often," I say to distract her from his reaction. "You're the only one who knows he's here." And if it wasn't she who told Cal, how in the world does he know?

"Would you like me to visit again?" Jayma rises from her crouch. She's smiling again, and I can only assume she's written off my brother's flinch as a by-product of too much isolation. If she follows through on visiting more, I'll figure out a way for him to wear something thick enough to prevent her from feeling through the fabric should his skin change to armor.

"Let's go." I tug on Jayma's arm. "People won't let us join the ration line if the guys have been waiting too long."

"You're right," Jayma says. "See you again soon, Drake."

"Great." He waves, puppy love radiating through his expression.

Jayma and I walk in silence through the building's narrow passageways—some formed by solid walls from the original structure and some literally paper thin. The only topics on either of our minds are ones we can't broach with our neighbors close by. Everyone suspects that Management has spies living in the Pents, and now that Cal's joined the Jecs, I know that it's true. There's at least one spy, one traitor, in our midst. Not to mention the Comps' cameras, but I'm confident most are broken.

Compliance tries to make us believe they're still watching, but most of the cameras, except near the Hub or Management buildings, don't move. Given how they've cut the rations for the rest of us, it's fitting that Management's suffering a few shortages, too.

After walking down sixteen flights of stairs, crowded with families who live on the landings, Jayma and I step through a narrow floor-to-ceiling gap, then start across a long suspension bridge to the roof of an adjacent building. Our route to the Hub isn't the shortest or safest—this bridge tends to sway—but it's the fastest. Less traffic than the surface.

My father told me that the bridges were built to ease congestion on Haven's streets—some suspended from steel cables hooked to the buildings, some made of ropes—and were never intended as dwellings. But my whole life, the bridges up in the Pents have been crowded. Scattered sporadically on both sides of this narrow bridge, families live in tiny shacks made of cardboard, fabric, newspaper—whatever building materials they could find. No habitable space is wasted in Haven, even these rickety bridges.

I see a new gap in the bridge, and after making sure Jayma noticed it, too, I step over and avoid looking down the sixteen-odd floors to the ground. The materials of the missing section of bridge are being used as the wall of a shack. I shake my head. What's the sense in having privacy if your floor falls out below you?

With a loud bang, a sheet of aluminum lands a few feet ahead of us, shaking the bridge. Shielding our heads with our arms, Jayma and I look up. This bridge is not only rickety, but it runs beneath two others much worse. A few heads peek out of shelters to investigate, and a boy of about ten runs to grab the metal and drag it home. He reminds me of Drake.

Even though my brother might have better air and more light for reading out here in the open, I can't imagine living on one of these bridges, or worse, on a poorly ventilated roof. Besides, it's silly to even contemplate requesting a move. Management would discover Drake.

Reaching the end of the bridge, I crouch and grab a rope, then climb down several floors. At the knot at the rope's end, I use both legs to push off the side of the building and swing from the rope to land on a metal platform jutting out from the next building. Vibrations penetrate my feet, rising up to my clenched teeth.

Jayma follows, and after landing she leans in close. "Finally. Now you can tell me. What happened up on the roof? I didn't want to ask in the crowds."

"Nothing happened." I glance around, checking for eavesdroppers. It's safe here.

"Come on," she says. "Since when do we have secrets? Tell me." Her voice lowers. "Why did you look so upset after talking to Cal?" She gasps and grabs my hand. "Does he like someone else? Is he getting a dating license?"

My heart pinches. "It's nothing like that. I was just in a hurry to check on Drake." It's not a total lie. But I'm confused about Cal, and my emotions are banging hard to get out, like we're in a physical fight I can't let them win. I'd give anything to tell Jayma my biggest secrets, give anything to be a Normal like her, give anything to turn back time to when our friendship was free and easy with no secrets, when we shared everything.

"Why are you upset then?" she asks. "Is it Drake?"

"I worry he'll get caught and taken to the Hospital."

Jayma's pale green eyes open wide with compassion.

"Some people say it's just rumors, but after Jack was taken to the Hospital . . ." Her eyes fill with tears. "I can't bear the thought of them taking Drake there."

Her big brother, Jack, caught the flu two winters ago and, after he missed work three days in a row, his supervisor reported his absence to the Comps. When they realized it was more than a cold, Health & Safety swooped in and carted him to the Hospital, later claiming he died of his illness.

Not likely.

Jack worked in Sky Maintenance, and it's a never-spoken truth that lower-level employees only go *in* to the Hospital—none ever come out. I shudder imagining the truth. His death is why I trust Jayma to keep Drake's injury a secret. She knows what Management does to the weak and the sick and the injured—not to mention Parasites and Deviants. Drake has three strikes. Big ones.

"Have you ever told anyone?" I ask. "That Drake lives with me?"

"No." Her eyes broadcast shock.

Air rushes out of my chest. "I knew you'd never." I don't want to talk about Drake or the Hospital anymore. Pretending to hear something, I raise a finger to my lips. She presses hers tightly together and nods.

Cal's news roused raw memories of the day my father killed my mother. We learned in GT that Deviants aspire to wipe out all Normals, but I'm proof that's not always true. I just want to fit in.

I shudder, wondering if something inside me lies

dormant, waiting to snap. If someday I'll change into a murderous monster. But if I dwell on the dangers I face, I could hurt Jayma, so I push the offending emotions down.

Stepping off the metal platform onto the building's foot-wide window ledge, I press my back against the bricks. This building's corridors are clogged, so it's faster to go around it than through. Taking controlled side steps, I rub my ring. It doesn't pay to dwell on the past.

CHAPTER THREE

THE HUB IS CRAZY CROWDED. WE STEP INTO THE SQUARE of light from under the crisscross of bridges, and I shield my eyes against the bright lights that bounce off the sky and glint off the glass of the highly polished towers. Rare in the Pents, glass isn't in short supply in the Hub—neither is light. Few individual citizens can afford more than one weak bulb, and with Management controlling and limiting energy from the windmills and solar panels, the Hub is the only bright place in Haven.

Above us, neon billboards blast messages from the Communication Department: Haven Equals Safety, Compliance: Your Key to Happiness!, The P&P — Your Safety Guarantee. The last ad has an image of two young men, one choking on dust and the other being chased by a Shredder. Its eyes bulge from its skull, and its human-shaped body is near skeletal and covered by skin scabbed with dried blood.

I wrinkle my nose in disgust. All around us people are grinning, talking loudly. The air's charged.

"All this for a lottery?" I say to Jayma and she shrugs.

Scout bounds up to us. "Someone's getting exed."

My stomach clenches. I'm so repulsed I can't look at Scout—excited when he should be appalled.

"Come on," he says. "We've got a great view of the screens from the line." He points ahead, and I turn to see Cal staring right at me. My body temperature rises, and I look down to my feet.

"Did you know?" I ask Jayma.

She shakes her head, and then turns to Scout. "Can you go back to the line and give us a minute? We'll join you guys soon. We're not finished with our girl talk."

Backing away, he lifts his hands, then heads for his older brother.

"I didn't know." Jayma grabs on to my arm and squeezes. "I'm sorry. I know you hate seeing these. Do you want to come back tomorrow instead?"

"We're here now." I smile to cover my churning nausea. "It's okay." It's not—at all—but it took us nearly an hour to cover the distance from home to the Hub, and now I know why so many people were crowding our route. An Expunging.

Jayma hugs me and I try not to stiffen.

"I'm so glad you're my friend," she says, and her body's so thin, I fear she'll snap if I hug her as hard as she's hugging me.

"Thanks. Me, too."

"Seriously." She pulls back and looks me directly in the eyes.

I let my gaze drift to the side but she dips her face around, forcing me to maintain eye contact.

"Tell me what's wrong," she says. "Let me help you for once. If it weren't for you, I'd be curled up in a little ball and crying half the time."

"You're the happiest person I know."

"Because I have you. Because you're so strong and brave, and you're always there for me."

I pull her into another hug. "You're always there for me, too."

The crowd roars, and everyone turns toward the huge screens that surround the square. I don't want to look up. I know I shouldn't, yet I do.

The man being exed is short and thin, his clothes embedded with grime. Over the booming speakers, the announcer tells us this man's a Parasite, having walked away from his work assignment four months ago—probably because he was asked to do something dangerous like external dome repairs. But the announcer doesn't mention the reasons and instead tells us how the man's been hiding, stealing food, and generally undermining Haven's economy, our safety. To hear the crowd's reaction to the man's crimes, you'd think he'd committed mass murder.

Expungings are televised in the Hub as a deterrent, but a good number of those exed are Deviants. Our crime is existing. Witnessing an expunging, the only thing I'm deterred from is admitting what I am.

Like everyone else, I grew up believing what I'd been taught: that all Deviants are a threat to Haven. And after my father attacked us and I learned he was a Deviant, I hated them more than most. But then I discovered Drake's Deviance, and later my own. . . . Now all I want is to learn there's a cure, and failing that, to stay hidden. If there were any way to get rid of my curse, I would.

Up on the screens, the cameras, mounted on the outside of the dome and on nearby poles, capture six Compliance Officers wearing dust protection suits and sealed helmets as they push the man through a door in the dome. A strong wind swirls the dust in huge sheets, creating an eerie sound, like someone whistling into a microphone. One Comp shoves the exed man, and he stumbles to his knees. Dust flies up around him.

Jayma gasps and grips my hand. The man covers his nose and mouth with his arm, but we all know it's futile. Outside without a mask he can't avoid inhaling the dust, and while his fate isn't certain, it's sealed. At this point he's lucky if he's destined to become a Shredder.

I feel the urge to shout at the screen, to tell him to bend down and pull in as much dust as he can, to let it clog his lungs. Drowning on dust would be better than being alive for the torture.

My hope doesn't last long, and a pack of about ten Shredders swarms in, teeth bared, their skin a deep maroon that resembles dried meat.

The Comps retreat and seal the door to Haven, and the man scrambles back and slams into the outside of the dome.

The Shredders surround him in a tight semicircle, and the biggest one—a creature wearing a cowboy hat—opens his mouth in what looks like a roar, but we can't hear over the squealing wind.

Four Shredders rush forward and lift the man like he's a feather, holding him by his limbs. The cowboy Shredder roars again and they drop the man, catching him just before he hits the dust. Leaping forward, the leader moves so quickly I don't see his knife until it's against the man's face.

The camera zooms in, and the man's fear slices straight to my heart. His eyes are wide and frozen in terror. The knife scrapes a layer of skin off his cheek, and the Shredder laughs and drapes the skin onto his own chest like a medal. The crowd cheers.

The backs of my eyes tingle with the threat of my curse. I can't let my emotions take hold.

The Shredders laugh and lunge at the man as the cowboy Shredder swipes the broadside of the blade across his biceps, adding a glistening layer of blood to his scabbed skin. I look away.

My chest heaves as I try to draw air, and I rub my mom's ring. I can't let my curse emerge. Too many people around. This is what awaits me if I'm caught, what awaits my little brother if I don't protect him.

This is what happened to my father. Monsters like this killed my dad.

I don't care what he did; no one deserves this kind of death. Shredders are crazy and sadistic and don't kill quickly. Some of their victims survive for weeks before the

Shredders finish tearing strips off their bodies and harvesting body parts for their nightmarish trophy displays.

I could almost understand Shredders if they actually ate their victims, if they were starving out there and saw people as meat. But they don't. Shredders live off the dust. They use the exed Haven employees for their amusement, and then leave their remains for the rats.

I shudder. I may have eaten a creature that once gnawed human flesh.

The exed man screams, and it's all I can do to keep from tucking into a ball and wrapping my arms over my shins. I frantically rub my thumb on my ring. It's not working, so I try to imagine my body flooding with icy light like the overhead bulbs at GT. But not just one light—hundreds, enough to erase my thoughts, numb my body, and freeze my heart. *White space. White space. White space.*

I can't find it.

Jayma touches my back. "Are you okay?"

I jump. I need to get out of here. Now. "Save me a place in line?"

Without waiting for Jayma's answer, without even looking at her, I run and push through the crowd that remains fixated on the screens' horror show.

Struggling to find a private place to recover, I spot a break in the ocean of bodies and burst into a dark alley I've never explored. From the look of the asphalt surface, it was part of a road BTD, but new walls have been built at each side, narrowing the alley to barely four feet across. At intervals, iron ladders hang down that must be the entryways to homes.

Nice ones, given their proximity to the Hub. I wonder if I'll get in trouble if I'm caught here.

I don't care. Not right now. I stop running and press my back against a wall that's cool and comforting, some kind of sheet metal. Closing my eyes, I wait for my heart rate to slow, for my emotions to come back under control so I can rejoin society and claim my rations.

Society. Ha!

Right now, I'm repelled by this society I'm part of—yet not. I may have an employee number. I might follow the P&P Manual—mostly—but since I discovered my curse I haven't belonged in Haven. As hard as I try, I'll never fit in, never be a Normal.

I almost wish I could become a Parasite and hide up on the rooftops out of sight, but I wouldn't be able to move Drake quickly enough if the Comps came. Plus, while I can do with less food, I'm less sure about the vitamin powders we get to prevent the spread of disease and to compensate for the nutrients from foods humans ate BTD. I'm already concerned that Drake and I aren't getting enough on half rations.

I draw long breaths. If Drake and I want to eat this month, I need to get it together and go back to the Hub. Who knows when I'll find more rats. The Comps might have already discovered the nest on our roof. For all I know, Cal reported them.

"Glory," a deep voice says—a voice I don't recognize. "I've got a message for you."

Turning, I see a boy who looks about my age, maybe

older. He's tall, even taller than Cal and much broader, more imposing.

I draw a sharp breath through my nose and wonder where and how he's managed to get enough protein to build muscles like that. Muscles that alter the shape of his shoulders and the width of his chest into a form rarely seen in Haven.

He's Management. Or a Comp. He must be—even though he's not only too young, he's not in uniform or a suit. His oversized coat, made of layers of heavy cloth, is belted loosely at his waist with a rope tied in what looks like a slipknot. Below the rope, the fabric flares out and brushes the tops of his boots.

It's too late to run—he's standing too close and knows my name.

"Who are you?" I ask, keeping my gaze from his eyes.

"Name's Burn."

"You have a message?"

He taps my shoe with his heavy boot. "Look at me."

He asked for it. I look up, and he's so close the heat from his body penetrates my skin. His hair is thick and dark and long, and there's stubble on his upper lip and jaw. He reminds me of a wolf or a bear or one of the other now-extinct creatures I've seen in books or stuffed at the museum.

My throat closes and I try to look away, but he takes my chin in his thick, strong fingers and forces me to look at him. "The message"—his voice is gruff—"is from your father."

I break free to run but he grabs my arm.

My heart races, my eyes tingle and sting. If I dare look into his eyes, I might kill him.

I *should* kill him.

"Let me go." I struggle against his grip, his hand a steel trap. "You're lying. My father is dead."

"No, Glory"—he meets my eyes—"he's not."

CHAPTER FOUR

"LIAR." I STARE AT BURN. "MY FATHER WAS EXPUNGED THREE years ago."

Burn pulls my face around, and he's so close it's impossible to look at him without triggering my curse. I can't do that. He might eat me.

"He's alive. And your brother's in danger."

I raise my chin. "I don't have a brother."

"Then who's Drake?"

My chest constricts. "Don't you dare hurt him." My words explode.

"*I'm* not the danger."

I jerk away, slam into the metal wall, and the vibrations clamber up my spine. My dad's coming back to finish what he started. To kill me and Drake.

But rejecting that theory, I banish my fear. This Burn guy

is lying. My father's dead and I hate how this boy has twisted my mind with such ease.

He runs thick fingers over his jaw. He could crush my neck with one hand.

"Your father sent me," he says. "To get you to safety."

"Safety? He tried to kill us." And he's dead now. Either dead or a Shredder.

Burn towers over me, but I square my shoulders.

"You're lying. What do you really want?" I narrow my eyes as my curse starts to build.

"Glory!" Cal's voice travels down the alleyway, and I spin to see his lean silhouette at the mouth of the Hub.

"Down here," I call out and he runs toward us.

I turn back to Burn but he's gone. Vanished. I spin and look up to see a shape near the top of one of the ladders, but it's impossible for him to have climbed so quickly. A shadow moves near the roof of another building. That can't be him, either, so I look farther down the alley. It's like he evaporated—or I imagined him in the first place.

The expunging must have brought back bad memories of my father, not to mention the shame and horror of discovering my own curse. I had to have been hallucinating. The alternative's much worse.

I'm still searching for evidence of Burn when Cal slams into me, wrapping his long arms around my body, engulfing me in his salty scent. Releasing built-up tension, my body collapses into Cal's, surrendering to his strength and support.

My mind and body are at war. My mind knows I have no one to rely on but myself, that I'm cursed, that I can't trust Cal—but my body wants to believe he can love me, accept me, protect me, share some of my burden.

"Are you okay?" he asks. "I saw you run off. I was worried." As he holds me, his hand strokes my back, comforting me like my parents did when life was normal. I don't want Cal to ever let go.

I push back. "Are you going to turn him in?" I blurt, then draw deep breaths to regain control.

"Who?" he asks.

I snap my gaze up. "My brother."

He reaches for my hand, and I let him take it into the warmth of his. "No, Glory. Of course not." He pulls me forward. "Is that why you ran off?" He shakes his head. "I would never turn him in."

"But . . ." I don't want to say too much. I can barely list all the policies Drake's breaking and certainly don't want to reveal them. My brother doesn't have a current employee number, he hasn't attended training for three years, and he's failed to report his injury to Health & Safety. Plus, he's a Deviant. All these broken policies are written in black and white in the manual, which we all had memorized before we could read.

I need to know how Cal found out about Drake, but must tread carefully. I've liked Cal ever since I was little—he never picked on the younger kids like some of the bigger boys in GT—and he's always formed a major part of my fantasy for the future. It's hard to imagine he'd willingly hurt me, but I'm no longer sure what to believe. When I woke this morning I wouldn't have believed he'd join the Jecs.

Cal tightens his grip on my hand. "I would never do anything to hurt you. Never." He looks down. "I trusted you with my secret. I want you to trust me, too."

"I do trust you." *I wish.*

"Why doesn't your brother go to GT?"

My throat closes. Before the Comps took him, the last thing my father told me was: never trust anyone. That, and tell everyone Drake's dead. Not that I felt any obligation to follow my murderous father's orders. The need to hide Drake was obvious.

"Is your brother a slow learner?" Cal asks. "Blind?"

Lips squeezed tight, I shake my head.

"Never mind. I don't need to know right now." Cal's hand is getting sweaty on mine, and he wipes the back of his other one across his forehead. "But I hope you'll tell me some day." He actually sounds worried, and I'm not used to that tone from Cal. "I'd like to meet him. I can't even picture the kid."

"Maybe." *There's no way I can take the risk.*

"And please, don't think badly of me about the Jecs." His thumb strokes the back of my hand. "Just because I want a better job, a better life"—his voice gets softer—"doesn't mean I'm going to turn against people I care about."

"You care about Drake?"

"I care about *you.*"

For a moment, I'm weightless. "You do?"

"How could you even ask that?" His expression softens

and, looking into his penetrating blue eyes, a feeling washes through me that's so foreign I can't name it. Everything around me is softer; hard edges dissolve and the air wraps me like a blanket.

Then I recognize the feeling. It's safety.

Cal cares about me. He cares about my brother because I do. He wants to protect us.

I'm wrong to be skeptical. Tension melts inside me and I almost lose my balance, but Cal slides his hand around me, pulling me close. His heart's beating strong and slow like a large drum, and my hands press into his back. I crush against his hard chest, and still I want to pull closer, to meld my body to his so I'll never be alone again, so I'll forget reality, so I can believe I've got the carefree life of a Normal.

His heat blurs the boundaries between us and my emotions build. But so far my eyes feel fine, helping me pretend that I don't have a curse, that there's no chance I'll hurt him, that we're officially dating, that he's someone I can trust. Warmth fills my chest, my belly, my heart. I haven't felt this safe for more than three years. Not since I had parents.

For a few glorious moments, I look directly into his bright blue eyes, and the way he looks at me tugs my insides. He presses his lips to the top of my head and I close my eyes, then his breath warms my neck. I tip my head farther to the side, inviting his lips to bridge the small distance that parts their heat from my throat.

Holding me close, his hands trace over my back, igniting fires I don't quite understand but don't want to put out.

His breaths grow heavier, faster, and his body tenses against mine. Then he pulls his head away and pushes me back.

I swallow the instinct to cry out.

He bends over, placing his hands on his knees, panting.

Terror threatens to take hold and stepping forward, I rub my ring. "Cal?" I was so careless, so selfish, so thoughtless. Wrapped up in my fantasy, I let my guard down. Emotions triggered my curse and I hurt him with these brand-new and very strong emotions.

He straightens and I step back, but he grabs my hand and holds it. His cheeks are flushed and two beads of sweat race down his forehead.

"I hurt you." My words float out on a breath, faint and steamy, before I realize I'm coming dangerously close to confessing my worst secret.

"Why would you think that?" he asks.

"You pulled away. You groaned. You seemed hurt."

A grin spreads on his face, then his eyes soften and he presses his palm against my cheek. "Glory, that's not why I pulled away." His thumb traces my cheekbone.

"Then why?" Fears spark and kick. Cal knows I'm a Deviant. He knows Drake is, too. He told me his secret to gain my trust and make me lower my guard. He's gathering evidence to turn me in.

I don't want to believe these horrors but for the moment, I do.

His tongue runs over his lower lip. "You really don't know what you do to me, how you affect me, do you?" His voice is gravelly, dark.

I step back, pull my hand from his grip, and stare at the cracked asphalt. If I run now, can Drake and I escape capture?

"One more second holding you and—" He blows out a breath on a low whistle. "We'd have been arrested for public indecency." He shakes his head. "We don't even have a dating license."

My gaze snaps up to his. Heat flashes onto my face, my chest, and I raise my hand to my lips. Embarrassed, I glance to the side as my cheeks rage with fire.

But pushing it all away, I straighten my shoulders. I feel so naïve, like a little girl shocked by her first Relationships & Procreation session in GT. Cal's only two years older than me, but right now the span seems greater.

"I didn't *really* think I'd hurt you." I swallow. "It was a joke."

"Oh." He steps toward me, a tentative grin on his lips. "So we're good?" He glances around the alley, then lowers his voice. "You trust me about Drake?"

I nod.

"I'm glad." He smiles and I risk a moment of eye contact.

"Glory." Cal takes a step forward. "Now that I've told you everything . . ." He runs his hand through his hair. Lifting his arm reveals a quick glimpse of his stomach that makes my heart squeeze. "Now that we have no more secrets. . . ."

I bite my lip.

"Will you—" He falters. "Can I take you out on a date?"

I suck in a quick breath.

I figured he'd ask who was with me when he entered the alley. But he hasn't mentioned Burn, reinforcing my conclusion that the strange boy must have been a figment of my imagination.

"If you'd rather not." Cal looks down. "I thought . . . I'm sorry."

"No—Yes." My mouth is suddenly very dry. "Sure. Yes."

Cal pulls me into another hug and I drift back into a dream state. One where I can pretend it's okay to trust Cal. Pretend I'm a Normal and safe.

I stick close to Cal as we step up to the counter in the Human Resources office. After we claimed our rations, Cal suggested we head straight to get our license since we were already in the Hub. Scout and Jayma got theirs today, too, and they left to celebrate.

The cheery green walls instantly make me think of the apple I had as a child when my father got one as a bonus. My mother cut the fruit into quarters, taking the smallest piece for herself. But thinking of my father and what he did to my mother makes me angry. Anger is the last thing I want to feel, so I rub my ring to erase the emotion.

The woman behind the counter looks up from her desk and smiles in a way that makes me think she likes her job— who wouldn't, working in a place that's been freshly painted in the last four decades? She pats the sides of her blonde hair, piled into a bun at least five inches high. "What a lovely young couple," she says. "Good luck with the approval process."

"Thank you." Cal puts his hand around my waist.

Every nerve inside me fires at once, but I don't pull away. His move is bold, considering our license isn't yet approved, but any indication that this isn't consensual might hurt our chances.

And I want our license approved.

My logical side knows this relationship is doomed before it starts—I can't have a future with Cal, or any boy—but I'm intoxicated by the idea of dating, intoxicated by Cal. I want, I deserve, a few brief moments of joy each week. Moments to pretend that I have a chance at happiness, a chance to be loved. Moments to pretend that I'm a Normal.

"Numbers please?" the HR clerk asks.

"3-24-63-11." Cal gives his employee number.

"3-87-42-25." I give her mine. Our numbers both start with three, signifying we're in the third generation of employees since Haven was founded by business leaders who took survival out of the hands of an ineffective BTD organization called government. The list of Haven's founding corporations and their presidents is on a plaque at the Hub. Our ancestors were among the lucky ones to be saved.

The woman types the numbers onto her laser-projected keyboard, and the electronic application forms Cal and I filled out at the kiosk appear. She drags a long fingernail over the details, reading the information line by line. The application forms ask for our employee numbers and work placements. Apparently there'd be more paperwork if we worked in the same department, but since I'm still in GT, that's not an issue.

"Everything appears complete," she says. "I won't be a minute." She spins on her tall chair and begins a series of sweeping and jabbing hand gestures in the air, pulling and pushing bits of information on and off her projected screens as she sorts through the database of Haven citizens, retrieving our genealogy records and performance evaluations.

She turns back and, looking at me, tips her head to the side. "Your parents are both deceased?" she asks me, although it's more of a statement.

I nod.

Your father is alive. Burn's words come back to me, but once again I choose to dismiss the mysterious boy as a hallucination. Even if he was real, what he said wasn't true. It couldn't be.

The HR clerk leans forward, the top of her bun scraping against the small window. "I hate to ask this, young lady, but it's my job. And given your family history . . ."

I keep still and trace my thumb over the inside of my ring.

"Are you a Deviant?" The last word comes out on an emphasized whisper.

I shake my head slowly, keeping my expression neutral and willing my heart rate to slow.

"No signs of any aberrant powers or abilities?" She probes again. "Because even the slightest abnormality—"

Cal presses his fingers into the countertop. "She's not a Deviant, okay?" His voice is clipped and hard. "I'm a member of—" He stops himself. "I've known her for years. If she were a Deviant, I'd know."

My insides warm, but at the same time I hate that Cal's defense of me is based on a lie.

I have no choice. Not if I want to keep Drake safe and avoid us both being tossed to the Shredders.

The woman straightens. "I'm just doing my job. If I don't ask"—she nods up to a camera—"I'll get demoted. Maybe even *downsized*." The last word comes out on a rasp, and tiny spots of color appear on her cheeks. She pushes her fingers along an image projected onto the counter and an electronic form appears before me. "Sign here."

I read the form and it's nothing to do with our license. Rather, it's a declaration that I'm not a Deviant. In big letters it explains that a false statement will lead to prosecution for fraud. I try not to laugh. If they find out I'm a Deviant, who cares about fraud?

People convicted of minor crimes are assigned the worst jobs, but the kind of job this woman fears doing if she's demoted from HR is probably better than the job I'm destined for. I pick up the stylus, sign, and then press my thumb onto the employee verification box.

"Now that we've got that nasty business out of the way"—the woman pulls back that form and pushes two more through the window—"please read and sign these."

I scan the details and try to hide my relief when I see no names listed under next of kin. My heart pinches as I press my thumb on that verification box, but my fingerprint doesn't mean that Drake doesn't exist. He's my brother, not an employee number or database record.

After a few more sections—ones in which we agree to inform HR should we wish to terminate this license, and pledge that we will not date outside this agreement or procreate before submitting to DNA tests—we swear to absolve Management of liability or sexual harassment claims should our dating agreement terminate unfavorably.

I sign the last section, then turn to Cal. He's already finished and smiling at me. His hand brushes mine, igniting a tingling rush.

The HR woman double-checks the information encoded on the metal, asks for our wrists, then clamps license bracelets on each. Now, not only are we bound together, but everyone can see it. It's almost as if I'm a Normal. As we walk from the office, Cal slips his arm across my shoulders and happiness lifts my heart higher than it's been in three years—maybe ever.

I have a boyfriend. I'm officially dating. If he knew the full truth, he'd leave me, turn me in—but I can hide my Deviance. He knows my brother's a Parasite, yet he hasn't turned him in. There is a risk that he might, that he's lying, but our dating doesn't alter that risk.

We're not yet outside the building when a tall man wearing a gray suit and a silver tie steps into the hallway, about twenty feet ahead. Cal's arm flies off my shoulders. My insides flood with terror, so I cast my eyes down and rub my ring to reinforce my emotional walls.

"Hello, Sir," Cal says. *Why is he drawing attention to us?*

We stop and the man continues forward, each step smacking the floor until his shiny black shoes are mere feet from mine—two dark harbingers of danger against the pale floor.

"Mr. Belando," Cal says. "I enjoyed your presentation to my committee."

The man nods. "Yes, you've joined the Ethics Committee. Good lad."

"Yes, Sir, and I'd like to introduce you to my—my girlfriend, Glory. Employee number 3-87-42-25."

A flash of joy at hearing the word *girlfriend* is squashed by the alarm that he's given this man my number.

Cal lifts his wrist to show off his bracelet. "We've just come from getting our license."

"My goodness." The man's voice is unexpectedly friendly. "What a joyous occasion."

"Glory," Cal tugs on my sleeve. "This is Mr. Belando. He's the VP of Compliance."

"Junior VP of Compliance," Mr. Belando corrects, like the junior part matters. Management is all that matters. Compliance is all that matters. The department the Comps and Auditors work for, the one that enforces the P&P.

"Don't be shy, young lady," Mr. Belando says. "Let me take a look at you."

Rubbing my mother's ring, I look up and smile. His hair is dark, except at the temples, where it's silver and so precisely cut it looks painted on with a brush. His skin is as bright as a newborn's, in spite of his obvious age. I've never been this close to anyone in Management and wonder if they all have such clear skin.

"Have you completed General Training?" he asks and I shake my head.

"She finishes GT this session and recently took the

Management aptitude tests," Cal says. I wish he'd stop drawing dangerous attention my way.

"Good for you." Mr. Belando smiles. "Just remember that less than 1 percent of M-Ap candidates qualify for Management training. But not to worry." He pats my shoulder. "One way or another, I'm sure you'll be assigned a rewarding work placement compatible with both your aptitude and Haven's current openings." He says this with no discernible irony and I wonder if everyone in Management believes we're happy to do whatever job we're assigned.

But I say, "Yes, I'm very excited."

"Do you have a preference?" Mr. Belando checks his cuffs.

"She'd make a great Tenant Liaison," Cal pipes in. "I think the liaison on our floor is retiring soon."

That actually *is* exciting. Tenant Liaisons are one step down from Management and such a great job is beyond my dreams. My mood brightens. If I land the liaison job on our floor, I could be near Drake every day and, better yet, avoid the risk that the new liaison might be more diligent than our current one. Maybe dating a Jecs has perks.

"I'll put in a good word," Mr. Belando says, then turns and strides away before I can thank him.

I turn to Cal. "You really know that man?"

"I've met him." He leans in close to my ear. "As soon as I become a Compliance Officer, the sky's the limit for us."

I smile but I've never understood that phrase. I'm well acquainted with the sky and it isn't a spectacular limit.

CHAPTER FIVE

I WAIT UNTIL VERY LATE TO COOK OUR RAT MEAT ON THE STOVE I share with the other residents of our floor. Anyone could see that the amount I'm cooking is far more than I have the ration points to buy. Rat teeth and claws are the most common cause of breaches to the dome, so the punishment for not reporting rats that have escaped the farms is severe. But not as severe as starvation, and most people living up here snag extra meat now and again. There's an unwritten rule that we don't report each other, but I can't be too careful. Cal has proven that I'm not the only secret-laden resident of our Pent.

Once the meat's cooked, I return to our room and wake Drake.

"What time is it?" He stretches his arms above his head.

"Two thirty." I set the meat on an oiled cloth to cool.

"Here, eat something." I crank the handle on our lantern so we'll have light to eat by.

"I'm sleeping." He turns to face the wall.

Resisting the urge to baby him—he can decide for himself—I tear off a chunk and chew the tough meat. Farmed rats live in cages, their faces pointed toward feeding trays, so it's no wonder the resulting meat is easier to chew. Their flesh must be as soft as my brother's legs.

Clearly unable to resist the scent, Drake turns over and snatches one of the rats.

"Sit up, at least." I shake my head. "You're dripping grease on your sheets."

Holding the meat in one hand, he shifts and pushes up with his elbow until he's sitting. He glowers, but Drake doesn't have to wash our sheets by hand in cold water. Grease is impossible to clean, and his sheets are spotted. I can't get them clean the way Mom could.

In the dim light, his jaw looks like our father's, and my insides twist. I crank the lantern to reduce the shadows.

"What are you staring at?" Drake cleans the meat off a leg bone.

"Do you ever think about Mom and—" I swallow the word *Dad*.

He tosses a picked-clean leg into our compost bucket, and then slides over on his mattress. "Why?"

"Someone got exed today." I shake my head, wishing I'd kept my big mouth shut. Today has already been too confusing. Drake not hating our dead father still shocks me, even though three years have passed.

"Stop dwelling on Mom's death," he says. "It was an accident."

I spin toward him. "Which is it, Drake?" My voice is sharper than I mean it to be. "Did he not do it, like you told Jayma, or did he do it by accident and you forgive him?"

Drake looks away. Good thing, because anger and frustration burn in my chest and behind my eyes.

"I'm just saying"—Drake's voice is quiet and deeper than usual—"accidents happen. Sometimes people don't know what they're capable of. Like when my armor showed up that day. Before then, I had no idea I was a Deviant."

"You're not making sense, Drake." I tear off another chunk of rat meat. "Are you saying that he's not guilty of murder if he didn't mean to kill her?"

"If I hurt you," he says, "you'd forgive me, right?"

I slide over to sit beside him and wrap my arm over his shoulders. "Of course I would." I imagine it every time his armor's up and he swings his iron-hard arms.

He taps my hand. "That's all I'm saying." He brings the rat to his mouth and tears off another chunk of meat. "Time to forgive Dad," he says between chews.

I don't respond. Our father was an adult, not a kid, and he attacked his whole family. It's different, but I don't want to argue with Drake anymore. Let him cling to childhood awhile longer.

Standing, I stretch and a yawn bursts out. I'm not sure I have the energy to eat any more, so after getting Drake's nod of approval, I wrap up the rest and stash it in our small food-storage box. There's a place in the box for ice, but we haven't been able to afford any since our parents died.

Without even removing my shoes, I climb onto the mattress opposite Drake and our lantern fades away to nothing. Soon Drake's breaths slow and I know he's asleep. My breathing slows, too, but I can't slow my mind.

Tomorrow night I have a date, and I can't help being curious and excited. I haven't been to a restaurant since our parents died and, even then, we only went once a year, alternating my birthday with Drake's. But as much as I'd love to forget my worries during our date, I still don't know how Cal found out about my brother and I can't relax until I'm past that hurdle. And yet, with so many important questions swirling through my thoughts, the one that surfaces over and over is whether or not Cal will kiss me.

Will his lips be soft or hard? Will his breath have the same spicy scent as his body? My insides heat and suddenly I'm scared. I've never been kissed. What if it raises emotions I can't control? I can't bear the thought I might hurt him—or that he'll find out what I am.

Uncomfortable in my clothes I kick off my shoes, then sit to take off my jacket. Checking my pockets, my fingers brush something I didn't put there. I pull it out and realize it's paper. Cal must have slipped it there during our embrace. Paper is expensive and that he used a scrap to express his feelings fills me with joyous anticipation.

I roll over and crank the lantern. Drake sighs and moves an arm over his face but doesn't wake. The paper is folded several times and I spread it out carefully and move it into the light.

Dearest daughter, the note reads. *I'm so sorry I haven't been there for you and Drake, but you were safer not knowing I survived. I've done all I can to protect you, but Drake is in danger. Trust Burn. He will get you both to safety. Your loving father.*

I drop the paper like it's on fire and back up against the wall. My heart thumps so quickly and loudly I'm afraid Drake will hear, even though I know that's ridiculous. He can't sense my heart like I can his.

This note cannot have been written by my father. It's impossible. But finding the paper confirms Burn wasn't a hallucination. I'm not going mad.

Although—given the idea that my dad is alive—going mad seems a better alternative.

CHAPTER SIX

AL'S CALLUSED FINGERS BRUSH THE EDGE OF MY CHIN AND nudge my gaze up to his. "Are you sure you don't mind?" he asks on a roof I've never been to before. It's nestled near the edge of the city, where the sky's low and sharply sloped, but not too close above us.

"This is way better than a restaurant." I roll to my side, facing him, and rest on one elbow. "How did you find this place?"

He smiles. "One of the Jecs works in Sky Maintenance. He spotted it."

Cal leans toward me and his biceps bulge. It's all I can do to keep my hand from reaching out to feel the hard, smooth slope of his arm, but before I can disappear into fantasy-land, I need answers.

He cuts a piece of cucumber with a sharp knife and lifts it to my mouth. It's strange to have someone feed me, but the cucumber is the freshest, coolest, most delicious thing I've ever tasted. Parting my lips I let him place the slice inside.

When I bite down, my eyes close. "So good." The skin is crunchy, tasting as green as it looks, and there are tiny slippery seeds inside the translucent flesh. "It's miraculous." I'll bet the cucumber cost a whole month's worth of ration points. I've never even seen one before.

"It was picked today at the hydroponic greenhouse. One of the Jecs works there." He shifts closer and puts a chunk of cucumber between his teeth. I can't keep my eyes off his lips as he chews.

I glance down. *Keep your focus.* "Cal," I say softly. "I've been wondering something."

"Uh-huh?"

"How did you know about . . . I mean . . . It wasn't Jayma who told you, was it?" I doubt she told him but I need to know.

He feeds me another slice of cucumber and smiles. "No. I didn't need your *friend* to tell me. It was obvious."

My stomach clenches. "Obvious? Why? What?" I snap my mouth shut to stop the stammer and then look for answers in his eyes, which are focused on my lips. Good choice. My lips don't kill.

He bends closer until I can't focus properly on his eyes.

His breath is hot; his lips hover over mine. "I've known for a couple of years, Glory. You aren't like one of those emotional drama-queen girls, but I could see what you were hiding."

"How?"

"You're pretty transparent."

"No, I'm not." I know I'm not. Either he's not making sense, or I've lost my ability to think straight. The latter grows more probable when his thumb brushes a hair off my cheek, and I feel sparks in my belly.

"You give off lots of little clues." His thumb sweeps my cheek, near the corner of my mouth. "When I catch you looking at me, you look away, and you blush." He pulls back a bit. "Am I wrong?"

I finally get it, and my entire body heats. "You're not wrong." He's misunderstood me. Completely. "I wasn't asking about that. About us." I reach for his hand, moving mine close, but not quite touching. "I meant—how did you know about my brother?"

"I don't want to think about your brother right now." He strokes my hair.

"Did Jayma tell you about him?"

"Jayma?" He shakes his head slowly. "*She* knows about your brother?"

I bite down on my lip, wanting to swallow my question. What have I done? I shouldn't have let my faith in Jayma slip for even a second. Now if Cal reports Drake, she could be named as an accessory to concealing a Parasite and for failure to report a serious injury—among other P&P violations. If Cal betrays me, I've signed my best friend's death sentence. "How did you know about him?"

"I saw his name on a list."

"What kind of list?"

"A database query. Unmatched, inactive employee numbers."

I snap up to sit. Thinking Management had no record of Drake was a huge comfort. I was deluded. No one just drops out of the System. "Who has the list? What does it mean?"

Cal sits and rests his hand on my back. "Don't panic. It's no big deal."

"Yes, it is." His warm hand is comforting, but doesn't erase my fear.

He shakes his head. "Your brother's a Parasite because he's injured, right? It's not like he's a Deviant."

Heart racing, I nod and he continues. "I saw the list by chance on the back of some Maintenance specs at work." His finger traces figure eights on my back. "The paper was recycled. Discarded. Don't worry. Parasites are low priority, and if the Comps plan a raid on our floor, I'm a Jecs now. I'll know about it well in advance. I'll warn you. I can keep you both safe."

"Really?" Assuming he's sincere, he's taking a huge risk. A huge risk for me.

"I admire how you take care of your brother." Cal's strong, warm arm slides over my shoulders. "If I get my wish, some-day he'll be my family, too."

My insides flip. "Your family?"

He cups my chin with his fingers, his thumb tracing down my cheek. "Of course. He'll be my brother, when we get married."

"Married?" My mouth dries.

"Someday. That's what I hope." He kisses my forehead, his lips both searing and soft. "I love you, Glory."

He loves me? It's what I've always wanted, but I can't respond, not with this huge secret between us.

His lips drift down and hover so close I inhale his breath. Knowing our lips are close to touching muddles my thoughts and makes my face tingle. I know I should stop him—if he knew what I was, he'd want me dead—but I don't *want* to stop him. I want to be kissed. I want to feel safe. I want to be a Normal. I want the horrors of my life to be over.

I tip my face up, and Cal's warm strong lips press against mine, igniting a sharp pinch in my chest that shoots down. His arms wrap around and pull me in tightly. His heartbeat penetrates my skin, thumps through me as our chests press together, and I hope beyond hope that the sensation's because he's holding me close and not because of my curse.

He inhales deeply and trails warm kisses up and down my throat then back to my lips. It's as if my body's an oxygen tank and he's Outside in the dust. Like he needs me to breathe. At any moment I'll forget my life. I'll drift into a dreamland where my problems are gone.

Emotions pop behind my eyes like a million tiny explosions and I fear what might happen should they join forces and escape. This is what I've always wanted but I can't lose control. Focusing on a spot of white light that's bouncing off a building in the distance, I will the brightness to surround me, to wipe out my emotions, to extinguish my curse.

I blink, and suddenly Burn is silhouetted on the far side of the roof, arms folded over his chest, his head slowly shaking. I stiffen.

Cal breaks our kiss and holds my head in his hands. "What's wrong?"

"I'm fine." I can't let him look behind us. Burn must be a Deviant, and while I have no reason to protect him, I feel compelled to.

Cal kisses me again, and this time his lips demand more but I can't enjoy it. Not with Burn near.

I push away and look past Cal. Burn's gone.

"I'm sorry." Cal drops his arm and he looks hurt. "I keep forgetting our age difference. I moved too fast."

"I'm sixteen. I'm not a kid." But he's eighteen, and I bet he's kissed other girls—with or without a license.

"Of course you're not a kid," he says with a soft smile. "I didn't mean it like that."

Seeing an opportunity, I stand. "This *is* happening fast. I need time to catch my breath. Can you give me a moment alone?" I gesture forward. "I'll take a quick walk over there."

"Of course. I'll tidy up this mess. We should get going if we want to make curfew." Cal wipes the knife clean of cucumber juice on his pant leg, and I force a smile before I walk to where I saw Burn.

A message is scratched into the roof's surface. *Meet me. One hour. Same alley. Important.*

Every muscle inside me trembles and I stagger back from the note toward Cal.

Burn is a ticking bomb I need to defuse, and there's no time for me to get home and then back to that alley. Halfway to our Pent, I stop Cal at the start of a bridge, then pull him onto a shadowed window ledge, stories above the ground. Clearly misinterpreting why I stopped us, he pulls me against him, drawing me in so tightly my feet leave the ground. Pressed against his hard, warm body, I almost forget why I stopped. Cal's assumption seems like a good plan and I melt into his arms.

A groan rumbles through his chest. "You make me so happy." He presses his lips to my neck and although it feels wonderful, I pull back. "Good night."

He laughs. "I don't think so." His lips slide from my neck to my jaw and then up to my lips, and I can't turn away— not without pushing against him—if I do that, one or both of us might fall from this ledge. Pleasure sparks at his kiss and I rub my mother's ring, needing to refuse what his kiss demands.

When his lips lift from mine, his cheeks are tinged red, his eyes are darker, and his breaths are fast and shallow. "Is something wrong?"

I shake my head, but wiggle back from him to put an inch of space between our bodies.

"Hey!" A loud voice booms from the bridge where it meets the ledge.

Over Cal's shoulder I see a Comp glaring at us. Cal presses his back against the building's wall beside me.

"What's going on here?" The Comp's metal armor clanks as he reaches for the shocker gun on his hip.

"We're licensed," Cal says as we hold up our arms to show the bracelets clamped on our wrists.

The Comp frowns. "A dating license does not excuse public indecency. Have you not read the P&P? There are children living on this bridge." He pulls a small computer from a pocket on his belt. "Employee numbers?"

I draw a deep breath. If I get arrested, Drake's doomed. I wish I'd left Cal behind on that roof and gone directly to meet Burn—strange that at this moment he seems less dangerous.

"Listen." Cal sidesteps toward the Comp. "Can you give us a break here?" He reveals the inside of his wrist.

The Comp pulls out a small rechargeable torch that doesn't seem to work. It casts a bluish glow on Cal's wrist, and the Comp snaps his head back and grunts. "*You* should know better," he says.

I fight to hide my surprise. Clearly Management stamps some kind of mark on the wrists of the Jecs.

"Yes, Officer." Cal straightens his shoulders. "It won't happen again."

The Comp snaps his computer back on his belt. "Haven equals safety. Observe the P&P. Set a good example." The Comp lowers his voice. "Especially in an area like this."

Cal nods and I wonder what the Comp means about an area like this. Sure, this is a densely populated bridge and there are kids, but the distaste in his voice was clear. If Cal and I had parents in Management, or lived in a better neighborhood, I expect we could kiss where we wanted.

"On your way." The Comp stomps onto the suspension bridge that's missing at least one of its original cables. The structure quakes under the combined weight of his body and heavy uniform. The few people who hadn't scrambled into their huts when they spotted the Comp, brace themselves against the vibrations.

I look over to Cal. "We shouldn't walk home together."

"Nonsense. He knows I'm a committee member." Cal's chest puffs a little but his eyebrows move closer together, and I can tell he's upset we were nearly arrested.

"I'm fine from here." I smile to reassure him and to quash the real emotions stirring inside me. "And clearly, I can't be trusted to behave."

He laughs and then rubs his fingers over his chin. "Maybe you're right." He lowers his head toward mine. "I hope no one saw me reveal my mark to the Comp."

"Mark?" I tip my head to the side, deciding it's better to pretend I didn't notice. "Why don't you go first," I say while he's considering whether to explain what he meant. "I'll wait until you're out of sight and then follow."

The Comp did me a favor. I don't know what this Burn guy expects to gain by forging a note from my father. And it has to have been forged. No one survives an expunging and I saw my father tossed out of the dome. The cameras shut off soon after the Shredders found him and if he's not dead, he's turned into one of them. A Shredder couldn't have written that note.

I rub my ring to calm down and think. Burn's motivation can't be blackmail. I've got nothing of value but secrets, and the way I see it, where secrets are concerned, Burn and I are at a stalemate. No chance that guy is a Normal.

I'll call his bluff. I'll tell him I know he's a Deviant; I'll tell him that I've got connections in Management—I'll make him see I'm a threat.

"Be careful. Keep safe." Cal bends to kiss me, but I turn my cheek to dodge his lips.

"I will, and thank you—for tonight, for the cucumber, especially. It was delicious."

He beams. "I thought you'd like it." He leans his shoulder into the wall. "I'll move up in the Jecs, and if I get through the Entrance Trials for Compliance Officer Training, we'll have plenty of fresh vegetables in our future."

"Great." My face hurts from the strain of smiling, and I can't figure out whether the nerves churning my stomach and skittering up my spine are from his talking marriage so soon, or my knowing it can never happen.

CHAPTER SEVEN

NERVES ON EDGE, I GLANCE DOWN THE ALLEY WHERE I FIRST saw Burn and assure myself that the danger of this meeting is lower than the danger of his following me around. I lift my hand to shield my eyes from the lights glaring from the far end, where the alley meets the Hub. No sign of movement.

I'm fifteen minutes late and he's nowhere to be seen. Worse, it's past curfew for employees still in GT, and if I get caught, I'll risk arrest for the second time tonight.

"You came."

I spin at the deep sound of Burn's voice, and the air rushes out of my lungs. I back up a few steps to increase the distance between us. How did he come up behind me without my hearing? I hate this guy for making me so uneasy, for proving I'm not as aware of my surroundings as I think.

Resentment builds inside me, igniting my curse. Instead of trying to extinguish the sparks behind my eyes, I look directly at Burn's and let my resentment build to anger. Focusing my thoughts on his stomach, I twist.

Pain flashes on his face.

Shocked, I look down, staring at the small hole above the big toe of my left shoe. Light-headedness threatens, but I win.

I did it. I hurt him. This confirms what I've suspected: I can affect more than rats' organs. My curse affects humans.

And Burn is a very large human.

He raises his dark, heavy eyebrows. "You're powerful. Hector was right."

I reel, my father's name a punch to my heart. I haven't heard or thought about my father's name for years, and I might have forgotten what it was until now. It was merely the name my mother called my father. I never thought of him as Hector, just Dad—then murderer.

My mother's name, Anna, flashes to mind and my thumb flies to her ring. I want to be like her, not my father, but to survive I need a little of both.

Burn steps closer, and as if sensing I might run, he grabs my arm. Smart guy.

"I *am* powerful," I tell him. "If you know what's good for you, never come near me again."

He pulls me forward. "I'm powerful, too, little girl."

His hand is tight, really tight, on my arm—so tight I might bruise—and I struggle against him and raise my chin higher to look into his eyes. "I am not a little girl. I've been single-handedly taking care of my brother for three years."

His grip on my arm loosens but he doesn't release me. "I know."

I swallow the fear that's pressing into my indignation. "Leave me alone." I look into his eyes, but this time he's smart enough to release me. I look away.

He takes a step back, reaches into his big coat, and puts on glasses that are darkened like the masks the Comps wear Outside. But these are strange, with dials at their sides, and they completely obscure his eyes.

"Listen." His voice is even and intense. "Your brother's in danger. I need to get him out of Haven."

Now I *know* he's crazy. "What?"

"You heard me."

"People can't live Outside. Nothing can, except rats and Shredders."

"That's what they want you to believe." His long dark hair falls against the side of his face, and he pushes it back with a strong, powerful hand. It's the scariest thing I've ever seen— and the sexiest. *What's wrong with me?* I want Cal. I love Cal.

"Who wants us to believe?" I ask, my voice breathier than I want it to be.

"Hush." He steps closer and lowers his voice. "The so-called Management of this place, that's who."

My heart thumps so loudly I can hear it, and it bothers me that he's so cool and calm. I need to seem as cool and calm as he does because I need answers—and I need to make him leave us alone. Although I've heard everything he's said, it's like my thoughts are a puzzle and none of the pieces he's offering fit.

I'm rubbing my ring so hard that it heats against my skin, but I have to admit I'm intrigued about the idea of life beyond the dome. Years ago, my grandparents were among the lucky ones hired to help build Haven, escaping certain death. Stories from BTD are vague, incomplete, and contradictory—such talk outside GT is against policy. Still, if the earth was once big enough that people flew through the air in machines, it doesn't make sense that we're the only ones left. The only ones who figured out a way to survive. "Why should I believe anything you say?"

"Believe me. Or don't. Doesn't matter." Burn towers over me and I catch my reflection in his lenses.

Fists form at my sides. I can't look away and wonder if this is how the rats feel when I've got them trapped. Burn knows *nothing* about my life, *nothing* about Drake, *nothing* about me. "Why would you claim my father's alive?"

"Because he is."

"My father was expunged. Torn apart by the Shredders."

"So they told you."

"Is my father a Shredder? Is that what you're saying?" I hate my father, but that's worse than thinking he's dead.

"No."

"Well, which is it?" I snap. "He's either dead or a Shredder. Once you're exposed to the dust, those are the only two options."

"Those are more Management lies."

"*You* lie. Give me one reason I should believe anything you say."

"Don't believe me then. Your father asked me to save your brother, not you."

My stomach contracts. "He doesn't need saving. I keep him safe."

He glares down at me and his strong jaw twitches, but he doesn't respond.

I want to hit him. "Even if I believe that my father is alive—which I don't—why should I listen to anything he says? He's a murderer."

He pushes his glasses onto the top of his head, and I risk a quick glance at his eyes, dark and intense.

My fingernails dig into my palms but I don't release my fists. Right now, I can use all the anger I can find. "I know people," I tell Burn. "Important people. People who could have you arrested and expunged."

The side of his mouth cocks up. "You mean your little boyfriend on the roof?"

He's mocking me. I stare into his eyes and lock my thoughts onto his heart, but he closes his eyes and shakes his head before I have a chance.

He reopens his eyes and glares. "Not as easy to kill as a rat, am I?"

I suck in a sharp breath. "Leave me alone. Stay away from me and Drake or you'll find out just how easily I can kill."

Looking him in the eyes, I focus my anger on his lungs and tune into the organs' spongy pockets. I squeeze, pressing out the air, and although he stays still and doesn't try to fight or look away, I can tell that he feels the power of my curse. His chest heaves in sharp thrusts as he tries to draw breaths.

"Stop it," he says low and hard. "If you kill me, your brother will die."

I look away to release him and he sucks in a few hard breaths as I rock, dizzy from using my curse, even if only for seconds.

He catches me before I fall. "Careful."

I pull my arm away. "I'm going to call the Compliance Department. In a few minutes this alley will be swarming with Comps."

He grabs my arm. "Don't." There's a fire in his eyes, and fear snakes down my spine. But I throw my shoulders back.

The veins on his temple bulge and his face reddens.

My back strikes the wall behind me before I realize I've moved. I thought Burn was intense when he was calm, but as his anger builds, it's like he's growing taller, wider, filling out the previously baggy clothes. Fear grabs hold of my chest, paralyzes me for an instant before adrenaline surges. I run.

But I slam into him—somehow he ran faster or leaped over me, and his huge body blocks my path. He lifts me by the shoulders and sets me down a few feet back.

"What are you?" I ask, my voice hardly as loud as a breath.

"Glory." He looks down, his eyes dark. "I have a gift, just like you. We were Chosen."

"Chosen for what?"

A beam of light shines down the alley.

"Who's there?" an amplified voice calls.

Burn wraps his strong arm around my waist. "Hold on." He leaps, holding me tight, and grabs a handle hanging above us. Something clicks and we accelerate upward. Air rushes against my ears, obliterating the Comps' shouts from below. My arms are strapped around Burn's neck, but I have no memory of putting them there.

Whatever he's holding pulls us up the side of the building so quickly that the surface blurs. We decelerate as we near the roof, and before we've fully stopped, he releases me onto a metal landing jutting out from the building.

"Get up." He unhooks the contraption that pulled us up and clips it under his coat.

I stand and he grabs me, crushing me against him. He jumps across the street to another roof. We land, hard, and loose gravel crunches beneath his boots.

His muscles flex against my body as he runs. I've never imagined a person could be as solid as a concrete wall, yet fluid.

"How?" My breath is gone and the word's barely audible.

"Up there. We've got him surrounded." Comps' voices shout in the darkness, echoing off the walls and the sky. I can't place their locations as searchlights bounce off buildings and bridges around us. Fighting to find my bearings, I spot the windowless gray walls of the Compliance Building to my right. We went north from the alley; my Pent is west and south.

"Ready?"

"Where are we going?" I ask, but without answering he leaps.

We land on another rooftop and he barely breaks stride. "Don't choke me," he says.

I release his neck and adjust my hold, unable to reach fully around his broad chest. He jumps and I cling, my fingers clutching his coat.

We land on another roof at least two stories down, and he grunts. My teeth ache from the impact.

But he doesn't stop. He runs and jumps again. We fly across another alley.

Midair, I slide several inches, terrified his grip will fail, but it doesn't. It's as if his arm's melded to my waist, holding me against the heat of his body.

We land. "I could use some help here." He adjusts his hold on me as he runs.

I lock my legs around his ribs and tighten my grip on his shoulders.

He leaps again, then again, then again, and I resist the urge to close my eyes as we move across Haven, virtually flying from building to building—so many I've lost count. I search for landmarks, no longer sure where I am.

A spotlight strikes us, blinding me for an instant.

"Crap." Burn skids along a rooftop, his boots sliding on the fine gravel as the building's edge rushes toward us. We're going to shoot off.

We stop. There's nothing between us and the narrow alley—many stories below. Burn teeters, madly waving the arm that's not holding me.

It doesn't work.

His muscles contract as we fall.

Plummeting, I open my mouth to scream but nothing comes out. I close my eyes tight and prepare myself for the end.

Instead, a clang then the shrill screech of metal against metal fills my ears. Trying to figure out where the sound came from, I begin to slip from his grasp. His arm tightens. Looking up, I discover we're dangling. Burn's other arm holds a ladder on the brick building opposite from the one we fell off.

"Can you climb?" He lifts me to the ladder before waiting for an answer. "Go. Run. Hide. I'll find you." And with that, he drops from the ladder.

A chill hits my body as he departs. Darkness engulfs him and I can't see where he lands or if he survives. My hands grip the ladder so tightly my knuckles turn white.

A spotlight sweeps across the building below me, and I climb the ladder then scramble into the first open space I find—a narrow corridor with doors every five or six feet. There's no light, but the smell of cooking meat means this building's residential. Not hearing any movement, I sit and lean my head against the wall, panting, resting my hands on the wooden floor.

What just happened? I've never heard of a Deviant as strong as Burn existing. My waist feels tender where he gripped me, but it's hard to deny that his intentions were to save, not to hurt me. Not that I trust him. I can't.

Rustling comes from behind a door across the hall.

I push to my feet and run forward. Something catches the

toe of my shoe. My stomach rises in my throat as I'm thrown forward and slam into the floorboards. Pain shoots up my arms and knees, but I can't afford to survey the damage. A door opens behind me, so I get up and stumble forward, hoping that I'll find a staircase or bridge at the end of the hall.

Another door opens. "In here." A woman beckons but I shake my head. She might be an Auditor.

Faint light comes in from an opening at the end of the hall. I stumble toward it. When I get there, I almost lose my balance. I'm at least fifteen stories from the ground. Above, the sky is high, sloping to the left and darkened for night. Given its height and slope, I must be about a quarter mile to the east of the Hub.

A thick rope lies at my feet, tied to a girder. Without other choices I bend down and turn, grabbing the rope and walking down the outside of the building. Two floors down, the building's shape changes, and I'm left dangling about five feet away from the wall. Even if I swing, I couldn't use the building or my feet to help my descent anymore. Hand over hand, I lower myself, searching in the darkness for openings.

My feet hit a knot and I rest for a moment before beginning to lower myself again, only to discover the knot is at the end of the rope. There's nowhere left to go. Using my arms, I pull myself up a few feet and scramble to find the knot with my feet, but my muscles won't cooperate. They burn and scream, and the skin on my hands is slick with sweat, or possibly blood.

I look around me. No openings. Then down. Nothing.

Hands cramping, I slip down the rope as my legs flail in nothingness. My throat tightens but I can't give up.

What use is a rope to nowhere? No use. And there's no piece of rope, no scrap of metal, no piece of fabric unused in Haven.

I spin my head around, searching. Surely if I swing, then push off the side of this building, there must be somewhere to leap to, but I can't see where. The next building is too far away and even if I could get there, it looks like sheer concrete.

Looking down, a sliver of light glints off a surface only ten or fifteen feet below. Blinking rapidly, then squinting, I try to bring it into focus but it's gone into the darkness.

My hands slip. I panic then let them slide until I'm holding the knot. My palms burn, my hands cramp. I close my eyes to think. Even if I can hold on until the sun's light reveals what's below me—doubtful—Comps will patrol at some point. There's no chance I can hold on much longer. Besides, I need to get home to Drake. There must be something below this rope.

I let go and drop.

Slam. My feet strike something with a loud clank. Pain shoots up from my ankle. I've twisted it but I've landed. And lived. My throat pinches. If I'd died or been arrested, what would have happened to Drake? I can't afford to dwell on that now.

Bending, I explore my surroundings in the darkness and discover slatted metal beneath my feet. I'm on a balcony, or a landing, jutting out from the side of the building. Crawling I find the wall, then a sheet of wood covering what used to be a window. It won't budge, and a chain and padlock explain why.

Great. Continuing to fumble, I crawl back to the balcony's edge and discover a lever. My heart sprints as I run my hands over what I'm quite sure is the top of a ladder that will drop down from this platform.

I pull the lever and the sound of clanging metal echoes in the quiet alleyway. With no way to silence it, I move down the ladder, hoping to race the noise and escape from whomever might hear. The last thing I need is for someone to come out to investigate, or call the Comps.

At the bottom of the ladder, it's still dark, but my eyes have adjusted to reveal the top of what looks like the door into the building. I must be near the ground.

I drop and land, knees bent, rolling to the side to absorb the impact. My ankle screams in protest, as do the scrapes, but I'm off the building; I've hit the surface. Relief floods my body, but I can't afford to rest. With all the leaps Burn made, I don't know where I am, but it won't take me long to figure that out. I have a fighting chance to get home. I wonder if Burn's been as lucky.

Who cares? It's safer for Drake and me if he gets expunged.

But I can't count on his being caught, and he must know where we live. I need a new place to hide Drake.

Worse, Burn's not the only danger we face. Someone in Management knows about Drake, and even if Cal believes he can warn us before the Comps come, I can't be certain. I can't risk Drake's life on Cal's assurances.

We are no longer safe.

CHAPTER EIGHT

SWEATING, HEART RACING, I'M OUTSIDE THE DOME, SUR-
rounded by Shredders. They've got me. I struggle to get free
but someone grips my shoulder.

"Hey," a familiar voice says. "You're dreaming."

I blink as light fills the space. The anxiety of last
night's escape from the Comps and my meeting with Burn
must have impacted my dreams. But I'm safe in our room.
It was Drake's hand on my shoulder. His shirt's off and a
cup of water and a cloth sit beside him. He's been washing.

As the puzzle pieces fall together, I keep my gaze on his
forehead and will my heart rate to slow.

"Are you okay?" he asks, concern in his voice. "I was
asleep when you came in last night."

"I'm fine." I look down and wince. My ankle is purple and
swollen, and my scraped knees and hands left blood marks

on my blanket. Those won't come out even if I wash them today, and I can't. I'm due in GT.

"You missed curfew." Drake reaches for his shirt.

"So?" I turn my ankle in small circles, trying to block out the pain and stifle the emotions brought on by my dream.

"Don't take crazy chances, Glory."

Anger rises up and my glare locks on his. Instantly, his armor appears like scales of iron covering his torso. Ashamed, I look down.

He drags himself back onto his mattress and turns from me, crossing his arms over his chest. "No need to hurt me."

"I'm sorry."

He spins around. "Sorry's not good enough. You need to learn to control that."

I leap to my feet, holding back a cry as my ankle protests. "Like you know how to control *your* Deviance?"

He squares his jaw. "I didn't just try to hurt you."

Guilt rises in my throat. "I'm sorry. You know I'd never hurt you. Let's drop it, okay?"

He nods and someone knocks. It's probably just Jayma, but what if it's Burn? It might be too late to move Drake.

"Who's there?" I ask.

"Glory." It's Cal. "Open the door."

I spin around but Drake is already pulling on his long-sleeved shirt, even though his armor has disappeared. He pulls his blanket over his legs, arranging them to look natural.

"Just a minute." I pat down my hair, and then scold myself. Who cares about my hair?

"Turn out the light," I whisper to Drake. When he does, I limp, taking short breaths, and then open the door a crack. Cal's leaning at the door's side, his shirt tight against his arm muscles. He moves to enter but I put my hand on his chest and push back, sliding out the small opening and into the hall.

"Hi." His voice is deep and husky, and the sound of it sends a thrill through me. I can't believe I want him to kiss me again under these circumstances.

"Why are you here?" I ask.

Hurt and shock flash in his eyes.

"Sorry. I didn't mean it like that. It's just that I need to leave for GT."

"You've got a few minutes. I need to tell you something." He glances around. "Let's go inside."

I shake my head.

His lips twist and then he says, "Come to my place then." He takes my hand and pulls me forward. "What happened to your ankle?" He stops. "I knew I shouldn't have let you go home alone last night. Now that we're dating, it's my responsibility to keep you safe. I failed."

"I hurt it *after* I got home." I'm shocked at how easily I'm able to lie to Cal. It's not right.

Bending, he pulls my arm up and over his shoulder, and then wraps his hand around my waist. I have to admit it's easier to walk with his support, even though it means we need to walk sideways.

After we turn into the next corridor, we run into Jayma, her sleeve pushed up, no doubt to make her new bracelet more prominent. Happiness radiates from her face. "Ready for GT?" She cocks her head to the side. "Aren't you working today, Cal?"

"Day off," he says. "And Glory might be a few minutes late for GT. Tell your instructor—" He pauses. "Don't tell her anything."

"You'll get in trouble," Jayma says. "If Mrs. Cona gives you a bad performance evaluation, it'll affect your work placement. That means the rest of your life." Jayma sounds so much like her mother sometimes, which makes me miss mine.

I wish I could ask Mom's advice now. She'd know whom I could trust, and she'd help me understand my feelings for Cal—how I can go icy-cold thinking about his joining the Jecs and yet buzz with heat when he's near.

"I'll be there soon." I reach out and take her hands. "I just need a minute to talk to Cal. You go on ahead. Don't worry." Right now, I wouldn't care if I got assigned to Custodial, Sewage, or the President's Office. With all that's happened the past two days, my career's unimportant.

She runs her hand over her dating license and a soft smile creeps onto her face. "I don't want to be late. I'll catch up with Scout."

"Jayma," I call after her, then turn to Cal. "Just a minute, okay?"

He nods and I step forward slowly, readjusting to the pain in my ankle.

"What happened to your leg?" Jayma asks.

"It's nothing." I wave my hand. "I need to ask you something important." I lean in close. "If anything happens, promise me that you'll take care of Drake."

She pulls back and stares into my eyes as if looking for the reason I'm saying this, and I wish I could tell Jayma about Burn and his claim that my father's alive. I wish I could tell her Cal's in the Jecs. I wish I could tell her I'm a Deviant. But I can't share all my secrets with anyone.

"Why are you asking me this?" Alarm registers on her face. "Did Cal go beyond the terms of your license? Do you need me to call HR?"

"No. It's nothing like that. Really. I just need to know you'd watch out for him."

"Of course." She squeezes my hand. "Of course I'd look after Drake. You know I would."

My heart fills with love for my friend.

"Are you really okay?"

I nod. "Go to class. I'll see you later."

She kisses my cheek and runs off down the hall.

When I turn, Cal has approached and lifts me into his arms. "We'll be faster this way."

"No"—I push back from his chest—"put me down. If I don't use my ankle, it'll stiffen up." Truth is, I love being in his arms too much and can't risk letting my emotions race out of control. Not after I've confirmed that my Deviance hurts humans.

He sets me down but keeps his arm around me as we walk through a maze of corridors across to the apartment he shares with Scout and their parents. He opens the door and I turn to him with a question in my eyes.

"No one's home." His cheeks flush and his hair falls in front of his eyes in the way that I love.

I step inside. Their apartment must be more than twice the size of Drake's and mine and is open at the side to the dome, giving a full view of the next building and the sloping sky above. Waist high, a railing stretches across the opening that must have once contained glass, and I hope the rail was placed lower when Cal and Scout were small. Fabric screens stand on opposite sides of the room, giving a little privacy to the spaces where the family sleeps. There's also a chair, with metal legs and a dark green plastic seat. What a luxury.

"It's beautiful," I say. "Speaking of apartments"—I draw a deep breath—"I need to move."

"Move?"

"Yes. Now that I know about that list you found, it's just a matter of time before they come for Drake. I can't let that happen." *I can't mention the other reason: Burn.*

"I told you." He puts his hands on my shoulders. "I'll keep you safe."

"I know you'll do your best but—"

He shakes his head. "You need to stay here. If you move, I won't be able to protect you."

"But—" I can't carry Drake on my own over much of a distance. It will be easier if he helps. "I'm moving. It's already decided. Will you help me?"

"Glory, you're safe here. I'm certain."

"How can you be certain?"

He drops his hands from my shoulders. "That's why I wanted to talk to you." He grins. "I'm certain because of Mr. Belando—you remember, the VP of Compliance we talked to?"

My heart thuds. I step back. "You told him about Drake?"

"No." His eyes broadcasting hurt, he continues, "I was going to tell you this last night, but . . ."

"But what?" I cross my arms over my chest.

"You know I'm not supposed to talk about Jecs business."

"Yet you expect me to trust you?"

Red flares on his cheeks. "Do you want to hear this or not?"

I nod, nerves racing.

"Yesterday, Mr. Belando gave a speech to the Jecs and made the department's priorities clear. There are no plans to actively seek Parasites. Not until we've contained the Deviant problem." He beams as if this is the best news ever and I chew on the inside of my lip. The words *contain* and *problem* rankle, even though I've heard words like that my whole life.

He traces his fingers down my arms to my hands. "See? There's no need to move."

I study Cal's face, searching for deception, seeing none. Cal believes he can protect Drake. But I can't relax—not while I'm still facing the danger of Burn.

He pulls me into an embrace. "Everything is falling into place. If I get into Comp Training, we can afford a posh apartment on a lower floor, where the air is cool and clean. Maybe we'd even have water on our level."

At this moment, in the relative safety of Cal's arms, it would be easy to drift into fantasy land, to trust him fully and believe he can keep Drake safe. It would be easy to believe I can have an easier life, a normal life, but I can't. An easy life is not in my future.

I will always be a Deviant.

CHAPTER NINE

BECAUSE I WAS TARDY, MRS. CONA MAKES ME STAY LATE at the end of the day. Jayma offers to wait, but I tell her to head home with Scout. Remembering they can walk together alone now, she doesn't argue for long, and I'm on my best behavior, helping our GT instructor clean chalk dust from the walls and gather up fragments from the floor so they can be reformed into new chalk sticks for future generations. When I'm finally released, I rush home.

With my brow sweating from the pain in my ankle, I open the door and pause.

Jayma's there. I slide into the room. Drake's sitting on his mattress, a look of alarm on his face.

"What are you doing here?" I ask her.

She shoots up from where she was sitting on the floor. "I've been talking to Drake. He invited me, remember? I came to tell him you were kept late, and he shouldn't worry."

"It's great that you came." I hug her hello. "I was just surprised, that's all."

Drake's still not sporting the huge smile I'd expect. Maybe he's disappointed I interrupted the only alone-time he's had with his crush? But his eyes look like he's trying to tell me something. Does he want me to go?

Jayma sits on the floor in front of my brother, then looks up to me, which seems to increase Drake's discomfort. His expression's tight.

"Drake has been explaining those geometry equations that I messed up on the last quiz. It's no wonder you do so well, Glory. If I had to repeat our lessons to someone every day, more might stick." She smiles. "Since he can't take a work placement, I figured Drake didn't need training." She cuts herself off and looks down.

Drake clears his throat and draws our attention. "Jayma, did I show you my new drawings?" He points to a place low on the opposite wall, and as she turns to look, he nods up to the ceiling while looking at me.

I glance up and gasp. *Burn.*

His back is to the ceiling. He holds himself suspended by pressing his hands and feet into the opposite walls of our five-foot-wide room. Facing down, he shakes his head then shoots his eyes toward Jayma. I drop to the mattress.

It's a small miracle she hasn't noticed him above her, and I'm thankful for our ten-foot ceilings. One advantage of the Pents. I need to distract her, to make sure she doesn't look up. I cough.

She turns and puts a hand on my shoulder. "I hope you're not coming down with something."

"Maybe you should go." I cough again and nerves buzz through me. "If I am sick, you wouldn't want to catch it." I rub my ring.

She pushes up from the floor and puts her hand on my forehead. "You're flushed."

"It was nice of you to stop by." I keep my tone bright and turn toward the door.

Her smile fades. "You're trying to get rid of me."

"I need to rest. My ankle hurts."

"I thought you said you wanted to keep it mobile."

"It's tired." My neck cramps, straining to keep from looking up.

"See you later, Jayma," Drake says. "Thanks for coming." Kicking Jayma out must be breaking his heart.

"I'll see if Scout's done with his chores." Jayma's lips smile but her eyes don't. She's hurt and I don't know how to fix it. Right now I have much bigger problems—like the huge, scary boy pressed against my ceiling.

Jayma pauses mid-slide through the door and whispers. "What's up with your brother?" Her forehead wrinkles. "First he wants me to come by more often, and then when I do, he acts all strange, like my being here is some kind of intrusion."

I slide out into the hall. "I'm sure it's nothing." I hope my voice doesn't sound as tight as it feels. "I'll find out."

Jayma squeezes my arm. "Don't forget to take care of yourself, too." She kisses my cheek and pulls me into a hug.

I want to crumple into her but I stiffen so she'll release

me, then I slip back into our room, terrified that Burn has killed Drake. But our intruder's leaning against the back wall as if he lives here.

Rage building, I glare directly into his eyes, but he's too smart and quickly looks away. "Leave my brother alone."

"It's fine," Drake says, as if Burn's being here is the most normal thing in the world. "Dad sent him."

"We don't have a dad."

Drake leans back on his arms and looks at Burn like they're long-lost friends who can't decide how to deal with me.

At the moment, *I* don't know how to deal with me and I stare at the wall, focusing on Drake's meticulous drawing of the streets and buildings around the Hub. How he uses a nail to scratch his intricate drawings, how he remembers places in such detail when he hasn't been there since he was ten, astounds me. As hard as it will be to leave these drawings behind, at least the walls in our new home might provide a fresh canvas.

Burn pushes off the back wall. "Gather all the water and food you can. Not much else. The moon is on the lowest cycle setting tonight, so there's good cover. We leave at 4:00 a.m., during the Comps' shift change. I'll carry Drake. Glory, you're on your own."

"Gather our stuff to go where?" I ask.

"I'll tell you later."

"You'll tell me now."

He ignores me and forgetting my ankle, I stomp toward him. "You're not our boss."

"Shit," he says. "When did you get hurt?"

Ignoring his language—using that word is strictly off-policy—I stand more solidly on my sore ankle. "We're not going anywhere with you."

"I'm going." Drake's voice cracks. He winces, and then repeats his words in a lower teenager voice. "I'm going with him, whether you like it or not."

"Don't be crazy. He'll kill you."

"I can't live the rest of my life in this tiny room."

I crouch and put my hands on my brother's shoulders. "So, you'd rather die?" I shake him a little but his upper body's so strong, I don't have much effect. Hopefully my words do. He'll see the big picture.

Drake moves a hand to my arm. "I need to get out of here. Even if I die trying."

My heart nearly breaks and I search his eyes for hidden meanings, all the while rubbing my ring for safety, but Drake seems sincere and determined to leave. *Why?*

I spin toward Burn. "Can you influence people's thoughts?" I have no idea about the bounds of Burn's Deviance.

He leans back, folds his arms over his chest and the muscles press against the fabric of his coat. "Can you?" He cocks an eyebrow.

I turn back to my brother and fight to keep calm. "Drake, why would you trust this stranger? I'm your sister. I'm the one who loves you. I'm the one who takes care of you. And you won't always be stuck in this tiny room. We're going to move to a new home. I found somewhere bigger, somewhere better, with a window and more light." At least that is my hope, not exactly the truth.

Burn grunts.

I spin back. "I've been taking care of my brother for three years. We don't need you."

Burn pulls a watch out of one of several pockets on his pants. I've never seen anyone below Management with a private timepiece. It must be stolen. "Four a.m. Be ready."

He yanks the door open, breaking the bracket, and strides into the hall, slamming the door behind him.

I rush to the door, but by the time I look out—mere seconds—he's vanished.

Bending over, I put my hands on my knees and suck in long breaths. Drake's right that he doesn't have much of a life right now. I should have recognized that sooner, but I can't blindly trust this boy who claims our father's alive. Not if I still have options.

Footsteps come from my right, so I crouch and pretend to brush dirt off my shoes, not even looking up to see who owns the passing patched brown boots that look like they've had several generations of previous owners.

I must find us a new place to live. Fast. I don't know who's more dangerous—the Comps or Burn.

Casting my eyes down, I plead with the man who controls the rentals on the roof.

"I only need a small space."

It's nearly ten, the sun's light faded hours ago, and I'm past curfew. I've run out of time—and money—handing over twenty ration points to even gain directions to this hellhole that smells like urine, soiled clothing and despair.

I can live with that.

"Got no vacancies." The man strokes his long, gray beard. "No space at all."

I glance around the cluttered array of lean-tos and boxes that pass as homes for the roof's inhabitants. "What about way over there, at the edge?"

The light there from the nicer building across the street would compensate for the lack of electricity. I've yet to discover how anyone cooks food up here. The prospect of raw rat meat is repulsive, but I'll cross that bridge when I come to it.

"Can't build there," the man says. "Too visible." He grabs my chin and forces me to look up at him. "You a spy? One of them Jecs kids?"

I shake my head as his rough fingers tighten on my face. I suspected this roof residence was undocumented and full of Parasites. Now it's confirmed.

He grabs my shoulders and his bony fingers dig into my flesh. "'Cause I'll toss you off this roof before I let you rat me out."

"I'd never." This man's kidding himself if he thinks the Comps don't know he's up here. More likely he pays some Comp on the take. Every year, more and more Haven employees are living in undocumented locations. There's just not enough room. The Comps largely ignore the off-policy dwellings, only clearing one or two of the many rooftops and bridge settlements each year to keep the fear levels spiked.

"You've gotta give me a reason to trust you, girly." The man's fingers knead my upper arms. "You ain't even scared."

I force my eyes to widen and my lips to tremble. Who knew there was a downside to my ability to hide my emotions? "Please, I'm an orphan. My last landlord, he"—I let my lips tremble some more—"he harassed me, t-touched me. I need to move."

Mr. Gray Beard loosens his grip but doesn't let go. I can tell that he's reconsidering, but it's not clear whether he's taken pity on me or whether he's hoping to sexually harass me himself. I'd kill anyone who tried.

He lets one hand slide down my arm to grab my elbow and then pulls me down a narrow gap between shacks. I stumble beside him, trying not to kick down the sides of anyone's dwelling. A few dirty-faced kids peek out between sheets of filthy draped fabric, their eyes like dull points of light in the darkness.

Stopping abruptly, he spins me and points to a gap about three feet wide and ten feet deep. "You can sleep here," he says.

"Th-thank you." I try to sound meekly grateful but already my mind's scrambling. We might be able to fit our two mattresses end to end in this space. Barely. And we'll forgo comfort and use our bedding to build a roof of sorts until I can scrounge something else. Keeping Drake hidden from the other tenants is priority number one. While I doubt there are any Jecs up here, I expect there are people desperate enough to gladly trade information about a boy with paralyzed legs.

I have no idea how I'll manage to get my brother onto this roof—the only route involves climbing a rope. While Drake's upper body is strong, he hasn't climbed one in years.

"I'll take it." I hand over the last of my ration points.

He grunts. "Not enough."

"I can get more. Lots more." I can't, but I can only tackle one problem at a time.

"Welcome home." He smiles with a nearly toothless grin.

CHAPTER TEN

WHEN I GET BACK TO OUR FLOOR, CAL'S STANDING IN THE open space near the east stairs, talking to someone around the corner and out of my sightline. His face is pale and sweating as if he's eaten rotten rat. I instinctively hold back, then move forward to assess the risk.

I freeze as soon as I gain an angle to see. Comps. Cal's talking to a group of Compliance Officers in full gear. From this angle I only see two, but I hear a loud clunk as another one shifts. Cal promised to warn me of any raids. He lied.

My body caves in, crushing my lungs, making it difficult to breathe. I slam back against the wall. He betrayed me. His attention was all a trick. I should have known better. Only silly girls lose their judgment around boys, and I've just proven myself to be one. Something I swore I'd never do.

One of the Comps turns toward me. "You. Come here," he says and I back away.

Cal lunges toward me but I turn and run.

"Glory, stop!" Cal shouts. "The officers have questions."

"Halt!" The Comp's voice follows me as I race away, desperate to get to Drake.

Not hearing them behind me, I slow down after I turn the next corner. It's either slow down or start pushing my neighbors aside. Clearly the Comps' presence is known, and many of my neighbors are milling in the halls, talking in hushed tones. I keep my gaze down and don't greet anyone.

Shaking, I slip into our room. Time to move Drake, although I'm not sure how. "We need to go," I tell him. "Now."

"Did Burn come early?"

"No."

"What's going on?" Drake's armor rises and he slips on his gloves.

My heart sinks at the futility of the precautions I've taken. As soon as the Comps walk in here, both my brother's injury and his Deviance will be spotted. It doesn't matter what horrors might occur in the Hospital; he'll never get there. He'll be expunged. A shiver traces through me as I imagine my little brother Outside, unable to run, defenseless against the dust and the Shredders. The best I can hope is we'll be exed together.

"What's going on?" Drake's voice is harder and deeper than normal. "Tell me."

"Comps."

His eyes snap open. "What do we do?"

"I found us a new place."

Drake grabs his water and our meat and stuffs it all into his pockets. He snatches his pillowcase and I realize it's already filled with nearly everything else we own, even though I haven't told him we're moving, yet. Did he really think I'd let him go with Burn?

I yank the ends of the blanket out from under the mattress beneath him, then pull the edges next to his hips. I spread his legs apart, turn, and crouch between them.

"Grab my shoulders," I tell him. "Now." I clutch the edges of the blanket.

He slings the pillowcase forward as he wraps his arms around my shoulders. Then, holding the blanket, I lean forward and pull him onto my back. He's on me, piggyback style but dangling, nearly choking me with his overlapped forearms, and he's so much taller and heavier than the last time I carried him. I tug the ends of the blanket forward, hoping and praying it's tucking around his backside and thighs.

I carefully secure his legs inside the blanket and tie it firmly in front of me. He slips but then grips with his elbows and pulls himself up higher as I lean forward and adjust the knot. This might work as long as I lean forward. Some people carry laundry and other bulky items this way, so as long as he keeps his head and limbs hidden we might pull this off. I still have no idea how I'll get up or down ladders or ropes, or what I'll say to anyone who confronts us, but I've run out of options. We've got to leave. Now.

I take the pillowcase and peek out the door. Cal's striding toward me. I slam the door shut.

"Glory." Cal pushes on the door. I push back.

"Let me in," he says. "Or come talk to the Comps. If you cooperate, they'll leave you alone."

Me, maybe. But Cal's assuming I'd sacrifice Drake, adding to the evidence I was wrong to trust him, blinded by my hormones, by my fantasy of us as a couple.

"Glory," he says through the door. "Let me in. I can help."

Not seeing an alternative—he's drawing attention—I open the door a crack and he slides inside. Cal looks scared.

My last puff of optimism rises. "Help me get Drake past the Comps?"

His jaw hardens. "Too late. There's no way past them." He looks guilty and nervous, which isn't like Cal, and I don't like the feeling, not at all.

I slam my fists into his chest. "You promised to warn me." I raise my fists to strike again but he grabs my wrists before they connect. The dating bracelet digs into my skin.

"Glory. I'm sorry." He drops my wrists. "I didn't—"

"Sorry isn't good enough." I make eye contact and latch on, but before I can do any damage, I chicken out and look away. I'm useless. How can I protect my brother if I can't even use my curse against those who've betrayed him?

"You said you'd protect Drake." My voice is strained and I'm in danger of letting my emotions explode.

Cal squeezes my upper arm. "Come with me. We'll talk to the Comps. You and me. If you run, you'll make it worse."

I bite down the retorts I want to hurl back and pull away. "How could this possibly get any worse?"

Cal wipes sweat off his forehead. "They haven't found

Drake yet and . . . maybe the Hospital's not so bad. I'll talk to Mr. Belando."

Drake tenses. His armor hardens and presses into the skin of my back.

"Leave!" I shout.

As soon as Cal's gone, I'll head in the opposite direction. I'm not sure how, or if, we'll get off the floor, but if the Comps came to arrest a Parasite with paralyzed legs, they might not have covered all the exits, especially the ones requiring ropes.

"Go. Now." My voice is solid ice.

Cal looks hurt and confused as he backs from the room. I don't care.

I close the door in his face and then Drake pokes his head out from under the blanket. "Put me down, Glory. Save yourself. Leave before the Comps come. Find Burn. He'll take you to Dad."

"Dad is dead." My words are sharp like freshly cut tin.

A scraping sound comes from the back wall.

I turn. A huge serrated knife slices through the wall, low to the floor. The Comps have us surrounded. They're cutting though the back of our apartment.

Drake leans over my shoulder and he's—smiling?

"It's Burn." Drake wiggles and then slips off my back, and I realize that while I've been so distracted he managed to loosen the knots of the blanket sling. "He showed me that knife before. It's super sharp and strong."

"What are you doing?" I grab for him but he drops to the floor in a heap.

"I'm going through that hole," he says. "You follow and pull the storage box in front once we're through." He grabs his packed pillowcase with his teeth and drags himself toward the wall.

His excitement seems unbelievably misplaced. Even if he's right and it *is* Burn making a hole in the wall, going through it will just lead to death by way of a different route.

But I hear the heavy footsteps of Comps in our hall and realize I'd do anything not to face them, do anything to prolong the time until Drake is captured. I can't give up.

With a thud, the section of wall falls into our room, leaving a hole. Burn's arms thrust through. He grabs the pieces of wall he cut out and pulls them into the room he's in.

Mind scrambling, I can't even think whose dwelling butts up against that wall, and the more I try to remember, the more confused I become. Spatial skills are not my strong suit and I'm still stunned and frozen in place when I notice that Drake is pulling himself by his arms toward the hole more quickly than I've ever seen him move—even when he had use of his legs. Before I can grab him, Burn has pulled Drake through the narrow hole.

"Wait." I dive onto my belly and slide toward the hole, grasping for my brother's feet. Burn's strong, hard hands latch onto my arms and pull me forward.

The second I'm through, I scramble over to Drake and put my arms around him. "Are you hurt?"

"Burn wouldn't hurt me."

"You're too trusting." I grasp my brother's shoulders. "You haven't seen enough of the world to know."

Burn grunts. "Like you've seen the world." He reaches back into our apartment and pulls the wooden box, which serves as both table and food storage, to block the hole. After standing, he grabs a huge piece of wooden furniture. It's taller than me and has doors on the front. He picks it up and sets it down to block this side of the hole.

"It will have to do." Burn strides over to the window.

I have no idea whose apartment we're in, but luckily, whoever lives here isn't home, or if they were, Burn scared them off. The tall cupboard-like thing that Burn moved isn't the only big piece of furniture in this place, and I start to wonder if maybe we're in the home of the Tenant Liaison. No one else living up this high could afford so many nice things. Against the wall a mattress sits on some kind of a platform raised off the floor. Overhead there are three light bulbs covered by a pretty glass case that filters the light to disperse it evenly, and against the wall lean wooden shelves stacked with rows and rows of books. The library only allows one book out at a time, so I assume these books must be owned. Imagine such luxuries.

While I'm distracted by the opulence—there's a rug on the floor!—Burn throws off his long coat, grabs Drake, and puts him up on his back.

"I'll carry him." I reach for Drake.

Burn ignores me and instead straps some kind of harness under Drake's backside, and then pulls it forward and back over his head. He tightens it across his broad chest. Burn dons his oversized coat and my brother's like a small appendage attached to his back. Where Drake covered my back and then some, he's more like a backpack on the much larger Burn.

Letting Burn carry him is more practical, but my nerves snap in protest.

Burn strides to the window and picks up a rope he's tied to a steel girder where the frame for a window used to be. He's pulling it, measuring out lengths, then, choosing a place to grab hold, he wraps it around his thick wrist. "Are you coming?" He glares at me but is smart enough to turn away before I gain focus. He steps over the girder and balances precariously on the edge of the building.

On Burn's back, my brother hangs helplessly out the window. If Burn releases those straps, or they break, my brother will fall to his death.

"Why use the rope?" I point to the adjacent building. "Why not jump across there?" I've seen the power in his legs.

"Too far down. Plus, too risky right now."

"Why?" Maybe if I reason with him, he'll step back into the room, instead of leaning out of it, and I can figure out a way to get Drake off his back. "If someone sees you taking Drake, what difference does it make if you're climbing down a rope or jumping through the air?"

"Stupid to advertise my gift."

"Gift?"

"Deviance." He says the word like it tastes bad, and then rechecks the straps holding Drake. Yanking the rope, as if to test its hold one final time, he looks up to me. "Are you coming or not?"

"Halt. Compliance!" someone yells and the door bursts

open. Three Comps, followed by Cal, crash into the room; their heavy boots boom against the wooden floors.

Burn grabs my arm.

"Let her go," Cal calls out. "Stop him."

Indecision grabs my belly. Should I stay? Trust Burn with my brother?

The Comps point their shockers but don't shoot, and I realize that if they hit Burn, all three of us will fall out of the thirty-two-story window.

"Now or never," Burn nearly growls in my ear.

"Glory, I love you," Cal says and my indecision vanishes.

Cal's a liar. He betrayed me. Betrayed my brother.

I'll miss Jayma, but beyond that there's nothing left for me here.

I nod to Burn, he clamps his arm around my waist and, holding the rope in one hand, jumps back.

My heart leaps to my throat as we fall.

CHAPTER ELEVEN

"**C**AN I AT LEAST MOVE?" I SHIFT AGAINST THE BULK OF BURN'S body. "Trust me. I won't leave without my brother."

For what feels like hours, he's had me pinned beside him in the corner of this tiny space he pushed me into after we dropped from the window. All I know is we're below ground level, underneath our building, in a small space that's dark and dirty. He's only cranked his torch once, just so Drake and I could see that we were both present and unharmed. I can hear my brother breathing, moving every now and again, but otherwise I'm blinded in the complete darkness.

It's fine for Burn. His strange glasses are special goggles that let him see in the dark. My skin crawls, thinking how he can see me but I can't see him. Having any boy so near right now turns my stomach, never mind one as scary as Burn. Over the past hours, I've searched for another explanation for the Comps' arrival on our floor, their pursuit, Cal's involvement—but I keep landing at the same conclusion.

Cal betrayed me and the weight of the truth is almost as heavy as Burn. Worse, every few moments his betrayal stabs me, poking holes in my confidence and belief in my judgment. Have I done the wrong thing again, by trusting Burn to help us escape?

"What is this place?" I ask.

"Bottom of a garbage chute." Burn's deep voice fills the space.

"What's a garbage chute?" Drake asks, sounding genuinely curious.

"Before The Dust"—Burn shifts, moving me—"people dropped their garbage down here from the upper floors."

"What's garbage?" Drake asks. While I've heard the word, I can't remember what it means.

"Waste. Scraps," Burn says. "Things people don't need."

"He asked an honest question." I poke Burn's hard arm. "The least you could do is give him an honest answer." I cross my arms over my chest and wonder if he can see my gesture in the dark. I have no idea which way he's looking. But if he wants me to believe there was a time when people simply threw things away, dropped them down some kind of chute, he really must think me gullible.

"What did they throw away?" Drake asks.

"Skins. Bones," Burn answers. "Pits from fruit. Old clothes. Things people didn't want."

"Wow." Drake sounds more like ten than thirteen. "BTD everyone in Haven must have been rich."

"Guess so."

"If they threw away food scraps," Drake asks, "how did they make soil?"

"Yes," I say. "Your story about garbage doesn't make sense."

"Soil just formed." Burn's voice is low and deep, but reveals no annoyance at our questioning.

"By magic?" Drake asks.

"No, not magic," Burn says. "Things in nature automatically decompose into soil."

"What's nature?" Drake asks.

"Plants and animals—but not on a farm. Okay, on a farm, too. But not like the farms in Haven. Farms in the open air, not inside factories."

"Cool."

Hearing Drake excited about Burn's stories, about anything, lifts my spirits and I start to relax. No longer straining against Burn's bulk, his weight pushing against me starts to feel more like a blanket than a burden.

"How long will we stay here in the dark?" Drake asks.

"Not much longer." Burn shifts his legs against mine. "We'll wait until they've stopped searching this area."

"How do you know where they're searching?" I ask. "Can you read the Comps' minds or sense their presence?" I intended this as sarcasm. But after saying it, I realize I have no idea what abilities come with Burn's Deviance. All I know is he scares me.

"I've studied the Comps' patterns, their routines," Burn answers calmly, not taking the bait my tone tossed out.

"When we get out of here," I say, "I could use your help getting Drake to our new home."

"New home?"

"I found us a new place to live."

Burn grunts. "That roof? You can't live there."

My nails dig into my palms. "You were following me?" Of course he was.

He doesn't answer.

"I suppose you've got a better plan?" I try to move my legs. "What is it?"

"You'll find out soon enough."

"I'll find out now, or we won't go anywhere with you." Frustration builds inside me, and I wish I could think of a way to escape this situation without relying on Burn. I don't trust him.

"He's taking us to see Dad." My brother sounds as if he's being taken on an adventure, or out for a treat.

"Drake"—I rub Mom's ring—"Dad can't be alive. On the off chance that he is, he's a Shredder. I'm sorry to be so harsh about it, but it's the truth."

"Is he a Shredder?" Drake's voice quavers.

"No." Burn's voice is low. "Your Dad's fine. Trust me."

Drake's hand lands on my foot. "We'll be a family again."

Not a family. Not without Mom. My insides cave in like I'm using my curse against myself. An aching pain traces through me, but I replace it with rage. "Even if Dad's alive, how can you be excited to see him? He killed Mom. He ruined our family. Ruined everything."

Burn whispers something I can't hear.

"What?"

Burn shifts. "First things first. We need to get past the Comps."

I grit my teeth, but he's right. This is no time to cry over what's lost. I need to be practical, think of what's ahead, even though it's veiled with uncertainty.

I move my arm and the dating license digs into my wrist. Suddenly, it's like the bracelet's made of acid. I twist and wrench, sliding it down. The pain's so intense I wonder if I'm breaking my bones, but finally I slide it off. Pulling my hand back, I start to toss the license but stop. I don't want to hit Drake with the offensive projectile and—I'm not ready to throw out the past.

I shove it into my pocket. In spite of my disappointment in Cal, my anger at Burn, and my determination to survive, sadness creeps inside me, pinching and poking into every available opening. I'm tempted to yield. To let sadness overtake me. To complain. To cry. But I won't. I've worked too hard to block my emotions, and dwelling on the past few days—how everything became so wonderful then horrible all at once—is dangerous.

Feeling sorry for myself won't do any good. I need a plan. And if Burn's not lying, if he really is taking us to see our father, I'll have a chance to confront him, to accuse him, to show him the depth of my hate and—a chill races through me—my hate kills.

"We shouldn't go this way," I tell Burn. "Too close to the Hub."

He turns toward me, a scowl on his face. Drake's still under the oversized coat, except now he's strapped onto Burn's chest, facing him, like Drake's an infant. I have to admit that unless I look closely, it's hard to tell he's there. It's more like Burn's even huger and bulkier.

Limping, I rush to keep up and then tug on his arm. "If we go to the Hub, we'll get caught."

Burn turns to me, fire in his eyes. "Quiet," he says, "and keep moving. Fast."

He turns sharply into an alley that's so narrow his shoulders rub on both sides. The light grows even darker as the slowly brightening sky is blocked by short bridges between the buildings above us. He turns another corner and I recognize this alley. It's the alley where I first saw Burn, and it leads directly to the Hub.

He stops and I slam into his back. He looks around quickly and then goes down on one knee.

"Don't be scared, Drake," I say. "I'm right here."

"Hush." With a swipe of his arm, Burn pushes me back against the wall, then scans the alley for movement. Bending, he rubs his hands over a rough spot on the road until his finger catches a small metal ring. Hooking the ring with his index finger, he lifts a huge iron disk as if it weighs nothing, right from the surface of the road. It reveals a deep, dark hole. Great. He's going to toss us into a pit.

"You first." He points to the hole and I try to shake my head, but my neck's seized in fear.

"Take the ladder," he says. "Wait at the bottom. Move. Now." His voice is quiet but comes out with cannon force.

When I don't move he adds, "You're not strong enough to pull the cover shut behind us, so if you're coming, you're first. Move—now."

My body sparks into action. I crouch down, and after verifying that there is, in fact, a ladder starting just below the road's surface, I reach for the top rung. But before I can get a good grip, Burn lifts me and shoots my legs down the hole. I stifle a scream, but he lowers me slowly enough to give me a chance to catch the ladder with my hands and feet. In seconds, the light disappears as Burn and Drake move into the hole above me.

Vibrations from the ladder buzz through my hands and arms and shoulders, so I quicken my pace to avoid having one of his huge boots land on my fingers. This is crazy. I'm climbing down into a bottomless pit with no light or end but it's not like the streets above are safer. Not for us. Not anymore.

My foot reaches down for a rung, but doesn't find one. Moving down, I stretch, my leg searching for the ground. What now?

Burn's pounding feet continue above me then stop. "Jump!" he barks.

Drawing a deep breath, I push off and let go, bending my legs in anticipation. The impact sends pain shooting up my spine and into my joints. My injured ankle screams in protest.

"Out of the way!" Burn yells.

I leap back and air rushes past me as he lands with a huge thump inches away.

"Drake?" I need to hear his voice.

"I'm fine." He barely sounds scared, and while I'm relieved, I almost want to be angry. Doesn't he know that he's strapped to the body of a crazy and dangerous boy who could very well plan to eat us for dinner?

Burn turns on a torch that reveals a small space. It's a miracle I didn't slam my head on the wall when I jumped back. Another few inches and I'd have knocked myself out. Burn loosens his coat and Drake lifts his face from Burn's chest.

"You okay?" Burn asks.

Drake grins. He actually grins.

"Once we go through there"—Burn gestures to a door I just noticed—"keep close to me and don't talk. Look like you know where you're going. We need to move quickly, make sure no one stops us to ask for our numbers."

"What's out there?" I ask.

"A mall. Only Management's allowed, but we need to cut through it to get to the tunnel's entrance."

"What's a mall?" Drake asks and I'm glad, because I want to know, too.

"A mall's a cluster of underground stores with a corridor down the middle." Burn turns to me. "Act like you belong."

I stifle a laugh. Since I discovered my curse, all I've done is pretend to belong. "Did you mention a tunnel?"

Burn nods without really answering. I know from Cal that Haven has a series of tunnels running outward from the main city like spokes. Since the city boundaries are fixed, there's no other way to expand, and from what I understand, most of them are used for storage and manufacturing. Burn must live in the tunnels.

"Keep close," he says gruffly. "And be quiet."

He opens the door, and then wraps his arm around my waist, pulling me into his side. I feel Drake's leg through the coat and hope we're not hurting him. He can't feel but he can bruise.

But any thoughts of protest are overtaken by the sights and smells around me. It's like we've walked out into an entirely different city, something from a story. It's well lit down here and the colors are overwhelming. It's not that I've never seen colors before, but these are so much brighter and stronger, as if everything else I've seen has been muted, painted over by a thin film of gray. My dingy jacket that I thought was green, looks brown.

And the smells. Fresh fruits and vegetables cover tables at the front of some shops—just sitting there!—and I wonder how the shopkeepers prevent people from stealing. I don't see any Comps, but there must be cameras. I look around but don't see any. A woman, dressed in a bright red dress and high-heeled shoes, made out of shiny black leather, studies an apple and then places it into a small basket along with a leafy plant that's as big as a head. She picks up something yellow that looks fresh and shiny with a green stem at its top, and then she steps up to the shopkeeper and hands him a card that he scans and passes back to her.

"Don't draw attention," Burn hisses in my ear.

A woman passes us with a question in her eyes. We stand out down here, especially if I'm struggling against his hold, so I stop doing that. I understand Burn's concern. We need to get through this mall place quickly, before someone calls the Comps to report us, but I can't help peering into a few shops.

A scent hits my nostrils and I almost stumble. My head snaps to the side to locate its source, and there's a store with long, light-brown lumps of something that smells better than freshly cooked rat. Even better than that cucumber Cal fed me. Above the shop window a sign reads Bakery.

"What's that?" I ask Burn as softly as I can.

"It's called bread. Keep moving."

I try but the variety and quantity of goods for sale, the brightness down here, morph my amazement to anger. What a contrast to the sad-looking rations we line up for each week. My friends and I survive on rat, rehydrated gruel, and, if we're lucky, one or two fresh things a pay period—yet this is how Management lives?

Adding insult to injury, this so-called mall, with its unbelievable riches, is hidden right below the Hub, where they dole out our gray rations and gather us to watch as our friends and neighbors and fathers are exed.

Another shop window captures my attention with its bright flashing lights, and I slip away from Burn to take a closer look. The shop is fronted with real glass. Behind that lies at least a dozen screens—just like the ones up high in the Hub but smaller. Displayed in front of each screen is a sign with a number, amounts that don't make sense as prices: ration points don't go that high. Surely these screens aren't meant for personal use? No one has a private TV. Imagine.

The screens all change at once—to a photo of Burn. The air presses out of my lungs. I'm in the next image. It's blurry, but it's clearly Burn holding my wrist and pulling me toward the window we escaped from last night.

Given Burn's long coat and the way his body's turned, at least the photo doesn't show Drake. Words under the image read: Promising Young Employee Kidnapped by Deviant Terrorist.

CHAPTER TWELVE

I BLINK AT THE SCREEN, NOT QUITE BELIEVING MY EYES. I'M not positive that Burn *isn't* a terrorist, but I'm shocked to learn that the Comps interpreted what they saw as a kidnapping. I can't decide whether this is good or bad news, and more to the point, whether it's the truth or a misunderstanding. But even if we have been kidnapped, I can't call for help. Compared to the Comps, Burn's our best bet.

He grabs my arm, and as I'm dragged down the hall, I focus on the shiny floor tiles to avoid showing my face to the crowd or possible security cameras. "Did you see those screens?" I ask quietly.

He doesn't answer, but his fingers tighten on my arm and he quickens his pace, keeping his head lowered, too. Footsteps race behind us, getting closer, and my heart pounds so fast and hard everyone down here must hear it.

The steps get louder and by the time they overtake us I'm

ready to explode. But they turn out to be from a couple of kids, younger than Drake but in much finer clothes, chasing each other through the mall.

My shoulders unclench and relief floods up my throat, making me feel as if I might cry.

Burn pulls me to the side and quickly types a code into a keypad against the wall. The door in front of us opens and Burn tugs me forward. It's quiet, except for the low hum of generators. The entire hall—walls, ceiling, floor—is made of gray concrete, scarred by watermarks and crumbling in places. This looks more like the Haven I know. It could be almost any street, except it's underground.

While chasing Burn down the hall, I sneak a quick look into one of the rooms, filled with boxes and shelves—perhaps storage rooms for the shops. He stops in front of a door, types in another code, and the room we enter is dark and full of big wooden crates. I follow through the box maze until we hit the back wall, but before I have a chance to open my mouth and ask the plan, he's tapped the corner of a crate. I hear a click.

One of the crate's sides drops to reveal a ladder leading down a deep, dark hole. But this ladder seems more ominous than the last, like it's leading me away from everything I've ever known—with no chance to return.

Burn rips his coat off and starts loading its padded compartments with weapons he grabs from inside the crate—Long daggers, huge heavy sticks, and various scraps of sharp metal.

"What are you looking at?" Burn asks with a gruff voice

and then grabs three filter masks from hooks. He slings the one lacking an eye shield over his head, its straps to the front, then passes another one to Drake.

My brother's eyes widen as he runs his finger over the filter covering the mouth and nose of the mask. "Why do we need these?"

"Just a precaution." Burn thrusts one toward me, then throws his coat down the hole, and it lands with a distant clank.

I run my hand down Drake's leg, the one that was squished between me and Burn. While I don't feel anything wrong, it's not like I could feel a bruise. At least nothing's broken.

Burn leans his head back and looks down toward Drake on his chest. "You okay, buddy?"

"He's not your buddy." Events are spiraling out of control, and I feel like I'm about to explode.

"I'm fine," Drake says.

Burn points at the hole. "You coming?" He won't look directly at my eyes. "Your choice, but if you ever mention this entrance, or the way we got down into the mall to anyone—especially your little boyfriend—I'll kill you."

Paralyzed by his words, I realize I do have a choice. My Deviance is easier to hide than most, and although I don't want to trust someone else to protect my brother, this isn't about what's best for me. It's about Drake. Burn can move more quickly without my sprained ankle limping along. The Comps think I was kidnapped, so it's possible I can still live in Haven as if nothing happened.

But something did happen.

My chest heaves in and out with quick, shallow breaths. Even if I stay, nothing will be the same. Cal's betrayal twists inside me and emotions fire behind my eyes, clouding my thoughts. To make this decision, I need to take emotions out of the equation.

Burn bends and ducks under the top of the crate. "Last chance."

I rub my ring, trying to clear the fog in my head, trying to locate logic through all the murk.

"Time's up." Burn grabs my dust mask, hangs it up, then steps onto the ladder. With Drake on his chest, he barely fits, and when he's down to his waist he turns to grab a rope that pulls the side of the crate back up.

"Wait!" I shout and grab onto the edge of the wood. He stops pulling just before my fingers are crushed.

"At least let me say good-bye to my brother."

Burn releases the rope and the weight of the wood falls onto my arms. As I back up, and Burn lowers the side to the floor, I hear the clink of metal hitting the ground behind me. I don't turn.

"Say good-bye then." His voice is gruff and hard.

"Come with us, please?" Drake reaches an ungloved hand toward me. He's frightened; his armor is up. Burn hasn't said anything in reaction, so I assume he already knew Drake was Deviant. Of course he did.

"Keep safe." My voice cracks. "Be careful. I love you." I don't know what else to say.

Out in the hall, something thumps.

"Time to go. Now." Burn looks me in the eye and I see

more depth than I expect. Along with the frustration and urgency, I see a hint of compassion.

I have no reason to stay.

"Out of my way." I grab the dust mask.

Burn's lips almost move into a grin as he climbs out enough to let me get past him and onto the ladder. As I descend, I see what made the earlier clinking sound. My dating bracelet is on the concrete floor outside the crate. My breath catches but I ignore the sign of regret. Good riddance is more like it.

Besides, it's too late to climb back out to get it. The box closes, and for the second time today, I descend into the unknown. And this time there's no going back.

CHAPTER THIRTEEN

DARKNESS PRESSES IN ON ME, CRUSHING, GRINDING, CHOK-
ing, and I stumble, tightening my grip on Burn's coat. He
stops, presumably to make sure I'm still on my feet.

"Can't we use the light?" I ask in a whisper.

"Not yet."

"Drake?"

"I'm fine." His voice is hushed but strong.

Burn might be leading us to our deaths but at least we're
still both alive. Hearing my brother's voice instantly makes
me feel better. I put my hand out and touch the wall of the
tunnel, damp and slimy, and so close. Even with his night-
vision goggles, I can't understand how Burn's navigating
without slamming into its sides or top. Our pace has been
so fast I'm panting, and I shudder as a drop of sweat slithers
down my back.

"Ready to move?" Burn asks. He doesn't wait for a reply

before his coat slips out of my hand. I lunge, grabbing into the near darkness to find it again.

Assuming he doesn't plan to kill us, is this my life now? Life underground in the darkness, in this dank, stale air?

Living in the Pents my whole life, I've been jealous of the children of Management who lived on lower floors, where the air was clearer and cooler. Although I never imagined places like that underground shopping mall existed, I did know there was a layer of Haven under the streets. I always imagined it to be a magical place. While the mall didn't disappoint on that count, in fact it far exceeded my wildest fantasies in the boundless luxury department, it never occurred to me that anything underground could be as horrible as this. In Haven, lower levels mean higher status. Not the case here.

After countless steps, Burn stops and I slam into his back.

A whirring sound, followed by torchlight, floods the tunnel.

"You need to rest?" Burn's body is a hulking silhouette, and when he looks back I shake my head no.

"Drink." He hands me a bladder of water made of hides that must be from huge rats, and I take several gulps before handing it to Drake. He's still strapped on Burn's chest but turned forward now, his legs dangling.

The walls of the tunnel are stone here, not concrete. And except for the occasional blast mark, they almost seem natural, not manmade with wooden or steel supports like they were right after we entered. And the strange iron rails on the ground have gone.

I've walked all the way across Haven more than once and it feels like we've been walking much longer than that, but I can't be certain because we've made so many turns. I have a poor sense of direction, even with visual cues. "Where are we?"

"The meeting point," Burn says as if that means something. Then carefully holding Drake, he undoes the harness and sets my brother down against the wall of the tunnel. "We'll rest here and wait. He'll be here soon."

My body clenches. "Who?"

"Dad?" Drake asks.

"You'll see."

I decide to ignore Burn's non-answer and crouch to check my brother's legs.

"I'm fine, Glory." He swats my hands away.

Burn shrugs his coat off. "You comfortable?" he asks Drake. Without waiting for an answer, he folds the coat shielding all the weapons and puts it behind Drake's back like a cushion.

Burn sets the torch on the ground but it's fading. I pick it up and turn the crank. He doesn't object, rather he leans against the wall with his arms crossed over his chest, so I shine the light ahead of us. While it doesn't project very far, I can't see an end to the tunnel.

"Put that down and get some rest," Burn says.

"Don't tell me what to do." I shine the torch into his eyes,

He scowls as he squints. "Stop that."

"I need some answers."

He swats at the torch, so I aim the light away from his face. "How old are you?" I'm not sure why I want to know that—why it matters, why I put it at the top of a gazillion more important questions—but he keeps bossing me around and it's making me crazy.

He doesn't reply and I'm not surprised. Of course he wouldn't share a personal detail. That would make him human, vulnerable. Can't have that.

"Sixteen, maybe seventeen." He shifts his bulk on the stone wall.

"How come you're not sure?"

"Never knew my parents." His shoulders twitch. "Sit, rest. Try to sleep. You'll thank me later."

"Thank you for dragging me into this tunnel?"

He grunts but it's almost a laugh.

I step forward, shoulders back. "Are you making fun of me?"

"Not a chance." His dark eyes flash a smile in my direction as the light from the torch fades.

My eyes snap open in the near darkness. *Rat dung*, I curse under my breath. I fell asleep.

Next to me Drake is still out, and I'm glad at least that Burn didn't murder us while we slept. There's neither a sun light nor a moon light turned on down here, so there's no way to tell what time it is, or how long I slept, but I sense it wasn't long.

Muffled voices drift toward me and I realize that's probably what woke me. I turn and see the faint light of a torch, surrounded by two male shapes farther down the tunnel. I press my back into the stone for a moment and draw deep breaths, banishing the fear threatening to invade.

Slowly standing, keeping pressed against the wall, I creep toward the voices, not sure of my plan, but knowing I can't develop one unless I know what I'm dealing with. Eavesdropping seems the best strategy.

The shape on this side of the tunnel is Burn, no mistaking his height, and the other shape isn't nearly as tall or as broad. The unidentified man bends one leg at the knee to rest a foot against the wall of the tunnel behind him, then runs a hand down his bent thigh and drums his fingers on his knee.

I raise my hand to my mouth to stifle a gasp. I'd know that gesture anywhere.

Dad?

Joy rushes through me, rising, building, making me feel like I'm about to burst. I rush forward, but then catch myself and stop.

What is wrong with me? This monster killed my mother, paralyzed my brother, and left us to fend for ourselves, and now I'm acting the same way I did when I spotted my parents after being lost in the crowded Hub at age four. I'm acting like a baby.

And that's far from the only problem. Besides the fact that I let myself feel such an inappropriate emotion, what happened to my plan to be stealthy? Rushing forward like a little kid won't keep me hidden, won't help me learn what's going on. I know better than that, and letting a murderer see me certainly won't keep me alive.

My heart thumps in my chest, but neither of them heard my near outburst, so I creep forward more slowly until I'm about ten feet away. Keeping to the darkness, I listen.

"She's mostly scared," Burn says. "And angry."

"Dangerous?" My father asks and I want to yell out that I am, but I don't.

"Nah," he says. "Not really. She's got great control."

My father nods. "Good. She's a smart girl. I hoped she'd find a way to deal with it once she understood what was happening." He lifts his hand to scratch his head. "I should have been around to help her, though." His voice is deeper than I remember, more filled with gravel, and if I hadn't recognized the way he drums his fingers on his knee, I'm not sure I'd know him. Now that my eyes are adjusting, his face is different, as if his skin is thicker and darker, like he's covered in tanned leather.

"We've kept an eye out since you were exed," Burn says. "I've been assigned to her for the past year."

"I know. Thank you."

He's had people spying on me for *three years*?

"She must hate me."

No kidding.

Burn shifts against the wall. "Drake's excited to see you."

"I can't wait to hold him in my arms."

Enough. No way am I letting this man get another crack at killing my brother.

Even if that's not his plan, he doesn't deserve Drake's unconditional adoration. And this casual chat between Burn and my father is more than I can stand.

I stride forward, pushing out of the shadows, too angry to care about hiding, too angry to think. "Did I hear you thank Burn for stalking me?" I shout at my father. "How long have you had me under surveillance? And why? So you could come back and finish off the members of your family you missed the first time?" If he thinks he can hurt me or Drake . . . "I've got powers now, ways to protect myself. So does Drake." Pressure builds in my ears as blood rushes through my ears.

My father pushes off the side of the tunnel and turns to stand in front of me, his posture awkward and stiff, every muscle taut. He's several feet away, and with the light from the torch shining down, all I can see is his shape— slight compared to Burn, yet bulkier than I remember. His hand stretches toward me then drops to his side. "Hello, Glory."

"That's all you have to say?" I form tight fists. If I could find his eyes in this light I'd finish him off right now, but they've turned one of their torches in my direction, blinding me, so I stare where I assume my dad's eyes must be.

I'll show him just how dangerous I am.

Not hearing screams of agony, I shield my eyes and step forward to improve my aim.

The beam of light from the torch drops, then changes shape on the floor of the tunnel as Burn steps toward me. "I'll get the kid."

"Leave him alone." I grab Burn's arm as he passes.

He leans in and growls, "I'm not going to hurt him."

In spite of his menacing tone, I believe him. At least I'd

rather have Drake with Burn than my father. I snap my attention back to the real danger.

Burn's menacing presence in my life these past few days—like standing under a massive weight held by a thread—seems suddenly comforting. I don't want him to leave me alone with my father, and I take a step back toward Burn and Drake.

My father must sense my fear, or maybe he's the one who's afraid, because he remains still, letting me increase the distance between us. His torch shoots light across the tunnel in front of him, and the fingers of his other hand splay. He's tense, too. Either that or he's getting ready to strangle me with those long fingers—or break my back, like Drake's. I don't even know the nature of my father's Deviance.

If he's just going to stand there, not saying anything, threatening me with his size and silence, then I can do the same. If he thinks I'm going to forgive him, even talk to him, he's got another think coming.

He reaches toward me and I stumble back a few steps.

"Glory."

"Don't touch me."

His hand drops back to his side. "You've grown so tall."

"It's been three years."

"I know and I'm so sorry. I wanted to send for you two sooner, but my life"—he stares at his feet—"I didn't want to take you away from your friends, from the only world you knew. . . ." His voice trails off.

"Sorry isn't good enough." I spit the words, and as they fly toward him I realize I've stepped forward. His long arms could span the space between us now but they don't.

His head drops and I watch as his fingers pulse at his side, stretching and relaxing in a constant rhythm, like he's resisting using them to kill me.

Studying my father's hand, I imagine the damage it could do, try to dig out the long buried memories, but instead of the ones I want, the memory that floods forward is one featuring that same pulsing hand on my back, its rhythmic movements comforting, stroking, brushing away my childhood fears when I woke from a nightmare. It wasn't just Mom who took care of us. He did, too. My throat tightens.

My father lifts his face and when our eyes meet his expression changes, but not to pain—there's a soft smile in his eyes, something tender. He reaches for me again.

I snap out of my nostalgia-induced happiness. I can't let one happy memory fog this moment's true and valid emotions. Narrowing my eyes, I let anger build and release my hate.

"Murderer." The word shoots from me with venom. Our eyes lock. I can sense his heart beating strong and fast. I squeeze.

His hand flies to his chest; the torch drops to the stone floor with a clatter. He groans.

I've hurt him—really hurt him—and although I shouldn't care, I do.

Breaking eye contact, I rush forward as he drops to a crouch. My hand lands on his back. He grabs me, rises, and pulls me into his arms. And the scent of his skin, like leather and smoke, brings back another rush of memories—memories that rouse emotions I don't want.

I push against him. "Let me go or I'll kill you like you killed mom."

His arms drop off me like we're magnets of opposite polarities and I slam into the wall.

"Glory, no," Drake calls out and my head snaps around to see Burn carrying Drake.

My mask dangles from Burn's hand. "Don't leave this behind—ever."

I grab it from him.

"Dad." Drake reaches out and our father pulls him from Burn's arms into his own. "I knew you'd come back for us." Drake, the foolish little traitor, buries his face in our father's neck.

"Let him go." I grab Drake by the shoulders and try to pull him away from the murderous monster.

"Stop." Drake glares at me. "Dad's not going to hurt me."

"How can you say that when—"

Burn plants his hand over my mouth, muffling the rest of my sentence, and raises the other hand to silence us all. He adjusts his harness and then grabs Drake and straps him onto his chest. "We've got company." He tips his head back in the direction we've come from. "Let's move. Quickly. Quietly. Now."

His voice comes out like a deep hum. He shuts off his torch, grabs my wrist, and directs my hand to the tail of his coat. The coat pulls me forward, and holding tight, I race behind Burn in the darkness, with the heat of my father's breath in pursuit.

CHAPTER FOURTEEN

URN STOPS AND, WITHOUT WARNING, LIFTS ME ABOVE HIS head and shoves me into what feels like a narrow cave, almost like a shelf dug into the side of the tunnel. Frantic, I reach out and find the back, roof, and one side with my hands, then the other side with an outstretched foot. The space is like a box carved out of the stone, about five feet deep and wide and less than four feet high.

"Glory?" Drake says softly, and I reach toward the voice and pull my brother in beside me, and then another body moves in, and I can tell from the smell it's my father. He touches my arm but I shrug him off, and he makes a soft sound, like I've slapped him.

There's a pause and I wonder what's happened to Burn. Is he going to hide somewhere else? Fight on his own? Or is this all part of his plan? Perhaps the people following us are his allies and we're stored here for dinner.

But soon I smell Burn's hot scent. With those goggles, he's the only one of us who can see and the only one with the strength to get into this high cave on his own. His presence heats the closed air as he arranges us until we're sitting, hunched over and in a row against the back wall. Drake is between me and our father and Burn's on my other side.

The footsteps draw closer and a faint glow fills the tunnel, revealing a junction. As well as continuing straight ahead, another tunnel branches off. We should have taken one path, giving us a 50 percent chance of escape. Trapped in this cave, we're dead if they spot us.

"Which way?" asks a voice and everything inside me lurches. It sounds like Cal but can't be. My insides crawl like my nerves want out, and I'm not sure whether I want to run into Cal's arms or kill him for his betrayal.

Burn's arm shoots across my body, pressing me back against the wall of the cave. He recognized Cal's voice, too.

"You're the one who thinks they came down here," a deep voice says.

"Wild goose chase," says a man with a gruff voice.

"All I did was find her bracelet." Cal's voice is even and strong.

My stomach flutters. Clearly, my stupid stomach has forgotten his betrayal.

"Where are they headed?" Gruff Voice asks.

"If I knew, we'd be there," Cal answers. "I didn't even know this tunnel existed."

Cal's helping the Comps track us, which confirms my worst assumptions. My throat tightens and I feel the signs of my curse building behind my eyes. I hate Cal. I hate him with all my heart, and if I could see into his eyes right now, I'd show him how much.

Something brushes my head, and I tense but soon realize Burn's putting his night-vision goggles onto my face. Once they're on, everything's bathed in a strange green light and I spin toward Drake. He's scared, likely because my father's arm is slung over his shoulder. How dare he?

But I'm kidding myself about the source of my brother's fear. Drake's leaning his head into the pit of our father's arm and is cuddled up to the man as if it's the most natural thing in the world. I choke down disbelief. The person who paralyzed him is not the reason he's scared.

Burn touches my arm and I turn back toward him. "Quiet," he mouths. He draws a finger across his throat.

One of the men moves into view and leans back against the tunnel wall, almost directly across from the cave near the junction. He's a Comp in full armor, and the light from his torch glints off his heavy chest plate. The mouth of our cave is level with his head, and if he raises his torch light a few feet, we'll be visible.

"Shine that light over here." Cal steps into view and points to the branched-off tunnel.

"You don't give the orders." Gruff Voice shoves him and Cal slams into the wall in front of us. His head is so close to the cave's entrance, if I slid forward and straightened my legs, I could kick him. For an instant I want to and then I come to my senses.

A Comp shines his torch where Cal was pointing.

"Look," Cal says. "Footprints, leading this way."

"Let's move," Deep Voice says, and the Comps and Cal march forward into the path on the right.

After what feels like hours but is probably less than a minute, Burn lifts his iron-strap arm from my body and I can finally draw deep breaths. But the air in the cave is rank and I want out.

"Can we leave?" I whisper.

"Burn," my father says, "give Glory and me a moment to talk?"

"No," Drake whispers hard and strong, and I'm so proud of my little brother for wanting to protect me from our monster of a father.

"No time for talking." Burn slides forward. He drops down out of the cave, cranks his torch, and sets it on the tunnel floor, pointing up and casting a dull light. "It won't take them long to figure out that the trail I left doesn't lead far."

Brilliant. Burn is smarter than I thought. Now we'll have a head start down the alternate route.

Burn grabs my ankle and pulls.

"Hey." I kick free.

He raises his hands as if in surrender. "Come out on your own then. Hurry."

"You go," my father says to me. "I'll hand Drake to Burn."

I let Burn help me down then he reaches back for my brother. Light from the Comps' torches bounces in the tunnel to the right, growing brighter. They're coming back toward us. Apparently they've already realized they were tricked.

Burn pushes Drake back into the cave, then bends to turn off our lantern.

I need to do something. Fast.

I dash to the entrance of the tunnel they're in and yell, "Help! You went the wrong way." My voice echoes down the tunnel as I head for the other fork and run. I'm not sure what I'll do once they catch me, and they will, given my bad ankle, but that doesn't matter as long as they don't find Drake. Burn will keep him safe.

Heavy footsteps pound behind me and I stumble in the darkness, my ankle screaming.

A hard, strong arm wraps around my waist, lifting me from the ground. It's Burn. I'm relieved and terrified at once. If he followed me, then my brother is alone with our father.

He stops, thrusts me forward, and my hands strike metal. "Climb."

CHAPTER FIFTEEN

As I CLIMB, A FAINT HINT OF LIGHT DRIFTS TOWARD ME. When I get to the top, the ladder meets an entrance to a small passageway, like a pipe or a chute, which slopes up at a sharp angle. Light glints off a chain extending down, so I grab it and start to pull myself through the narrow space. It's too tight for me to fully rise onto all fours, but I do my best to use my legs to speed my ascent.

My knees scrape along the rough surface as I focus on the ring of light. The only place outdoors I know that's this bright is the Hub, but it doesn't make sense for us to be there, so this tunnel must exit into some brightly lit room.

At the top, I push on the exit's cover. It doesn't budge. Burn's heavy breaths follow behind me as he grunts and pulls himself through the chute. "Wait."

"Why are you following me?" I hiss down.

He pulls himself up using the chain, unable to get onto

all fours, until he's half on top of me. The weight of his body presses against me in the tight, sloped space. "Quiet." He pushes up until his mouth is next to my ear. "We can't surface here. We're not Outside yet."

That confirms it. We *are* still under Haven. If I go out, Burn won't follow. He's a wanted kidnapper, and based on the amount of light behind this seal there will be no hiding once I exit. Burn will go back and save Drake; he'll have to. My brother's right. It's time to trust someone else.

"Go back to Drake," I tell Burn.

He clamps his hand over my mouth.

Voices drift toward us but it's hard to make out the words. Burn's weight lifts off me and he moves slowly back, presumably to hear what's being said or to gauge a safe time to climb down and into the tunnel. He slides down the angled chute to the ladder.

Still leaning against the cover, my hand strikes a spring-loaded clamp at its edge. It's now or never. I flick the lever and the clamp releases. Falling forward out of the hole, I roll onto the surface a few feet below.

It's so bright I can't open my eyes, but wherever I am, it's dirty—and hot. Running my hands over the ground to determine my surroundings, grit presses into my palms and knees. Have I landed in a furnace of one of the factories?

No. It's not that hot. With my eyes squeezed shut, I try to place the sensation using only touch, but the closest I can come to the texture is our vitamin powder but that's not right, either. I try to open my eyes a slit but they sting at the bright light's assault. There's no time to let my pupils adjust, so I keep my lids squeezed shut as I scramble away from the exit.

"Your mask!" Burn shouts and something strikes my back and bounces to my side. Still on all fours and unable to open my eyes more than a slit for a split second at a time, I grope for whatever hit me. It's my filter mask.

"Go back and save Drake!" I yell, and shading my eyes I squint to see Burn forcing himself through the tight hole—with his mask on.

"Put it on!" Burn yells and I finally identify the gritty substance under my hands.

Dust. But I thought he said we weren't Outside?

Panic squeezes my chest, choking me. At least I hope the choking catalyst is panic—not dust. I pull the mask on and adjust the straps to tighten it over my face.

The mask's darkened eye shield provides a relieving break from the brightness and I turn to see the outside of Haven rising in the distance, shiny panels covering it in no discernible pattern. Between me and the dome, windmills stab up from the landscape of dust and ruins. I can't stop staring.

Even uglier from the outside, the so-called dome is not as domelike as it's depicted on the Haven standard that flies in the Hub. It's an irregular shape, curved in places, sharp edged in others. Even more unexpected, the dome has tendrils reaching out that lead to other domes and structures. Nothing matches the picture I have from inside.

Between there and here, scraps of rubble jut out from a landscape that's not just a vast sea of dust. Shells of ruined buildings thrust out, like broken bones reaching up through the surface. Everywhere twisted chunks of metal punctuate my view. Given how much went into building Haven, I'm surprised there's anything left out here. That our city was salvaged from ruins has never been more obvious to me than while seeing its haphazard exterior.

Spanning the distance, I'm slammed by the utter hopelessness of my situation; the utter failure of my plan. Comps or not, we need to go back into the tunnels. Burn grabs my arm, then pulls me against him, picking me up off the ground and trapping both my arms against my body, under just one of his. "What were you thinking?" His voice is distorted through his mask, like he's speaking through water.

"You said we weren't Outside."

"Outside that."

Burn spins me and I see a huge wall in the distance. It must be fifty feet high, fabricated from concrete and steel and other materials I don't recognize. Dust has drifted up its sides, like fingers stretching to get out.

There's a wall around Haven? Why? I can't judge the distances out here. Even from the roofs of tall buildings inside Haven I've never seen such vast spaces stretching before me.

The wall must be there to keep Shredders away from Haven and, given there's never a shortage of the monsters, I shudder to think how many must be on the other side of that wall. And *that's* where Burn was taking us?

"Stop struggling," Burn growls in my ear. "We need to get back into the tunnels before they find us."

"The Comps?" I didn't realize I was struggling and let my

body go slack. I almost slip from Burn's grip as I realize who he means by *they*.

Shredders.

He drops me into the dust and it rises up in a cloud around me. I lift my hand to cover my mouth and nose, forgetting about the mask until my fingers strike it. The heat is even worse out here than at the highest point of Haven, and I realize the heat is coming from the same place as the bright light. I look up and there's what looks like a huge ball of fire high above us. Bright yellow, it's hard to look at, even with the eye shield.

"Where is the light coming from?"

"The sun."

"It shines outside Haven?"

"The *real* sun," Burn says flatly.

"Really?" I'm embarrassed by my breathlessness, the awe in my voice. But for my whole life "sun" has meant the light that reflects off the sky during daytime hours in Haven. This monstrous light, so high I can't see what it's hanging from, gives a new meaning to *sun*.

"Shit," Burn says and I spin toward him. He leaps ahead, practically diving for the large metal disk covering the entrance to the tunnel. Before he gets there, I hear a loud clank.

Waiting for Burn to open the cover, I watch, stunned, as he continues to curse and kicks the door repeatedly with his boot. One kick from that boot and my back would be broken, my ribs shattered, my skull crushed.

The hole we came out of is at the side of a concrete structure that's low to the ground and covered by dust. Now that the dark metal door is closed, it's hard to even make out the round shape. Burn gives up kicking and slumps down beside it.

"What's wrong?" I try to hide how frantic I feel.

"It's locked."

"Why did you close it?"

He leaps up and charges toward me so quickly I fall back onto the ground, my hands stinging as they hit the dust.

"I didn't close it." He looks into the distance, turning to see all around us.

I struggle up and look, too. "How do we unlock the door?"

"We don't. Unless you set the spring first, it closes on a timer. There's no way to open it from out here. Precaution against the Shredders getting in."

"There must be a combination, a lock." Combinations can be broken; locks can be picked. I rush over and run my hands over the steel cover, but feel nothing on its pitted surface.

I spin back toward Burn. "It must open."

"The access codes are embedded into the Comps' gloves. We can't open it. Trust me."

I don't trust him. Not anymore. "If you knew it would lock, why didn't you block it open? You were out last." My breaths come too quickly and steam forms on the inside of my eye shield. My brother is down there, alone with our monster of a father and the Comps. Both want him dead.

"You're the one who raced off." Burn stomps toward me. "You're the one who opened it. You're the one who didn't set the spring for reentry."

"How was I supposed to know?" My voice is weak because he's right. This is my fault. And I left my brother behind.

"Look," Burn glares down at me. "Your little stunt was reckless but it might have worked. The Comps followed us, but went past that ladder. Hector and Drake have a chance. Now, let's move."

"No." I bang on the door to the tunnel, run my fingers around its barely visible edges. "I'm not leaving my brother."

"You already have." Burn grabs me by the arm and pulls, but when I resist he lets go and I fall back against the door. "Stay then!" he shouts. "I don't care. Fifty-fifty chance whether the Shredders or Comps find you first. Good luck, either way."

My heart races, my brain feels oxygen-starved. I can't think.

Burn strides off, heading away from Haven and toward the wall. I spin back and forth, taking in my surroundings and keeping him in sight. Haven is closer than the wall and every instinct tells me to stay near the dome, near the only home I have ever known.

Right now, Haven does not equal safety.

Even if it did, getting there means facing Shredders—means torture and death. The Comps might find me first, but that seems a long shot, and they certainly won't get me back to my brother.

Choosing the devil I know, I race after Burn, stumbling over and around debris stabbing through the dust. Even though my ankle's not as sore anymore, it takes me over a minute to catch up with Burn, and when I do, he doesn't even acknowledge my presence.

Drake must be scared—assuming he's still alive, assuming our father hasn't already finished the job he started three years ago. I can't give up hope. I need to believe he's alive. Until I learn otherwise, every fiber of my being will be dedicated to ensuring Drake's survival.

"Where are we going?" I ask Burn, trying to catch my breath. He doesn't answer, so I grab his arm and try again. "There's another way down to the tunnels, right?"

"No point in going back down there now."

"But my brother—"

"They'll come out on the other side of the wall."

"Why go there? Where are you taking us? Where's Drake? How will we find him?"

Burn pulls his sleeve from my hand and trudges forward, scanning our surroundings, acting like I'm not there.

"Where"—my voice rises—"are we going? Tell me."

He stops for a moment and rearranges weapons in his flared coat.

I'm done with him holding back his plan, not telling me anything. How dare he get angry when I couldn't have possibly known I was making a mistake? I will not be ignored.

Turning his back on me, he starts to walk. I race toward him and jump onto his back, wrapping my arms tightly around his neck. I hang back, let my weight pull against his throat. Maybe I can choke some answers out of him. "Answer me!"

He twists sharply and the violent movement tosses me off like a fly.

"Please." The desperation in my voice is humiliating. "I need to get back to my brother."

He stops and his shoulders lift then drop. "Hector knows where to meet us."

A huge noise distracts me and I spin back toward it. About halfway between us and the closest edge of Haven, something, or someone, is moving quickly toward us. A shriek rings out across the dust and the shape falls. Other shapes follow behind the first, a moving wall of black.

"Run!" Burn yells and sets off. "Shredders!"

CHAPTER SIXTEEN

MY LUNGS AND LEGS ARE ON FIRE. I LEAP OVER A TWISTED and charred piece of steel, then stumble. All around and under us are pieces of the old city from BTD. Burn stops to let me catch up and when I reach him, he swings me onto his back.

"It's faster this way." He runs before I can answer, and I cling to him with no idea where we're headed. I don't care as long as it's away from the Shredders. The wall looks impossibly far and with no experience judging open distances, I don't know how long it will take to reach it, but we don't seem to be making much progress.

To our right, a building's skeleton rises higher than the rest of the debris. I have no guess how high this building was BTD, but steel girders and blocks of concrete rise from the dust to at least three stories, more in some places.

We reach the ruin's edge; I slip off Burn's back. Gripping

me around my thighs, he lifts and pushes me up above his head. "Grab it."

I stretch and barely snag the edge of the girder of the first floor above ground.

"Pull yourself up." His hands slide down to my ankles and push up as I pull with my arms.

When my belly touches the girder, he lets go and the steel digs into my gut. I swing one leg over so I'm straddling the foot-wide beam. Burn grabs one of the vertical supports and scales it without effort, the soles of his boots walking up, while hand over hand he grips the girder's edges like he's walking on all fours but straight up. I can't take my eyes off his powerful upper body as it presses back against his coat. Reaching the top, he swings onto the end of the girder I'm perched on.

He beckons with one hand, and then walks quickly along a narrow beam of steel until he reaches a six-foot-high concrete slab. He pulls himself up on top of it. Holding onto the girder, I swing my legs up behind me and land in a crouch. The Shredders are closer now, yelling loudly, and I wonder if they're following our scent. Can Shredders smell?

I stand and struggle to keep balanced as I walk toward Burn, turning at the corner and following toward the slab. The Shredders are close enough to see us now, and I hear a roar from below.

Looking down, I expect to see Shredders but instead see a man, huge chains wrapped around him and attached to blocks of concrete. Has there been a second expunging this week? Considering the weight he's pulling, he's moving quickly, but his pursuers are rapidly closing the distance. He's close enough now I can see he's wearing a mask, a big, black one like the Comps' wear but it's damaged. He stumbles onto his knees, inciting another loud roar from the throng behind him as they narrow the gap.

I should feel bad for the man but I don't. I'm too consumed by relief at knowing that the Shredders have another victim to pursue. Maybe we'll have time to get away while they're distracted by ripping him apart. That the Shredders might not have even seen Burn and me is too much to hope.

Lying on his stomach, Burn reaches down from the concrete slab and pulls me on top. Stairs head up from its side and ahead of us are the remnants of another flight down. We're on what was once a landing between floors. The first stair below us seems relatively intact, but steel rods stick out from the second and below that there's nothing.

"Are we climbing up farther?" I ask. The stairs seem functional up to the landing above us and higher seems better. As far from these monsters as we can climb.

Burn shakes his head and raises a finger to the mouthpiece of his mask.

The man is on his feet again and about twenty-five feet from the ruin. He looks up. I think he sees us but Burn ducks down, flattening himself on the surface and I do the same. When I lift my gaze, the Shredders are on top of the man— literally. They push him face down onto the dust and four of them hold him there, their boots on his limbs. The man strains his neck to keep his face out of the dust but another Shredder bends down and rips off his mask. They all laugh as the mask is tossed aside.

At least six blocks of concrete lie scattered around the man, attached to him by chains that also bind his arms to his body, yet he moved so quickly. His Deviance must be speed and I assume the Shredders used the chains and concrete to slow him down.

Laughing, one of the Shredders breaks off a long chunk of chain, as if he's snapping a thread, and binds the man's ankles and knees together. Even if he could get back to his feet, there's no chance of his running now, and he grunts loudly as he strains against the chains. He can't break them.

"Get up!" one of the Shredders yells, the sound grating my ears. "I want to see your face while we skin you alive."

Shock grips my mind. I had no idea Shredders could talk. His voice is horrible, loud, and scratchy, but I understand the words. Grunting and laughing, the other Shredders pull the man up and drag him to a girder that's jutting up from the ground not far from this building's entrance. They bind him to the girder and one of them plunges a knife into the man's thigh. Blood spreads on his dusty gray slacks as another Shredder draws the point of his knife down the man's cheek, leaving a thin trail of blood in its wake.

A pounding noise comes from farther back, and I look up to see Comps, seven of them all in their heavy black armor and face-obstructing filter masks, half-running half-marching in tandem. Their equipment and guns bounce with each step—thump, thump, thump, thump.

My body seizes. Even if this man was expunged, surely the Comps are here to save him. But even as that thought flashes through my mind, I realize I'm wrong. The Comps broadcast torture in the Hub, and it's more likely they've come to drag the show back into camera range.

At least I hope there are no cameras out here. A shiver runs through me but I ignore that fear and brace for the battle. As badly as I want to see these Shredders taken down and the man saved, I hope the scene won't be too brutal.

A few of the Shredders look back toward the approaching wall of Comps, but they barely react and turn back to tearing the clothes off their victim and making small slices in his skin with their knives. One of the Shredders has a necklace that clatters as he moves. I realize in horror that it's made of teeth—human teeth.

I swallow bile and close my eyes, but I can't leave them closed. Not seeing this scene won't make it go away, and it feels safer to know what's going on and at least be prepared if we're spotted.

The Comps stop in unison.

The one in the middle, clearly the captain, steps forward. "Give us our chains."

"No." The big Shredder with the tooth necklace pushes the Comp captain's chest. "Finders keepers."

Confusion slams through me. I don't know what's more surprising: that Shredders can talk with what seems like intelligence, or that they seem to have been working *with* the Comps all along.

"We slowed him down for you. The chains are ours," the captain says and the other six Comps draw their guns—the biggest guns I've ever seen—and point them at the Shredders.

The main Shredder laughs and it's about the most chilling sound I've ever heard, like metal on metal but deeper.

"Your fault he took off." The Shredder spreads his legs wider. "This one should've been hobbled from the start."

The Comp captain lifts two fingers, and then twists them around in some kind of signal.

Bang.

One of the Comps shoots a Shredder, and the blast sends the monster flying back and onto the dust. There's a gaping hole in what used to be his chest, but very little blood.

The other Shredders look up for a second then get back to poking their knives into the Deviant man, just enough to draw blood. They laugh when he screams.

The captain points his gun at the Shredder with the tooth necklace. "We're taking the chains."

The necklaced monster lifts his knife to the Comp's throat, which seems pointless given his armor. The Comp at the other end of the line shoots the Shredder. He falls, his macabre necklace swinging up to the side then landing on what used to be his ribs.

I've never seen anyone shot. Never seen a real gun used. Inside Haven they only use shockers, and even then only rarely. Even in my worst nightmares I never imagined guns could do the kind of damage that's been brought upon this Shredder, blasting away half of his torso.

The captain raises his hand, flicks his wrist, and the Comps open fire. Raising my hands, I cover my ears against the sound as Shredders fall in broken heaps onto the dust. The Deviant man passes out from the pain, or the loss of blood that stains the dust at his feet. He slumps, held upright by the chains.

My breaths come too quickly; I can't pull oxygen deep enough to reach my lungs. Every part of me wants to tear off the mask so I can draw in more air. I press my arms into the concrete to prevent my hands from doing what every part of me, except logic, thinks is a great idea. One of Burn's arms lands across my back. The heavy weight is comforting and helps me slow my breathing.

The Comps gather their chains, winding them up and stashing them into bags strapped on their backs. When the last chain is pulled from around the man's chest, he drops from the girder and collapses into a heap on the ground.

One of the Comps bends to pick the man up, but the captain shakes his head sharply. "Leave him. Another pack of Shredders will find him soon enough."

The Comps return to formation. The captain lifts his fist, twists it abruptly, and on that command, the group of seven spins on a dime. They march in a slight V shape, the captain at the apex, back toward Haven.

The Deviant man isn't moving. Is he alive?

When the Comps dip down below the crest of a dune, Burn leaps to his feet, runs to the girder he used to climb up, and slides down it like a pole to the ground. When he reaches the man, he turns up to me. "Get down here. More Shredders will come. We've got to get moving."

I stand and will my leg muscles to function, drawing a deep breath to force back my fear. The injured man will slow us down but there's no way we can leave him.

CHAPTER SEVENTEEN

MY ASSUMPTION THAT WE'RE SAVING THE MAN IS QUICKLY quashed. Burn forces the stranger's nose into the dust, and I tug on his arm, trying to pull him away. The man looks up at me, his mouth and nose coated in dust. I don't recognize him and I'm glad.

Fear tightens my throat. The man's eyes are crazed, his lips twisted in a tortured grimace. He's drowning on dust, going crazy in his attempt to escape Burn. The poor man barely escaped being skinned by the Shredders.

I pound my fist on Burn's arm. "Don't kill him."

"Get off me." Burn pushes me away. "We can't waste time."

Burn can so easily overpower me, there's no point in fighting. I back away and sit, leaning against one of the girders of the skeleton building.

Just as I started to trust Burn, just as I started to believe that underneath he could be an actual human being, he does something like this. Acting like he's about to save a man then killing him. Maybe this is more humane. Perhaps it is better if he drowns on dust, rather than being left for another pack of Shredders who won't take kindly to finding him surrounded by pieces of their dead friends.

But I can't watch Burn kill this man, so I look up to the sky. It's so high. And so blue. If this is what they were trying to emulate when they painted the inside of the dome, they fell a few hundred miles short. I push the sleeves on my shirt as far as they'll go, and the heat from the monster-sized sun light strikes my skin. The warmth is comforting and makes me smell different. Kind of salty but something else, too—almost sweet—and it reminds me a bit of the smells that came out of that shop called a *bakery*. I almost forget that Burn's killing a man not twenty feet away.

"That's enough," Burn says gruffly.

I gasp. The man's still alive. And even stranger, Burn's now pulling the struggling man away from the dust. The man wants more. His arms battle for the ground as Burn holds him back.

I run over. "Let him die if he wants to."

Burn turns toward me. "What?" He wraps his arms around the shorter and much older man's chest and holds him as he flails, reaching toward the dust at his feet.

"Why else would he want to inhale the dust?" I ask. "First you force it on him, then you take it away."

"Hey, buddy." Burn squeezes the man and lifts his feet from the ground. "You've had enough. Calm down."

The man relaxes in Burn's arms and Burn lets his feet touch down.

"Here." Burn takes one arm off the man and reaches down for his broken mask. He takes a long piece of cloth from one of the pockets inside his long coat and stretches it across the broken filter. "Might be hard to breathe through, but it should keep out the dust."

He puts the mask over the man's messy gray hair. He's calmed down enough now for Burn to release him completely.

"What's going on?" I'm not sure when or if I've ever been so confused. I had just come to grips with the idea that Burn was killing the man in an act of mercy. Perhaps Burn was testing him to see if he'd turn into a Shredder?

"Thanks, kid." The man claps Burn on the arm then bends over, his hands on his thighs, and the pace of his breathing slows to a more normal rate. He straightens. "I'm Gage. From Haven." He gasps for breath between each short sentence. "Exed today. What are you . . . kids doing . . . Outside?"

"I'm Burn." He points to me. "This is Glory. All her fault."

"What?" I stomp over and punch him in the arm. "You drag me and my brother away without a word about where we're going, or why, and it's my fault we're Outside?"

Burn glares at me. "If it weren't for your stunt, we'd be safely in the tunnels, probably beyond the wall by now. But you can't follow simple directions, and here we are. In danger of being torn apart by Shredders or—" He stops and shakes his head. Based on the look on his face, I don't even want to ask him what he'd planned to say after the *or*.

"Then I guess I owe you a thank you, little lady." Gage lifts his mask a few inches, smiles at me, and then fastens it back into place. Burn grunts.

"I still don't understand." I shake my head. Gage puts what's left of his torn clothes back on, and his cuts have stopped bleeding. Some are scabbing over, but it seems too quick for that. It's hard to be certain when there's so much blood.

"Your cuts." I have so many questions I can't even form full sentences to express them.

Burn looks off into the distance. "We've got to move." He turns to Gage. "I assume you're fast?"

"Very." Gage runs his fingers over one of the worst cuts on his chest and doesn't even wince. "At least before I got cut."

Burn pulls a huge knife out. "Once the pain goes, you'll be good as new."

I tug on Burn's arm. "I don't understand." Is part of Gage's Deviance fast healing?

"I'll explain later. We need to find somewhere to hide until dark. Then we'll head for the wall." Burn turns and, holding his knife at the ready, heads through the open ground level of the building we just hid in. "Stay close."

"Why is the sun falling?" I ask. The lower half of the sky is pink and orange and more beautiful than anything I've ever imagined. "Where is it going?"

Burn, sitting next to me on a raised concrete slab, doesn't answer. I nudge him with my leg, not wanting to take my eyes off the sky for a moment. The sun has turned into a fiery orange ball and the colors of the sky keep changing. If it weren't so spectacular, I'd think the world was ending.

Gage is across from us, sleeping. I turn to shake Burn.

He grunts. "I was sleeping. You should be, too."

"Won't the sun set the world on fire?"

Burn's shoulders and chest shake.

"Are you laughing at me?" Trying not to care, I turn back to the view.

He puts a hand on my shoulder. "It's called a sunset. Happens every day."

"But how?" Yes, every day in Haven, the sun gets softer and goes out, to be replaced by the bluer and dimmer moon light at night, but I've never seen or even imagined anything like this.

Burn pulls his legs up and leans forward, putting his arms over his shins. "The sun is a star."

"Stars are tiny pricks of LED lights on the night sky." My father explained them to me and told me how there were more of them when he was a kid. They're growing sparse, especially over the part of Haven we live in, no longer replaced as they burn out.

"*Real* stars." Burn takes off his mask and turns toward me.

"Your mask."

"I'll be fine," Burn says. "Take yours off if you like.

There's no wind tonight and no dust up here." He runs his hand over the surface we're hiding on until dark. I have no idea what this building was BTD. Now it's just a ruin, and it strikes me as a miracle that anything is still upright with all that's been salvaged to build inside Haven—not to mention that wall. We're higher this time, at least three stories up from the ground and much closer to the wall. I wonder if Drake's already out of the tunnels on the other side. I can't let myself think that the Comps or Shredders found him.

Gage's wounds started to bleed again after the climb. Remembering his deranged expression when he was breathing in dust, I run my hand over the filter that covers my mouth.

Burn reaches over to take off my mask. The air feels great on my face, cooling and comforting, evaporating sweat as the heat from the sun wanes. Without the dark plastic distorting the colors, the sky is even more spectacular. The soft yellow light it casts warms the tone of Burn's skin and softens his hard edges.

He's studying me, too, which makes me uncomfortable. Smoothing my hands over my hair, trapped by the mask all day, I focus on the sunset.

"They didn't teach you about the stars or planets in school?" Burn asks.

"School?"

"GT."

"Yes, but I never imagined anything like this." They did teach us something about the planets and stars when they were explaining what made the dust come, but I'm beginning to realize that much of what we learned was based on what Management wanted us to know, rather than the truth.

"Stars are balls of fire, millions of miles away." Burn's voice is deep but the gentlest I've heard it. "The sun is the closest star to earth, so it looks bigger. It heats our planet and provides light."

"And the moon does that at night," I say to show him I'm not quite as ignorant as he thinks.

He shakes his head. "The moon's light comes from the sun. It's just bouncing off."

I furrow my brow but don't question him. This doesn't make sense, but even if Burn's lying or making this up as he goes, he clearly knows more about Outside than I do.

"Was it a star that struck the earth? Is that how the planet caught on fire?"

He stretches out his long legs. "No. Asteroids. Lots of them. They're more like huge rocks."

"Then how did the fires start?"

"Volcanoes. Earthquakes."

"Oh, right." That's what we learned in GT. "The asteroids hit so hard they shifted bits of the earth, right?"

He nods.

"Then the atmosphere filled with ash and dust, changing the climate, blocking air travel, jamming communications—then the dust fell." This is what we learned, and Burn doesn't correct me. "What was in the dust? Why did it change us?"

He shakes his head. "Don't know. I'm not sure anyone does. Something came on the asteroids, I guess. Or out of the volcanoes . . ." It's the first time I've heard him unsure. He leans back. "Doesn't matter."

And he's right. It doesn't matter. It's not like we can turn back time, take away the dust, and make the Shredders go away—make either of us a Normal.

"What's happening to the sun?" It's no longer round—it's cut off at the bottom and the orange color has intensified.

"Don't worry." He leans and nudges me with his shoulder. "Nothing's happening to it. We're turning away from the sun for the night, that's all."

Once again I'm confused, but that doesn't matter. "It's beautiful."

"Yes." His voice is huskier than normal, and I look over to find him staring at me. When our eyes meet, he turns back to the sunset.

"Where's my brother?"

He shifts, bends one of his legs, and grabs his shin as he turns to me. "There's a door in the wall. We'll go through it after dark."

"And Drake's on the other side?" My chest collapses under the fear of not knowing if he's safe, under the guilt of not taking better care of him, under the shame that I've let anything but finding him invade my thoughts.

"Hector will keep him safe," Burn says. "Don't worry."

My father's name brings on more fear, but curiosity pushes it aside. "What's it like on the other side of the wall?"

"Not that different than this, at first. But farther away there are fewer ruins, less dust."

"Less dust?"

"The wall traps the dust. Holds it in close to Haven. It blows around in here and drifts up the wall." He rubs his chin. "Some claim they bring more dust in on purpose, but I've never seen them do it." He shrugs. "This is only the fourth time I've been aboveground in the hot zone."

"The hot zone?"

"This Shredder-infested space around Haven."

"How do the Shredders bring dust in?"

"Not the Shredders. Management."

"But . . ." Implications flit through my mind like sparks from a bad electrical plug. Management purposefully brings in more dust? I have so many questions I don't know which to ask first. "When we first saw Gage, it looked like the Comps were working with the Shredders."

"They were."

I was certain there'd be some other explanation. "But the Comps killed the Shredders."

Burn grunts. "Yeah. Over chains." He shakes his head. "Chains they used to slow Gage down to make it easier for the Shredders to catch him." He laughs. "I wonder how much of Gage's escape got caught on camera. Management will be pissed they didn't get their show. They probably shut off the feed the second Gage ran, then told everyone that dust got into the camera."

"So Management . . ."

"Likes having Shredders around the dome. Keeps you Haven people scared and compliant."

"And the Shredders? Why are they so sadistic?"

"Too much dust." His eyebrows rise. "Plus, they're recruiting."

He says this as if it's obvious, and I'm not sure I can digest any more information right now. Everything Burn says sounds crazy if I take each piece on its own, but it's starting to hang together into a consistent pattern. A pattern that shows how we've been lied to in Haven. Constantly.

CHAPTER EIGHTEEN

LIGHT AND SPARKS RISE FROM BEHIND A LONG, LOW BUILDING close to the wall. Burn says it's a Comp outpost for storing food and weapons, but Comps must not be stationed there tonight given all the Shredders. Shouts and screams pollute the night air and it's hard to guess the exact number of monsters based only on shadows and occasional silhouettes. We climbed as high as we could, but still can't see to the other side of the outpost, beyond which lies the Shredder camp, then a door through the wall.

With my mask at my side, one hand resting on its straps in case the wind picks up or we have to run, I shiver in my thin jacket. I was warm enough while we were moving—given the effort of walking quickly over the uneven and soft surface of the dust, not to mention climbing obstacles—but since we stopped, the night air has been biting through my clothing, chilling the light sweat I worked up on the run.

Burn looks toasty in his thick coat, not seeming to notice I'm cold. He did give one of his sweaters to Gage, and the garment hangs halfway down the thin man's thighs as he leans against a partially intact ruin wall.

Gage turns. "How far to the next way out?"

"Don't know," Burn answers. "I don't know for sure there *is* another way."

"So we just wait until those Shredders leave?" I ask. A whole day has passed since we were separated, and Drake must be terrified.

"They don't exactly look like they're planning on leaving." Gage pushes away from the wall, bends down, and whispers to Burn.

I jump up and move closer. For all I know, Gage is suggesting they offer me up as a sacrifice. I wouldn't put agreeing past Burn. "What are you talking about?"

Gage looks at me and shrugs. "I was just saying that I'm fast and could run along the wall's perimeter to look for another way out."

"Too dangerous in the dark," Burn says.

"Not with your goggles." Gage points to the night-glasses Burn has pushed onto the top of his head.

Burn doesn't reply, but his brow furrows in the moonlight and it's clear he's not going to give up those goggles for anything. He stands and walks to the edge of the raised platform.

"I'll find out what we're up against." Burn leaps from the ruin, down fifteen feet to the dust.

I almost shout after him, but a loud voice might attract

the Shredders' attention, putting Burn in even more danger, so all I can do is hope and wait. Keeping low and sticking to the shadows, he moves swiftly and soon I've lost sight of him.

"Will he be okay?" I ask Gage.

"Don't know." He leans against the partial wall again, and pulls a shaking hand under the cuff of the borrowed sweater. "He should have loaned me his goggles. Your boyfriend has trust issues."

"He's not my boyfriend." My cheeks heat. "And if you took the goggles, how do we know you'd come back?" That part of Burn I understand. If they were mine, I wouldn't trust anyone else with them, either.

Gage shifts his position against the wall, then groans.

"You should sit down," I tell him. "You're obviously in pain."

He turns toward me and his skin seems nearly transparent in the moonlight. "It's not that bad, considering."

I step closer. "Don't try to be brave. I saw them cut you."

"My cuts are healing, fast. Some of the small ones are already closed." But he sits cross-legged on the concrete, leaning back, and I drop down a few feet away.

"Is healing part of your Deviance?"

He shakes his head.

"Then how—?"

"I'm not sure, to be honest." Gage runs his fingers through his hair, making it stick up even worse. "From the little bits I got out of your boyfr— Burn—the dust helped me heal."

"Really?"

"That's what he claimed, while he was forcing my face into it."

I grip my dust mask. "What was it like"—I slide closer—"inhaling the dust?" I almost ask if he's changing into a Shredder, but the question seems insensitive, intrusive. Plus I'm not sure I want to hear the answer.

Gage is quiet for what feels like several minutes, and I assume he isn't going to answer, then he turns to me. "Breathing the dust was amazing. It was like inhaling pure energy. As if I'd been turned on like a light bulb." He fumbles with his mask and stares down at the ground longingly. "I want more. It's all I can think about."

I stare at him, incredulous, fumbling over what to say. "But dust is lethal." I regurgitate what I've been taught. "People choke to death on it. I've seen it happen." But even as I say it, I'm not sure I've witnessed actual deaths. Maybe I've heard the stories so many times I can picture them, and I never had reason to question it.

Gage draws a long breath. "I've seen it, too." He shakes his head. "Clearly, it's not always lethal for Deviants."

"Or Shredders," I add. That must be why Burn stopped him from taking more in. For all I know, Gage might be one lungful away from turning into a Shredder. I inch away from him.

He lifts his head and I instantly feel bad for moving away. I'm trying to figure out Gage. One minute he's a nice guy and I'm grateful we have an adult with us, but the next he seems to unravel. I can't clear my mind of his crazed expression when Burn was feeding him dust.

"Is your Deviance speed?"

He nods.

"How did the Comps find you?"

"I told someone that I was a Deviant." His voice is hard, cold. "She turned me in."

"Someone you trusted?"

He nods.

That was his first mistake. Trusting someone. "Someone betrayed me, too."

Gage's wipes his glassy eyes with the sleeve of the sweater he borrowed from Burn.

"Who was it?" I ask quietly.

He shakes his head and his expression hardens as he stares into the night.

"Do you have a family back in Haven?"

He shoots to his feet and starts pacing. His face twists into a grimace and I can't tell whether he's in pain or upset by my question—or both. I stand, hoping he'll stop, but his speed increases, each pass across the twenty-foot-wide slab taking mere seconds.

I'm getting dizzy, and worried. "Are you okay?"

He stops and spins toward me. "No, my cuts are hurting. I need more dust." Gage grabs me and his bony fingers dig into my arm. "Get me some?"

"More dust?" Even if it heals, this doesn't seem wise.

"Please! Just a little."

I shake my head and pull my arm from his grasp.

"Help me." He lunges and I jump back. "I can't go down there right now, not like this. If Burn sees me taking more dust . . ." His eyes are open too wide, he's sweating and his whole body's shaking. "He warned me. I don't trust myself. I'll take too much."

He drops to the concrete and starts punching his thighs so hard it would hurt even if he weren't cut.

"Stop that." I grab his arm. "What are you doing? You're going to hurt yourself." Fresh blood seeps through his pant leg—he's not as healed as he claimed—then he curls up in a little ball, tucks his face into his knees and moans. The sound's low and creepy, and although part of me thinks I should try to comfort him, I can't bring myself to do it. Instead I move away, as far from him as I can get on the platform.

Gage is the adult here—Burn and I are kids in comparison—and it's too much for Gage to expect me to look after him. Besides, I'm not qualified. Look at the mess I made of looking after Drake. I was a sorry replacement for our mother.

Sadness lands on me like a fallen sky panel and I drop to the floor, the weight of the last few days sapping my strength.

Hoping to conjure her presence, I rub my mother's ring, but I'm beyond comfort, beyond saving, beyond hope. Cal betrayed me, I lost my brother, Burn deserted me, and now Gage has gone insane. I'm all alone, surrounded by darkness and dust and death.

Gage sobs and his clear self-pity pulls me from mine.

I can't sit here and do nothing. And no way will I cry.

Burn has been gone for too long. I stand at the edge of the slab and look ahead, scanning for him but I can't see him. Whether he's deserted us or needs help, I can't just sit here listening to Gage's moaning. I need to do something. I need to see what we're facing for myself.

I don my mask. Immediately the world grows much darker, so I unsnap the eye-shield and flip it up to the top of my head. Not even saying good-bye to Gage, I grab on to the girder at the side of the platform and swing around until I'm hanging from it in a crouch, my feet braced on the rusty metal. Hand over hand, taking some of the weight with my feet to slow my descent, I lower myself until I'm close enough to the ground to jump.

Dust rises to my knees and I'm glad I put the mask on, even though I already miss the crisp night air. My ankle didn't scream when I landed. Must be adrenaline. Can't be the dust.

I don't believe what Gage said about the dust healing— and I don't want to. A shudder runs through me. If I inhaled enough dust to mend my ankle, I'd be one step closer to becoming a Shredder. It was easy to see how crazed it made Gage.

As I slowly move toward the Shredder camp, searching for Burn, the noise rises along with my fear. Reaching a pile of twisted metal, instead of going around or over, I carefully climb through it. Midway a sound makes me jump. A rat scurries in the corner and my shoulders relax. At least now I know where to come for a meal.

I duck under a beam. The sharp edge of a metal sheet glints in a sliver of moonlight and I lean to avoid slicing my face. The light's brighter ahead, and I'm almost out of this bizarre den-like structure.

Reaching the edge, I start to flip down my visor then stop. Without a fully covered face, dust might sneak under the filter's edges or enter my body through my tears, but I need the extra visibility.

The outpost building is about fifty yards straight ahead, but shouts and screams from the camp make it seem much closer. Their fire casts an orange glow on the dust and the building's sides. Various piles of concrete and steel jut out at intervals—some in light, some in shadows—but there's no way to tell whether anyone's lurking behind one. Even Burn. The nearest hiding place is at least twenty yards away. As soon as I move, I'll be completely exposed.

My best option is to sprint to one of the piles that's far to the side. From there, I'll gain a vantage point to peer around the building. Burn might have been captured, but for all I know he's in cahoots with the Shredders, maybe making a deal to turn Gage or me over, in exchange for safe passage.

I don't really believe that, but I'm in the dark, in more ways than one, and need information to form a plan.

Focusing on the shadows, watching each potential hiding place, I choose a direction then keep low and run. Reaching my target, I press myself against the far side of the crumbling concrete.

The distance was short yet my chest heaves, and I concentrate on pulling in air through the filter to get my breath back. Pressed against the slab to minimize my shadow, I move to its edge and look.

At least twenty Shredders are gathered around a huge

fire. They're all male, as far as I can tell. And on the far side of the fire, two Shredders are shouting at each other in hideous, grating voices that assault my ears with noise, but no detectable words. The smaller of the two picks up the big one and tosses him into the fire.

The burning Shredder roars and my hands fly to my ears, certain my eardrums have shattered. He crawls out of the fire, but as he rolls on the dust to extinguish the flames, he bumps into the legs of another Shredder who kicks him back into the fire.

My stomach revolts. There's still no sign of Burn. I crane my neck to see more of the crowd. A few are stretched out on the ground, and another fight has broken out between six or seven Shredders between the fire and the building. It might be a trick of the light, but it looks like one of that group has metal spikes protruding from the backs of his hands. Not from gloves, from his actual hands.

Nausea rises in my throat and fear grabs my chest. On the far side of the fire, a man—or a Shredder; it's hard to be certain—is strung up between two posts, his limbs bound. Is he alive? Someone shifts and the flickering firelight illuminates the captured man's body. I back away, hiding my face behind my concrete barricade.

Dead. He must be, seeing how his insides are hanging out.

My back pressed against the concrete, I bend at the waist, pull off my mask, and heave for air, struggling to regain my composure. If I don't, I'll be their next victim.

Recovered, I replace my mask and slide to the other side

of the concrete, where I'm better hidden. Burn wasn't around that fire. From here, I could race to the wall in minutes, but not without being spotted by the Shredders, and I have no idea whether or not the door will be locked. Plus, I have no idea how to find my brother once I'm on the other side. Like it or not, I need Burn. I need to go back. Maybe he's already returned.

I'm working up the courage to run when a huge shape— like a monstrous boulder—lands in the dust between me and the Comp building. A cloud of dust rises around the shape, but I can't figure out what it is.

More shapes appear from around the far side of the out-post, and they're easier to identify: Shredders. I press against the concrete, keeping as much of my body behind the slab as I can, yet still being able to see.

The three Shredders head toward the lump. When they draw close, the lump expands and rises. It's man-shaped. But huge. At least seven-and-a-half feet tall and wider than any human I've seen—even Burn. The shape raises its arms and turns in a slow circle.

I gasp. It *is* Burn.

At least this huge monster-like creature is wearing Burn's clothes. His normally loose coat, which I've seen brushing the tops of his boots, now strains to contain his body and hits above his knees. The creature's palms look ten inches across, fingers thick and menacing.

Burn leaps forward and brings his arms, the size of steel girders, down on the shoulders of one of the Shredders. Its body crumples under the blow like its spine was snapped.

The Shredder falls to the ground, but the others continue forward, flinging weapons.

Burn roars and bends to pull what looks like an ax from his leg. He limps forward, grabs the ax-throwing Shredder, lifts him above his head, and throws him nearly twenty feet. The Shredder's body slams into a concrete wall and slides down in a seemingly lifeless lump.

The previously crushed Shredder gets up and throws a metal spike that lodges in Burn's shoulder blade. Burn roars again and tries to reach around to pull it out, but the bulk of his thick arms blocks his attempt. He runs forward, grabs the Shredder's head and twists, ripping the monster's head off of its shoulders. He tosses it aside like a ball.

I cover my mouth to capture my scream.

The last Shredder's more cautious and steps forward, carrying a long chain like the ones I saw wrapped around Gage, but thicker. Each time Burn steps forward, the Shredder swings the chain. Burn grabs for it but, with his thick arms and huge hands, he seems less coordinated and can't catch the flicked chain.

When Burn gets close, the Shredder turns and flings the chain so it wraps around Burn's body, binding his arms. The Shredder drops a loop at the end of the chain over a piece of steel sticking up from the dust. Burn tugs and strains, and I almost think he might break the chain, but his pulling only tightens its hold. The Shredder takes another long metal shard from a sheath on his back and hurls it toward Burn.

Distracted by the chain, Burn doesn't dodge the sharp-edged projectile, and it lodges in his upper left arm. Before my eyes, Burn shrinks back to his normal size. As he shrinks he struggles against the chain and it tightens around him, holding him fast. If he'd stood still as he shrank, the chain might have dropped from his body. But he didn't.

Burn is as good as dead.

The Shredder pulls out a long knife, but instead of plunging it into Burn, he picks up the end of the chain and tugs, yanking Burn down onto his face in the dust. The metal shard sticks up from Burn's back. The Shredder seems amused by this and drags Burn toward the wall.

I gasp, realizing what's about to happen. Right now, Burn is facing one Shredder—the one he threw against the wall hasn't risen and one's missing its head—but if the Shredder pulling him manages to get Burn around the building, he's dead.

I run toward Burn as fast as my feet will carry me.

With his heavy load, the Shredder isn't moving quickly, but I need to do something to draw his attention. It's too dangerous to yell, so I stop to pick up a brick. Taking careful aim, I wind up and throw as hard as I can. It misses the Shredder but lands on a nearby pile of dust. He stops and turns toward me.

I continue to run, gathering my hate and anger. This stupid, sadistic creature will not kill Burn. He will not kill my chances of getting my brother to safety.

"Go back," Burn says when he sees me, and the Shredder tips his head back and laughs.

"You look tasty." He mouths a kiss and my anger builds.

I remove my mask and step forward. "Let him go."

The Shredder smiles at me and the edges of his nearly black lips break and crack. Then, he makes a mistake.

He looks directly into my eyes.

I lock on, and let my anger and hatred build. Fear invades, too, but I'm not sure if that's useful, so I focus on my anger, my rage, my utter disgust.

The Shredder's head tips back a few inches and the tendons in its dried-out neck strain as it tries to look away from me, but I won't let that happen. Its heart beats slower than a rat's or a human's, and its blood seems thick and slow. I grab on to its heart with my curse and squeeze. Blood rushes to my head. I'm dizzy but refuse to stop.

The Shredder drops to his knees. The world darkens and fades like someone threw a blanket over the moon, and my breaths come so quickly that my chest nearly vibrates. I can't do it. I can't stop him. The Shredder's too strong.

But then I feel it. The creature's heart stops.

I squeeze one final time. Everything goes black.

CHAPTER NINETEEN

I OPEN MY EYES. IT'S DARK. I'M TRAPPED. I'M BOUND BY HEAVY ropes surrounding my body. I can't move. They'll skin me alive.

I struggle against my bindings, fighting with every ounce of power and energy.

"Hey, hey, hey, easy," a deep voice growls in my ear, and I realize I'm bound not by ropes or chains, but a heavy, warm body—Burn.

We're sitting inside the den of twisted metal I crawled through earlier. He's leaning back, and I'm curled up between his legs, pulled in tightly against his hard body, with his oversized coat wrapped over us both. But that's all I can figure out.

"What?" I can't form a full question. My voice is weak and hoarse and my head pounds. I can't remember what happened.

"You hurt?" Burn asks.

"I don't think so." I shift slightly and his hand slides from my shin to the side of my thigh. I feel the heat, but he moves it off quickly. I feel so safe, so warm, and the sensation of being held is at once familiar and foreign. Like I've come home to a place I'd forgotten.

"What happened?" I ask.

Burn picks up the hem of his coat and pulls it back over my shin, resting his hand there. "You're safe."

"But . . ." My mind's thick and foggy, like the air near the top of the dome in the hottest months.

"By the way . . ." Burn's voice is strangely soft. "Thanks."

"What for?"

"You saved my life."

"What?" I pull back to see if he's kidding.

"You killed him," he says.

"Killed who?"

"The Shredder."

My heart rate increases. "No." I can't remember what happened, but it can't have been that. I remember watching some Shredders attack Burn—not much else. Is it possible? I wish I could remember what happened. Another downside of my curse.

I rub my temple but it increases the pain. "How did I end up here?"

"I carried you."

"When?"

"Six or seven hours ago. It's almost morning."

Through the dim light I see a blood-coated shard of metal and the remnants of a homemade spear. Images from last night flash in my mind. "You were hurt."

"I'm fine."

"But I saw . . ." What *did* I see?

"Gage helped me get the metal out of my back. I'm okay."

"How is that possible?" The shard is blackened with blood. "You were badly wounded."

"Took in some dust."

I turn, leaning into his chest. "Does the dust heal?"

He nods.

"How? Tell me."

"Don't know how. It just does."

I shake my head. "Dust kills." My mind's a muddle.

"Too much kills some people, not us."

"Deviants?"

He stiffens. "I hate that word."

"Chosen, then." I sort through Burn's words. "If the dust doesn't kill the *Chosen*, then why bother with masks?" I pull forward, looking for mine.

"It's over there." He pulls me back. "You don't need it now. You're fine."

But I'm not fine. I'm confused and utterly exhausted even though I just woke.

Burn leans his head back on the metal sheet. "The Chosen can take in some dust. Small quantities heal, make us stronger. Why do you think your ankle got better?"

I look upward to see if he's joking, but he's not. Not that I can tell. I'm not sure of much anymore.

He puts his hand on my back. "Important thing to remember with dust is: don't take too much."

"What happens then?" I ask softly. "Will we become Shredders?"

"Too much gives you dust madness," he says. I take that as a yes. A yes that neither of us wants to dwell on. A yes that means both of us have the potential to be monsters.

My body tenses as a memory floods back—*Burn as a monster.* "Is that what happened to you last night? Dust madness?"

"No," he says sharply. "That . . . It's . . . It happens sometimes." He straightens his leg and bends the other one. "When I lose control, I become a monster."

He says this as if he's ashamed and on some level I understand. But if he's got an inner monster, I'm glad the monster's on my side. "Is what happened . . . I mean, how you changed . . . is that your curse—I mean gift?"

"Yes." He remains silent for several minutes. My body rises and lowers along with the pace of his breathing.

"How do you—" He pauses. "How do you control it?"

"Control what?"

"Your gift. That thing you do with your mind."

I twist to see his face to confirm he's teasing, but unless I'm reading this all wrong, he isn't. He's serious. There's blood on his cheek and I resist the impulse to reach up and clean it off. "You think I can control it?"

"Better than I can."

I sit still for a moment. He's so wrong but I don't want to argue. My headache's subsiding, but I still can't remember what happened, not fully. "Did I really kill a Shredder?"

He nods.

I shudder. "You think I can control what I do, but I can't. I don't even remember what happened. I can't believe I killed a Shredder. I've never killed anything bigger than a rat."

His mouth twitches. "You graduated from rats."

I wish I could remember more, but what's past doesn't matter. I need to regain focus. "Will we find Drake today?"

"Don't know." Burn's voice is back to its normal gruffness. "First, let's see if Gage comes back."

"Where did he go?" I look around and then twist to see the top of Burn's head. "Where are your night-vision goggles?"

"Loaned them to Gage. Figured his plan to look for another door was worth a shot. My plan didn't go how I hoped."

"What *was* your plan?"

He shifts behind me. "Thought if there weren't too many, I could sneak us around them."

I haven't known Burn long, but I can't imagine what I'd do if he'd died. "It was dangerous to head for their camp by yourself."

"You're one to talk."

He's got a point there, but I couldn't just sit and hope for the best. The light filtering through our metal cave has grown brighter but doesn't have the tone or sharpness of yesterday's sun light. I'm too embarrassed to ask Burn what kind of light's turned on now. "What if Gage doesn't come back?"

"He will." Burn tightens his hold on me, and I'm shocked to realize I don't mind, even though I'm not cold anymore.

"How long will we wait?"

A gust of wind raises the dust outside, and I raise the edge of Burn's coat to cover my face.

Gage crawls toward us wearing his half-broken mask and carrying Burn's goggles. "I found another door through the wall." He jerks his head toward the camp. "Shredders here are sleeping. We've got to move fast."

There's nothing slow about Gage. He disappears in a blur and reappears somewhere else seconds later, repetitively retracing a path ahead of Burn and me as we run.

Gage appears. "Still clear. Can't you move faster?"

Dust flies up in a trail behind Gage as he runs off again.

"Can you run faster?" Burn asks.

"Can you?" I sprint as fast as I can on the dust, but Burn passes me in seconds.

He stops and I smash into him.

"Get on my back." He bends over.

"You're wounded." I resist the urge to put my hand on his back where that shard of metal sliced into him last night.

"It's healing and bandaged. Get on."

My jaw's tight. I hate that I can't keep up on my own, but I put my hands on his shoulders and jump. The instant I land, he runs. Air rushes past my ears, cooling my skin against the sun that's transformed the sky from pale gray to pink and now blue, like some kind of miracle Burn called a sunrise. After he explained the whole earth/sun/moon thing again, I think I understand.

Gage reappears, says it's not much farther, then disappears in a blur. Burn increases his speed and I hold more tightly to control the bounce. Then, in what seems like an instant, Gage is back. "We've got trouble."

Burn stops. "What?"

"Comps."

We aren't moving so there's no need to stay on Burn's back, but his hands grip my thighs.

"Did they see you?" Burn asks Gage.

He shakes his head. "They were close though, right in front of the door. Must have been in the outpost when I was there the first time."

"What now?" I ask.

Burn drops one of my legs, I swing to the side, and he sets me down. I should feel relieved that I'm no longer under his control, but instead I feel vulnerable and small and find myself standing closer to him than I mean to.

"Can you jump the wall?" After what I saw last night . . .

"No." He stares at the massive wall stretching up beside us. "And certainly not carrying either of you."

"Can't you grab on to those?" I gesture up to what look like pieces of metal jutting from the wall.

He shakes his head. "They're booby-trapped with sharp edges on their tops; they'll slice off your fingers if you try to grab on." He looks down. "Seen it happen."

I shudder.

Burn reaches for me and before I can resist, he's swung me up on his back. "Let's see what we're facing."

Two Comps stand between their outpost and what's clearly a door through the wall. The three of us hide at the side of the shelter, out of their sight line, with Gage crouching at the corner of a tall concrete slab, and me on Burn's back, ready for a quick escape. The Comps have huge guns strapped to their backs—guns longer than their torsos—even bigger than the ones that did so much damage to those Shredders yesterday.

"I'll go after the one on the left," Burn says. "You kill the other."

I tense on his back.

"Me?"

"Same way you took out that Shredder."

"Good plan," Gage says. "I'll open the door while you kids take care of the Comps."

Acid rises in my throat. They're right. We need to get to that door. While I have no idea what's on the other side of the wall, I do know what's on *this* side—certain death. But what Burn's suggesting . . . Even if I did kill a Shredder last night, I acted because it was about to kill Burn. That's different than killing this human just doing his job.

"I don't know how I did that last night, or if I could do it again."

"You can do it." Burn shifts me on his back.

"That's not the point." My heart pounds in my ears. "And what about their guns? They think you've kidnapped me. They might shoot first, ask questions later."

"You got a better idea?" Burn's voice is low but tense. Beneath me, his back expands and contracts like he's trying to exhale impatience or frustration, and I want to do my part for the team but I don't want to die—or to kill.

"Why don't we wait until they go back inside?" I like my plan. "They've got to sleep and eat sometime, right?"

Burn grunts.

Gage straightens and turns toward us. "I'll get their attention, then run. They'll follow me. You two head for the door."

Burn nods.

"What if they shoot you?" I ask Gage.

His mouth slides into an awkward, forced smile, and he puts his hand on my shoulder. "Don't worry, darlin'. I can outrun bullets."

I doubt that's possible, but given how fast he moves, he does have a chance of avoiding the Comps' aim.

"How will you get out?" I ask Gage.

He runs a hand through his hair. "You kids leave the door open behind you."

Without a word of debate, Gage dashes off. At the other side of the outpost, he stops and yells at the Comps, "Is this the way to the Hub?"

The Comps leap from their relaxed positions and point their guns, but Gage disappears in a flash. A blast strikes the other side of the building—probably where Gage was standing—and concrete fragments fly. Another blast strikes a few hundred yards farther away and I duck.

Burn runs and the Comps follow Gage as predicted. He appears again, taunts them, and they shoot. By the time they pull their triggers, he's moved again. At least I hope so. I didn't see him fall.

We reach the door and Burn drops me to the ground. He winds up and kicks the door hard with his boot. The sound vibrates my stomach. The Comps don't turn, but the door doesn't budge.

"Find me a rock. Something." Burn kicks the door again

and I glance around, pawing at the dust, suddenly wishing I'd put my mask back on. Although it's just slung around my neck, there's no time, not right now.

I uncover what looks like a block of concrete but I can't get it out of the ground.

Burn crouches beside me. "That'll do. Back off."

I let the block go and fall. Dust flies up around me and I scramble to put my mask on as Burn easily pulls the huge chunk of concrete from the ground. He lifts it high above his head and brings it down hard on the keypad lock on the door. The block breaks in two and the keypad sparks; a piece falls off.

Burn kicks the door again. This time it swings open. He reaches down and pulls me off the ground and up onto his side in one motion. My body slams into his and then we run through the door, leaving it open for Gage.

The entire world bounces to the beat of Burn's gait, and I struggle to take in my surroundings. Just like inside the wall, the ground is covered in dust and riddled with ruins and obstacles, but I have trouble comprehending the distances stretching before me. To the left, the ground rises up, and I wonder if that's another wall or the edge of the world.

But no. I know the world is round and couldn't end there. It's like the earth has some kind of ridge or bump, and I remember reading stories that spoke of hills and mountains.

Ahead and to our right, the entire horizon's filled by a long strip of dark green. It can't be a building, at least not like any building I've seen.

Burn slows and looks behind us toward the wall. "Keep

your eyes on the door. We've got to make it to the forest."

I nod—even though I don't know what *forest* means—and keep watch for Gage, or any Comps, while Burn runs. It's hard to focus with the bouncing and my mask's visor.

Something flashes. The door closes. "Gage got out," I tell Burn. "At least I think he did."

The door bursts open again and a Comp steps through. "Gun!" I shout.

Burn drops me then flattens himself on the dust, draping his arm over my back. Ahead of us, a block of concrete explodes, scattering dust and debris.

"Stay down," Burn says and he's not going to get any argument.

I twist my head to see what the Comps are doing. They're pointing their guns to the left of us, and then something explodes. A blur of gray and green flashes between us and the explosion. The next instant, dust flies up around us and Gage is next to us on the ground.

"We've got to get out of here," he says.

Burn twists to look back. "Stay low." He creeps forward on his belly and I do the same.

Gage gets up, disappears again, and returns a few moments later. "I'll draw them away, if I can." He disappears and a blast hits the dust about thirty feet to our left—the same direction Gage ran. Ahead of Burn and me, a ruin rises out of the dust. It might shield us from gun blasts, but crawling like this, the Comps will overtake us first. And assuming that long, green strip is the forest, we've got a long way to go to get there.

I hope Burn's got another plan that won't lead to our being shot in the back.

The ground trembles.

Aftershock. Decades after the earth died, we still get them.

The Comps stop coming toward us and race back to the wall. I spin the other way. A metal monster is heading toward us.

"What is it?" I ask. It scared away the Comps. That can't be good. Plus, it's causing the trembling I mistook for an earthquake.

There's panic in Burn's eyes. My heart almost stops. Burn doesn't panic. The expression disappears and he moves his head near mine and whispers, "A tank. A military vehicle from BTD."

"What will it do to us?" It's rapidly moving on what look like wide bands of articulated metal plates, crushing every obstacle they encounter.

"It won't do anything." Burn lifts an arm, waves, and the tank monster stops. "But what's inside it will."

Men emerge from the top of the tank, dressed in dull, dark green clothes with irregular spots of other shades of green and gray, and they're all carrying guns as big as—some bigger than the Comps'.

My first thought is relief. We're saved. But Burn frowns. His jaw is tight.

"Follow my lead," Burn says before they get close. "Keep your mouth shut."

CHAPTER TWENTY

"ON YOUR FEET!" A MAN YELLS AND KICKS DUST. THE DUST settles over us and the man's boots. He's obviously the leader, flanked by two other men, and their clothes don't look like anything I've seen inside Haven.

Burn slowly rises and I do the same, keeping close. In the distance past the tank, Gage appears, but when he spots us, he shakes his head and takes off.

For an instant I'm angry—he's deserted us—but it's not like he could help. These men have guns, not to mention their big metal machine that Burn called a tank. Loss tugs inside me. Will we ever see Gage again? His bandages need changing, and I wonder who'll help him and how he'll survive out here on this own.

"Masks off," the man yells. We obey, holding them at our sides.

Pockets cover the men's clothes, and what look like

metal caps sit on their heads. Like Burn's, their masks only cover their mouths and noses. The eyes of the man who spoke are angry and bloodshot. Fear builds inside me. Sparks threaten the backs of my eyes. I drop my gaze to the dust.

"You come from in there?" The man points to the wall. "Did you escape from those dome people?"

"We were never behind that wall or under that dome," Burn answers quickly. He spreads his stance wider and crosses his arms over his chest, letting his mask dangle from one hand. "My wife and I came up from the South."

I snap toward him at the word *wife* but keep quiet. I have no idea where South is either, but Burn seems to have a plan and I certainly have no idea how to deal with these people, or their guns. Their existence confirms Burn's earlier claim that people exist in the world beyond Haven.

"You traveling alone?" The man narrows his eyes.

"We heard there was fresh water up here," Burns says. "Everything's gone dry down south."

The man shifts his gun from one hand to the other. It makes a crunching sound that sends shivers through me. I've never seen a gun so close.

"Why were they after you?" He nods toward the wall, and I glance back to see the Comps head back inside. Clearly they don't want to tangle with these men and their big metal tank monster. A shudder traces through me. Are these men worse than the Comps?

"Those men spotted us taking water from the big lake." Burn lies so easily. "We ran around that wall and thought we'd lost them, but then they came out of that door and sur-prised us."

"Sarge," the man on the right says. "Permission to exe-cute. Him, anyway—there's not much meat on the girl."

Meat? Fear ignites my curse behind my eyes, so I keep them cast down, not wanting to use them as weapons. Not yet. Even if Burn's right and I did kill a Shredder, even if I could bring myself to kill a human, I could only kill one of these men at a time. Chances are we'd be shot before I got started.

"Either of you got skills?" The one in charge asks, com-pletely ignoring the man behind him.

"Skills?" Burn asks so convincingly I'm not sure whether he understands the question. I don't.

"Can you take in the dust?" He narrows his bloodshot eyes. "Can you do anything, *special*?" He sizes us up and grips his gun tightly like he expects an attack.

Are you Deviant? That's what he wants to know.

"No." Burn lifts his mask in demonstration, and all three men tighten their grips on their guns.

"Let's test them," says the man who asked to execute Burn. "Let's cram their faces into the dust and see if they choke."

Burn backs away. "Don't kill us, please. We've come so far. My wife and I just want to find a safe place to settle."

If I didn't know Burn better I'd think he was actually scared, actually pleading for his life. But I sense that this is an act—he's pretending to be frightened and definitely wants to hide that we're Deviant.

The man who wants to kill us picks up a handful of dust

and shoves his glove into Burn's face. Burn spits and chokes, bending over at the waist then twisting, trying to get his face away. He's doing an amazing acting job. I *think* it's acting.

"Don't hurt him," I cry out. Even though Burn told me not to talk, it seems like the natural thing to say. I put my hand on Burn's heaving back. "Please." I look up to the boss. "He'll drown."

He narrows his eyes, and then says, "Corporal, that's enough."

Burn's released but continues to cough and spit.

"Please," I say to the sergeant, realizing it's a title, not his name. "There's so much dust here. May we put our masks back on?"

"You won't need them where we're going," the sergeant says, and the other two men point their guns straight at us, the dark metal as ugly and ominous as the unpainted panels of the sky above Haven's Pents. "March."

"Search them," the sergeant yells after we've marched at gunpoint to the tank. The corporal grabs the small pack off my back, finds my remaining stash of now rancid rat meat, and tosses it to the ground. He pulls out my knife, laughs, straps it to his belt, then throws me my pack.

"Take it off." The sergeant points to Burn's coat. Once it's off, he grabs it.

"Give it back," Burn says in a deep, booming voice and a vein pulses at his temple. "I need my coat."

The sergeant laughs, tosses it to the ground, steps on it, and grinds the fabric into the dust.

My insides lurch, knowing the coat's lining and hidden pockets are loaded with weapons, but the men seem more interested in searching Burn's body. The corporal puts his gun directly under Burn's chin as the other man binds his hands behind his back. Burn stares at his coat as the corporal pats his hands over Burn's chest and back, searching for weapons. Discovering the bandages, the man purposefully pushes on the wounds underneath.

Burn's jaw hardens and muscles on his cheek twitch as he pulls in a long, slow breath. The man checks Burn's legs and when he reaches his calf, grunts and tugs up his pant leg.

"What have we here?" He pulls out a long knife. Grinning, the corporal narrows his eyes and puts the knife into a sheath on his own back.

"We need our knives to skin rats," I say.

"Not anymore." The corporal turns to the sergeant. "They're clean. I confiscated their weapons."

The third man picks up Burn's coat and checks the obvious pockets, finding only empty water bladders and various objects he deems harmless, then he dons the coat. The other two laugh as it engulfs him and drags on the ground. Face reddening, the man takes it off and tosses it aside.

Burn stares at the coat.

The corporal pulls a dark fabric hood over my head. I can only assume someone puts one over Burn's head, too. After binding my hands behind my back with rope, someone roughly grabs my shoulders and pushes me forward.

My instincts scream, "Run. Find Drake," but terror overrides instinct. Terror is smart. Obeying these men is the only way to survive for the moment, especially with my eyes covered by a hood that's tied around my throat.

Burn grunts beside me. I'm afraid that the men have hurt him and hope that his still-healing wounds don't open. The men force us into the metal monster. It roars to life. When it moves, I fall over, striking my head on something hard. The tank bounces and lurches and I slam from side to side, until I find something to grip behind me, a rail of some kind.

The noise inside the moving tank is deafening, but with my hands bound I can't raise them as a buffer. It's all I can do to keep a grip on the rail. The tank bounces. I lift from my seat then land hard. Through the roar and clanks of the tank, I hear laughter. These men are lucky my eyes are covered, or one of them would end up dead.

Feeling lost and alone, I'm not sure where Burn's sitting, and suddenly I'm not even certain he got into the tank. I try to calm myself. My fear must be nothing compared to what Drake is feeling, alone with our father, not knowing where I am. In spite of my father's claim that he wants to help us, how do I know he won't suddenly snap like before?

Tears threaten, but refusing to let them rise, I blink them back. I will not give these men the satisfaction of seeing tear tracks streaked though the dust on my cheeks. My teeth ache from the constant bouncing, my ears hurt from the deafening roar and clanks, my hands cramp, and my shoulders are so tight they feel like they might tear each time I'm tossed to the side.

I need to relax, to stop fighting against the movements, but I dare not release the rail long enough to feel for Mom's ring. I try to imagine I'm up on a rooftop in Haven, talking to Jayma, laughing about the way Sean Cowen makes faces behind Mrs. Cona's back in GT. For a moment it works, but thinking about Jayma makes me think about Scout, then Cal. I was so stupid. Never again.

What feels like an hour later, I'm tossed hard to the right as the tank stops. My ears buzz with the comparative silence.

"Get them out of here." The sergeant's voice fills the small space. "They can walk the rest of the way."

At least Burn's still here. I hear shuffling, then hands grab my arm and force me to my feet.

"Up you go, girlie." The corporal's voice sounds drenched in slime close to my ear. I don't think I've ever hated anyone so instantly.

He pushes me and I step forward. My entire body aches.

Burn grunts, the sound muffled, and I hope he's not hurt. I'm pushed onto a metal ladder, start to climb, and hands press up on my bottom and squeeze. I jerk my hips to the side and resist the urge to kick the corporal below me. I know it's him.

Back outside we march, the sun heating the air under the black hood, making it difficult to breathe. My mask's still over my shoulder and I hope the fabric filters the dust. Walking over an uneven and unseen surface, my legs scream. Each time I fall, I'm punished by the sting and burn of new scrapes and bruises.

It's all I can do not to ask where we're going, but Burn made it clear I shouldn't talk to these people. I lose count of how many times I stumble in a hole or knock my leg, but each time I hit the ground, I'm prodded by what I assume is the gun, or sometimes one of the men's boots. Based on what I hear, Burn has fallen a few times, too.

I'm about to drop from fatigue and thirst, when someone yanks my arm to stop me and I hear the jangle of metal against metal and then a creaking hinge. I'm pulled forward, then metal clangs behind me.

The surface below my feet becomes harder, more even, and other voices and sounds penetrate the cloth bag. I struggle to make sense of the noise but I can't. The smell of cooking meat strikes my nostrils. I inhale deeply but suck the cloth into my mouth and nostrils. Choking, I cough, repelling the dry cloth from my tongue and lips, then draw shallow breaths.

Someone grabs my shoulders, yanks me back, and loosens the rope around my neck. As the heavy fabric lifts from my face, I squint against bright light. The sergeant grabs my arm and starts walking, pulling me along. Ahead of us, the corporal pushes Burn, who stumbles, his hands bound behind his back. At least he gave Burn his coat back—in a fashion. It's covering his head like a blanket, but doesn't fully hide a deep red stain spreading out from his shoulder blade. Even with the dust he's taken, that wound hasn't healed.

Best I can tell we're in a small city, but not one like Haven. I was right to suspect that others survived Outside, and if there's a place like this so close to Haven, I wonder how many other people are alive. Are there parts of the earth that weren't destroyed? There couldn't be, or surely they'd have come to help us.

We turn onto a wider road. A smell twists and growls my belly. Someone's cooking meat over coals. The buildings are smaller than those in Haven. They're made of concrete bricks, and the top of the city is open to the sky—the real sky. A few people are carrying masks, but not all, and I wonder how they keep the dust out of this town without a dome. Many of the men are dressed in the same faded gray-green uniforms of the men who brought us here, and I still can't decide whether we've been saved or captured. Both, I suppose.

This street must be nearly twelve feet across. Even the roads leading into the Hub aren't this wide. The tank could fit down this street. Burn and the corporal fall in step next to me, but I'm not sure if Burn knows where I am. His head's still covered.

Directly in front of me, a boy of about ten walks backward—a slight skip in his step and swinging a short stick, he scrapes on the road with each pass. His hair's cropped short and he's missing one of his front teeth. My throat tightens. He's about the same age Drake was the last time he walked. But Drake was never this hard, this scrawny, this dirty.

"Do they got skills?" the boy asks the sergeant, and I wonder if they've got General Training centers for the employees of this town. The boy hasn't learned proper grammar.

"Don't think so." The sergeant's grip on my arm tightens. "But we aim to find out."

The kid prods me in the belly with his stick, stopping me in my tracks.

"Hey." I wish I had my hands free to grab the kid's weapon.

The sergeant tugs me forward and laughs. Burn struggles against his captors and the boy whacks me in the shin with his stick.

I jump back at the sharp pain. "Ow."

Laughing, the men stop, and one of them takes hold of the kid by his collar and lifts him onto the toes of his scuffed boots.

"Just testing her," the kid says. "Don't seem like she's got skills, though." He strikes me in the arm. My skin burns.

"Please." I keep my eyes cast down. "Why are you hitting me?" I turn to the sergeant. "Why are you holding us captive? What is this place?"

Muffled noises flow from under Burn's coat and hood. They gagged him. He probably doesn't want me to ask these questions—any questions—but I refuse to stay in the dark.

The sergeant turns toward me. "Where did you say you came from?"

"South."

His eyes narrow. "And how long have you been living off the dust?"

"I am not a Shredder." I assume this is the response that will keep me alive. They must expunge Deviants here too. "Dust kills humans."

"Not some it don't." The kid pokes me, again. "Some got special skills and protects us from the Shredders."

His words freeze in my chest but I hide my reaction. "These people with skills must be very brave."

The sergeant narrows his eyes. "Dangerous, more like it. Their handlers are brave." He gestures ahead. Three men are pulling a wheeled cart that's carrying an iron cage. Inside is a man, clearly Deviant, with huge claws where he should have hands. His skin's the same color that Drake's turns when he's threatened.

Nausea builds and I stop, but the sergeant jerks me forward, his grip hard on my arm.

"That one has skills," Sergeant says, studying my face. I'm careful not to make eye contact. "They're part human, part Shredder," he continues. "When they're in danger, or angry, their monster nature takes over. Some are strong enough to kill Shredders." He squeezes my arm. "If not, their screams provide us with an early warning system outside the fort."

As the cage is wheeled past, the men pull Burn and me to the edge of the road and I look into the Deviant man's eyes. He's scared. Terrified.

Who wouldn't be?

I understand why Burn lied. If our captors discover what we are, what either of us can do, we too will be caged.

Used as Shredder bait.

CHAPTER TWENTY-ONE

E'RE LED INTO A BUILDING, THEN DRAGGED DOWN A NARrow corridor until we reach a steel door. From a hook on the wall, a broad man grabs a metal ring holding a series of strangely shaped metal sticks. The sticks jangle, sliding together on the ring, and he pushes one into a hole in the door. He turns it and the door opens. Some doors in Haven have holes like that, but they're never used, and I assume it must be some kind of primitive locking device.

We're pushed down a narrow, dark corridor and then stopped in front of a wall of iron bars. The man with the ring uses another metal stick, and part of the barred wall swings open on screeching hinges.

The corporal shoves Burn, whose shoulder strikes the edge of the door, making him spin and stagger into the stone-walled room. The sergeant cuts the rope from my wrists and I'm shoved in after Burn—his hands still tied, coat still draped over his hooded head. The door of bars clanks closed.

The only light in the room comes from a small window, high on the back wall, and a low bench stretches across the left side. On the other side of the bars, the sergeant crosses his arms over his chest, his two lackeys at his flanks.

"Can I untie him?" I nod toward Burn and the sergeant shrugs, which I take as a yes.

Burn's arm muscles flex when I touch him, and I carefully remove his coat first, the weapons well buried under layers of thick cloth and padding. Then I reach up to loosen the knot that holds the black hood over his head. Clearly sensing I'm having trouble reaching, Burn goes down on one knee so I can get a better angle for the knots. I remove his hood. He squints against the window's light as I untie his gag.

He stands before I get the rope off his hands and strides to the bars of the cage. "Why are you holding us? What did we do?"

"Shut up." The sergeant slams his palm into the bars. "I'll ask the questions."

The corporal stares at me with what looks like amusement as I work on the knots trapping Burn's hands. My scraped fingers sting on the rough rope but I manage to loosen the bindings enough for Burn to break his hands free.

"We don't have any skills," I say. "We're Normals." But I'm not sure my lie is convincing, or if Normal means the same thing here as it does inside Haven.

"I'll be the judge of that," the sergeant says gruffly.

"I'll test them," the corporal says.

The sergeant spins toward him. "You're not killing them. Not yet. Skills or not, these two could prove valuable to Fort Huron." He narrows his eyes. "Especially her. I'm calling the general."

The sergeant turns and strides out of sight, the other two men following closely behind. What would make me valuable? This doesn't make any sense, because he couldn't possibly know about my curse—I haven't hurt anyone since we were captured—but so little makes sense right now, I add his last comment to my heaping pile of uncertainties.

"Where are we?" I ask Burn as soon as the men leave. "Who are these people?"

"Keep your voice down." Burn looks around the cell, studying every inch and running his hand over the walls.

"What are you looking for?"

"Cameras."

I help, looking into the corners, but I don't see any. From what I saw walking through the streets, this place doesn't have the same technology as Haven. There weren't any screens and, I realize, no signs of electricity. But something must have made that tank move. Burn lifts and turns over the bench. He runs his fingers along the underside and then stands on it to run his fingers over the junction of the walls and the ceiling.

Finally, he moves the bench to the back of the cell.

I sit down beside him. "Can you get us out of here with . . ." I look at his coat.

He shakes his head.

"Then why were you so eager to get it back?"

He spins toward me. "Because I need it. Because it's mine."

I take a step back. We glare at each other before I avert my eyes. "I should check your bandages."

Without answering, he removes his loose-fitting sweater and then his T-shirt. I bite my lip. His arm looks fine, but blood has soaked through the bandage wrapped over the gash on his shoulder blade. There's no water to cleanse his wound but I unwind the cloth anyway.

"Do you have anything clean I can use to rewrap this?"

He shakes his head. "Just find the least grimy section."

Reaching around him to pull the fabric back, my fingers accidentally brush across his chest. He sucks in a sharp breath, as if the wound's there. He turns toward me and I look into his eyes, his gaze so dark and intense my cheeks heat. Then the rest of me heats, too.

I glance down.

Something is wrong with me. I barely know Burn, but touching his skin, feeling the hard muscles rippling beneath its surface, smelling his scent, I want to press up against him, want to run my fingers over every inch of his broad body.

I don't understand what I'm feeling or why. Just days ago I felt sure I loved Cal, and although his betrayal is still sharp and fresh, I'm shocked that I'm feeling this way around Burn. What happened with Cal should have taught me never to trust such feelings.

Rubbing my ring, I wipe the emotion and restore my

sanity. I need Burn's help. That's it. He saved me last night and made me feel safe and protected. I'm grateful. Letting other feelings invade is not only unnecessary, it's dangerous.

His bandage off, the wound doesn't look infected, but it needs stitches, and I wonder if these people have medicine. "You should keep this arm still and shifted back." I touch his left shoulder. "Every time you use that arm, you pull the wound across your shoulder blade open."

"Should have inhaled more dust out there," he says, "but didn't want to risk it."

Finding the cleanest-looking part of the filthy fabric, I carefully fold it so that it will pad the gash, then rewrap his chest, trying my best to keep my hands off his skin.

"Why did you tell them I'm your wife?"

"Not too tight." He takes the end of the cloth and finishes wrapping it himself.

"But, if it's not tight, it'll slip off."

He rewraps the bandage loosely but loops another piece diagonally to hold the first one in place. Then he puts his T-shirt back on and leans back against the wall. Motioning me closer, he leans his lips close to my ear, so close I can feel his breath. "Whatever you do, don't let these people know you're a Deviant."

"I thought you didn't like that word."

He doesn't say anything.

"Do you know where we are?"

He nods.

"How far are we from the place where we're—"

"At least a two day's walk." He cuts me off before I can finish. "Maybe more. Getting hauled here didn't help."

"But my father will wait."

"Not sure."

Sadness and defeat settle inside me, stinging my eyes.

Burn releases the tension in his shoulders. "We'll find them. If they don't wait they'll head on to the Settlement and we'll find them there."

"Settlement?"

"It's where we're headed. It's safe."

I want to believe him and there's no point in assuming the worst. I can't permit myself to think that I'll never see Drake again, never find out if he's safe. "Why did you tell them we came from the South?"

"Survivors migrate up here. There's not much water down there so it's hard to grow food."

"How many people live here? How many others survived the dust?"

"I don't know. We stay clear of the people here at the Fort."

I can see why. "Did Management build the wall to keep the migrants out, because there's not enough room in Haven?"

He laughs. "You give them too much credit."

"Then what?"

"That wall is to keep Shredders in. To keep dust in. Didn't you see how it drifts up the sides?"

"But why?"

"To keep you all scared. To keep you from trying to get out."

Anger stirs inside me. If what Burn's saying is true, Management is preventing employees from leaving, from even knowing it might be possible to live Outside, even with masks. The dome keeps us safe from the Shredders, but while they clearly exist out here, we haven't seen any Shredders since we got to this side of the wall.

Burn puts his sweater back on, then reaches for his coat, even though it's plenty warm in this room. Dressed, he sits again and I lean in close.

"What you're saying doesn't make sense. Haven is overcrowded. Why wouldn't they want to let us out if we wanted to go?"

"Think about it." Burn leans back against the wall. "Without their employees, how would Management maintain the dome? How would they create all their nice things?"

"People earn rations at their assigned work placements. That's the way the economy works." I wrinkle my nose. I'm practically quoting the P&P.

Burn moves his lips close to my ear. "Management controls Haven through fear. If people knew they had choices, Management couldn't force them to work."

I'm not sure this makes sense, but we don't get a chance to argue, because a man strides into the space in front of our cell. The way he looks at us makes my blood chill.

"I'm General Phadon," the man says. "Step forward so I can see you."

Burn's already standing. I do the same.

"We're travelers, looking for water," Burn says.

"Liar." The general slams the bars and the sound jangles my ears. "You're trespassing in my fort."

I grit my teeth. His men found us out in the open and brought us here. But arguing does not seem smart.

The general is tall and thin and his hair's cropped so short it's more like day-old whiskers, and a ragged red scar runs diagonally across his face, twisting his lips into an unnatural shape. "Girl, let me look at you."

The hair on the back of my neck rises as I step forward.

"Closer," he says. I look over to Burn, but he's staring at the wall like he hasn't heard the general's demand. Burn must have a plan. Maybe he'll wait until the man's distracted and then attack him with one of his weapons.

I continue forward but stop before the general can touch me. His teeth are crooked and yellow, and my stomach roils as his hand reaches through the bars.

"You'll do," he says and I shudder.

"She's my wife," Burn says softly but he keeps his eyes cast to the ground.

"Not anymore, son." He laughs. "We've got a shortage of females. This one looks healthy enough to bear children."

I spin toward Burn and my ponytail whips around. The general grabs my hair, yanks, and I stagger back to stop the pain.

"As commanding officer of Fort Huron"—his voice is low and deep—"I get first pick of the childbearing females and it's your lucky day, girlie. You get to be one of my wives." He cups the side of my face, drags a callused thumb down my cheek, and his skin's so rough I wonder if it's scraped me.

"Let her go," Burn says, but his voice is quiet and controlled, like he doesn't care. His indifference jabs me, but I can't afford to yield to emotions. I force away the pain.

"You look strong, Boy," the general says to Burn. "Play your cards right and I'll let you serve in my army. Play them wrong and you'll end up invited to Sunday dinner—as the roast." A horrible grin spreads on his face, revealing more of his smelly teeth. "Either way's fine. Lots of protein on you, even if you'll need to be tenderized."

Trembling builds deep inside until I must be visibly vibrating. As horrible as Management might be, no one in Haven eats other people—I don't think—and even if physiologically these people here are like the Normals in Haven, they seem more like Shredders.

"Look at me." The general grabs my chin and lifts my face toward his, but I keep my eyes diverted.

The familiar stinging and tingling builds. Rubbing my ring doesn't help. If I look into this evil man's eyes, he'll discover the truth. I'll be caged and dragged outside this fort to ward off Shredders. If they discover my "skill," these people won't ever let me leave. If I can't leave, I'll never find Drake.

"I said—look at me." The general tightens his grip on my face. "As one of my wives, you'll soon learn obedience."

I twist away but I'm too close to him now, too close to his rotten-meat breath. I gag. He grabs my lower arm and pulls me hard against the iron bars. The rusty metal digs into my cheek, and he presses his hand against my breast and squeezes so hard it hurts.

A roar erupts from behind me. The general drops his hand and I turn.

Gasping, I press my back into the wall at the side of our cage. Burn has turned into the monster. He's expanded at least a foot in height and more than that across his shoulders and chest. The fabric bandages I wrapped around drop to the floor in a bloody mess, and his sweater stretches and strains against his expanded width.

Veins and muscles pulse and bulge from his arms, his neck, his chest, and his face twists into a terrifying grimace. Eyes red, full of rage, his expression floods me with fear. I barely recognize him. I'm glad it's not me he's mad at. I hope not.

He roars again, kicks the bars, and the metal screeches as it surrenders to his foot. The force pushes the general back and he falls to the ground. I should want to cheer, but I can't feel anything but shock as I watch Burn wind up and kick again. The metal bars twist and snap.

General Phadon, on his knees, grabs a gun from his belt. But before he can raise it, Burn forces his way through the bent and broken metal bars. He stomps on the general's arm.

As the man shouts, Burn stomps down on his chest, and I cover my ears against crunching and cracking.

Burn killed the general. I don't care how horrible he was, I can't process what happened.

Fear and horror wind up my chest and into my throat. I'm losing control. If I make eye contact with anyone he'll die.

"Burn, think about what you're doing." I keep my eyes down as he strides toward me.

Without saying a word, he grabs me, wrapping a huge arm around my body and crushing me into his side. My ribs crack. I can't breathe. My mind hazes with pain, and when something sharp and hard scrapes along my back, I realize I'm through the bars. The door at the end of the corridor bursts open. The man who first opened it comes through.

Burn roars, kicks him, and the man flies back. Footsteps pound toward us. Burn leans over, lifts the man, and gripping his waistband, holds him in front of us. The guard's arms wave wildly as several other uniformed men appear holding guns.

But they don't shoot and I realize Burn is using the guard as a shield. He plows forward, crushing me against him with just the top of one arm, swinging the guard in front of us with the other.

The men and their guns back away and I shield my head and face as Burn steps through the building's door and onto the street. Sirens blare in my ears and canopies unfurl above us, covering the streets and blocking the sky. All around me, people don masks, but mine's strapped over my shoulder. I can't put it on with my arms pinned, not with Burn spinning and thrashing me around.

At least I'm doing better than the man being held up by his waistband. As Burn slams him into other people and buildings, his body grows slack and I wonder if he's dead or passed out.

A man in a window to our right points a huge gun straight at us. Gathering my fear, I focus the stinging pain it brings to my eyes, then force myself to look directly at his. We make eye contact, but he blinks, breaking my chance to get a strong hold. Yet he drops the gun, grabs his head, and backs into his house.

Burn leaps onto a huge bin, leaps again, and we land on a roof just as the canopy covers the street below. From this vantage point, I can see most of the fort. It looks to be about a quarter the size of Haven, made up of low buildings that are surrounded on all sides by a wall made of stone, concrete, and steel. In the distance I see a long, green strip like the one I think Burn called a forest.

Most streets are covered by canopies now, and I understand why. The wind builds. Dust strikes my face, stinging my skin and forcing me to squint. I try to cover my mouth and nose with my free hand, but it's impossible to hold that position as Burn leaps from roof to roof. I know he's saving me, but he's holding me so tightly, he's killing me, too. The pain's blinding.

The tank appears on the other side of the wall. Its gun points toward us. Burn sets me down on a roof, grabs two guns from holsters on our man-shield, then tosses his body off the building. The guard lands on one of the canopies, lifeless. A huge boom sounds and Burn grabs me and leaps over the wall of the fort, down into the dust.

Whatever projectile was shot from the tank lands inside the fort, and I hear screams and smell smoke. Burn drops me to the ground and I gasp, realizing that I'm pulling in dust. Pain spikes my chest when I move, but I fight it. Burn climbs onto the tank and bends its big gun to the side. He's strong normally, but that's crazy-strong. Inhuman. Deviant.

Remembering my mask, I reach for it, but he jumps off the tank, grabs me by the arm, and leaps again. Feeling as if my arm might come out of its socket, pain sears through me and the world goes white. Behind us, there's a huge explosion. The men in the tank must have tried to fire their now-bent gun.

Burn leaps again and I dangle, almost striking the ground when he lands. He shifts his hold. My chest screams in pain as he binds his arm around what must be broken ribs, but at least I'm more secure. He runs so quickly the wind and the dust are like shards as they strike.

"Burn," I call out. "You're hurting me." But he can't hear as he runs across the dust, leaping over obstacles, landing hard.

Weak from the pain, I fade in and out of consciousness, until I realize he hasn't landed from his last leap—we're falling.

I open my eyes and we've dropped down a huge hill of dust. Burn hits the ground first and we roll, over and over, but he doesn't let go.

We stop in a heap, me on top of him, and I struggle to make sense of what I'm seeing and smelling. It's like we jumped from a high dust dune into the stretch of green I saw earlier. The dust isn't blowing down here, and the scent filling my head is like nothing I've experienced before. Sharp but pleasant, the scent washes through my sinuses, reviving me for a moment. A canopy of green stretches overhead, supported by thick-stemmed plants—some several feet in diameter—each with a rough surface.

I'm pulled from my dumbfounded awe by the sight of Burn. He's not moving. His grip on my body has loosened, so I tentatively shift my position, wincing at the sharp pain my movement fires. My vision blurs from the pain. I'm going to pass out.

"Burn?"

He's shrunk back to his normal size. I can't tell if he's breathing. The cut on his arm is bleeding, and I can only imagine what's going on with the much worse wound on his back.

"Burn?" I shake him, but moving hurts so much I'm not sure I can rouse him. I slide off his body and land on the ground. Pain spikes from my chest to my brain; my vision blurs and blacks.

CHAPTER TWENTY-TWO

THE SUN CASTS YELLOW LIGHT FILTERED THROUGH A CANOPY of green and brown. Without trying to sit, I crane my neck to discover Burn crouched about ten feet away. That same strong scent I smelled earlier clears my head.

The fort. The general. Burn. The monster. Escape. It mostly comes back—I think. My ribs feel broken but at least I can breathe.

Burn doesn't move but raises his gaze in my direction. "You okay? Because if you are, we need to move."

I draw a deep breath. It pinches, but the pain isn't as bad as I expect, and I remember how much dust I must have breathed while we escaped. Turning from him as I sit, I lift my shirt. My abdomen and side are bright purple, magenta in places, and I tentatively poke my ribs. While I was sure they were broken, they must be just bruised. Or maybe the dust healed them. I shudder.

At a sharp intake of breath, I look up. Burn's standing over me, his eyes on the bruises. I cringe, pulling down my shirt.

When I stand every inch of me cries out, but I try not to show it.

"What happened?" he asks. "Who did that to you?"

My head snaps up. Is he kidding me? His eyes look sincere and concerned, but he hardens his expression as if I've caught him in a look he didn't intend.

"You don't remember?"

He shifts the goggles resting on the top of his head. "Last thing I remember is that asshole general putting his hands on you." His lips twist. "Did he"—he looks down—"did *I* do that to you?"

I nod.

He stomps away, and the brown, stick-like things covering the ground fly up around his boots. "I don't remember. I can't control it."

"You saved me." I take a step toward him.

His jaw shifts. "I hurt you." His voice is low and broken. "I'm a monster." He raises a hand toward me.

I jump back, instantly ashamed by my behavior, but Burn scares me and now that I've seen what he can do, what he becomes, my fear's much worse.

"What triggers your"—I stop myself—"your gift."

"Rage," he says, low and hard. "At least based on what others have told me."

"You're not sure?" I ask, wondering if his curse will shed light on mine. "Can you feel it coming on?"

He stays silent for a while, and then turns toward me. "How did you learn to control yours?"

I shake my head sharply. "I told you, I *can't* control it. I can't control *anything*." An understatement these past days and I realize my previous sense of control over my life, over Drake's safety, over anything, was illusion. Our survival these past three years wasn't due to my precautions. It was dumb luck.

"I've seen you control it." He stands but keeps his distance. "I've seen you hold back. I've seen you stop."

I spot my mask on the ground, pick it up, and pull it tightly to my chest. "It doesn't feel controlled." Burn's brow wrinkles and there's such deep pain in his eyes.

"Did I"—he looks down—"did I *kill* anyone?"

I nod slowly—at a minimum Phadon and probably the guard he used as a shield. Maybe more men when that tank exploded.

Burn's shoulders lurch forward like someone punched him hard in the gut.

His imposing figure exudes danger and malice, but all I see in his eyes is anguish. Even if he's not very good at expressing himself, he's deeply sorry that he hurt me, sorry he caused anyone's death. If he could have gotten us out of that fort, saved me in any other way, he would have.

"Killing the general was an accident. You didn't mean to. You said yourself that you can't control it."

"That's no excuse." He looks down and stomps, shaking his head like he's arguing with himself. "I never, ever want to turn into that monster again."

"You saved me," I say softly. "If you hadn't stopped him, I don't know what General Phadon would have done."

"I do." He grunts and his eyes narrow, but then he looks overhead. I don't want to talk about this anymore, either. Thinking about the general yanks emotions to the surface, sparking the backs of my eyes. If Burn thinks I have a modicum of control, he's wrong.

"What is this place?" I change the subject. "What are these?" I put my hand on one of the thick-stemmed plants we saw earlier.

"Pine trees." He gestures around us. "We're in a forest."

I look up and spin. "I've heard of trees, and I know there are plants in the farms and the air-scrubbing factories inside Haven, but I never imagined . . . They're so tall." The tallest must rise forty feet. I look down and realize the ground is covered by bits of the trees that have fallen.

"Did these come from the trees?"

He nods. "Needles. They turn brown and fall off to make room for new ones to grow."

Ignoring the ache in my ribs, I bend and pick up a handful of the brown pine needles.

"How did the trees survive the dust?" Every living thing outside Haven—whether man, animal, or plant—perished when the dust fell. That's what I learned in GT, but in the past twenty-four hours I've learned how much I don't know.

"See these?" He lifts an oddly-shaped brown thing off the ground. "It's called a cone, and it contains the seeds. When it's in danger, it closes up and only opens when it's safe for the seeds."

Just like my little brother, I think but don't say. Instead I rub my hand on the surface of the tree, then over a grouping of needles. The lovely scent definitely comes from these trees. I can't imagine a more glorious place and wonder if Drake's been here, too.

"How soon until we find my brother?"

"If we walk through the night, we might catch up with them tomorrow."

Joy spreads inside me.

"What's it like?" Burn leans against a tree and looks down.

"What?"

"Having a family."

"You don't have one?"

He shakes his head, and I remember how he told me that he doesn't even know his birthday. "What happened to your parents?"

He doesn't move.

"My brother is the most important person in the world to me."

"That's why you took care of him after your parents . . ." his voice trails off.

"Yes," I say quickly. "Drake is funny and smart and a really talented artist, and even though he has so much to complain about, he almost never does."

"He's lucky to have you as a sister."

"No." I shake my head. "I'm lucky to have him." But my joy hardens. Family is a loaded concept for me, the bad hidden in the good like a terrorist's bomb.

Still, I can't wait to find Drake—even if it means facing my father.

We're slower with my walking, but Burn hasn't offered to carry me, and frankly it's a relief. We move without talking, our progress only interrupted when Burn hears something and raises his hand to signal me to stop. The light from the real moon is prettier than the fake one in Haven, and Burn explains why the moon's such a funny shape, like someone's taken a bite from a circle.

I'm not sure what I expected, but the world outside Haven is varied and vast. We leave the pine forest soon after dark, pass through other areas much like the ruins near Haven and then enter another pine forest even larger than the first. After the forest, we follow a deep rocky path that's almost like a road. Burn says it used to carry water down to the big lake near Haven, but that doesn't seem possible.

Just thinking of water makes my tongue stick to the roof of my mouth. Drake was carrying more than his share of our water, and the last of the three rat-skin bladders I had is now nearly empty. At least the sunlight's not so hot when it's bouncing off the moon.

Burn holds up his hand. I stop, then move closer to him. An eerie howling fills the air, followed by snorting. Rocks roll down the banked surface to our right.

"Behind me. Get down." Burn reaches into his coat and yanks out the bigger of the two guns he stole from the guard. He drags part of the gun against itself and it clicks. Then he waits and waits and waits. My muscles twitch, desperate to run.

A hairy monster jumps over the edge of the bank. Scrambling down on four legs—like a rat—it's much bigger and covered in dirty, matted gray fur. Nearly yellow eyes spark in the bright moonlight and I suck in a sharp breath. I saw an example of this supposedly extinct animal once as a child. It's a dog or a wolf. But opposed to the stuffed version in Haven's history museum, this wolf has foam around its snarling teeth and several huge gashes caked in dried blood on its body.

Burn fires the gun and the creature flies back, half of its head blown off. Then it rolls down the rest of the hill and lands with a thud, about fifteen feet away. Burn retrains the weapon on the hilltop, as if convinced another will follow.

He's breathing quickly. His shoulders rise and fall with each shallow breath as he holds the gun aimed and ready. After what feels like ten minutes, I raise my hand but stop short of touching him. We haven't touched since our escape from the fort. Not really.

I slide my hand onto his back.

He jumps, then relaxes and lowers his gun. "Shredder dog," he says without turning. "Even worse than the humans who turned Shredder. Pack animals didn't need dust madness to give them the instincts to hunt and kill."

"Are there many animals out here?" I try to remember the other beasts I saw stuffed in the museum, some much bigger than wolves.

"Not many." He finally puts the gun away and turns toward me. His face is slick with sweat.

I step toward the carcass and my stomach pinches. "Can we eat it?"

"Too dry and tough."

I cringe, thinking of the chunks of flesh that flew off the Shredders the Comps shot, and how little blood there was. "If there are Shredder animals, are there *Deviant* ones, too—like us?"

He shakes his head. "Not that I've seen. No normal ones in the wild, either. Any born must get killed."

"Born?" I try to speculate how this is possible. I never thought about why the Shredder population hasn't died out. "Can Shredder dogs—can Shredders—have babies? Normal ones?"

"Yes." Burn's short answer is so cold and dark, I'm afraid to ask for more details. I try to focus on a less-terrifying, less-repulsive subject than Shredder sex.

"How much farther until the meeting point?"

He looks down and doesn't answer.

"What aren't you telling me?" I step into his path.

"We passed the meeting point four hours ago." He looks me directly in the eyes and I glance away quickly, his words swirling around my head and stealing my balance. I stagger to the side.

We passed the meeting point. They weren't there.

I've lost Drake.

If my father hasn't already killed him, he'll be tortured by Shredders or torn apart by one of those wolves.

"Let's go." Burn starts walking.

Then I remember. Burn mentioned a Settlement. "We can still find him, right?"

Burn stops and points down. "Look." He steps to the side and points down to the rocky surface of the riverbed.

I rush to his side. "What am I looking at?"

"Footprints," he says. "We've been following them since the meeting point. They look fresh, so if we hurry, we'll catch up with them before day breaks."

My heart swells and my eyes open wide. I lean over the supposed footprints. "How do you know it's them?"

"I just do."

CHAPTER TWENTY-THREE

BEFORE THE SUN RISES, THE SKY TURNS PINK. THE SECOND sunrise of my life and it's even more miraculous out here in the open. We've been walking for over fifteen hours, but every time Burn asks if I need to rest, I quicken my pace. My side aches and the bruises have grown darker, but I refuse to even look at the small caches of dust I've seen stuck between rocks. So close to finding Drake, we can't afford to stop, and I'm terrified of dust madness.

The trail of footprints disappeared miles back, but we've been walking over rocks and through forests and can't even spot our own footprints behind us most of the time.

"Why isn't there more dust around here?" I ask Burn.

"Not much for the dust to stick to. It all blew away."

I nod. He's right that not much sticks to these rocks, and I marvel at the determination of each grouping of trees we pass, finding something to cling onto in this beautiful but rugged world.

We cross through a narrow band of trees and then the rock surface ahead seems to round off and drop into nothing. Getting closer to the edge, I see it plunges about a hundred feet, and beyond that—it looks like water.

The sunrise strikes the water, painting its deep blue surface with a coating of shimmering pink. My jaw drops.

"It's a lake." Burn sits on the edge of the rock and stretches his legs. "Water used to come up to there." He shows me a line on the rocks about twenty feet down, where the surface changes color.

"What happened?"

He turns toward me. "Earth got hot after the dust. Changes in the upper atmosphere. Plus with the quakes, cracks opened up and a lot of lakes went dry."

"Can we drink it?" I shake my water bladder—it's down to its final drops.

"Sure," he says. "But we'll lose a lot of time getting down to it. The Settlement is another full day of walking, if we're fast."

"Do you really think Drake is already there?"

He shakes his head. "No."

"No?" My throat tightens and my heart rate increases. "What happened to him?"

"I think they're somewhere around this lake." He leans out, shields his eyes with his hand, and looks to each side. "Problem is, I don't know which way around they took."

About half of the lake is ringed by trees, but the far side

is barren rock which must drop off, because beyond it I can't see a thing.

Finding them seems impossible, then my heart lifts. I have an idea. No matter which direction my father took around this nearly circular lake, assuming he's following its edges—and why wouldn't he?—he and Drake can see down to the water as easily as we can. If I head down there, into the open, Drake will spot me.

Walking out to the edge where Burn's sitting, I look down. It's not quite as steep as I first thought. The rock's not entirely smooth. There are places to put my feet.

I can do this. I know I can. Without even mentioning my plan, for fear he'll stop me, I sit and slide down the top of the steep edge, keeping my center of gravity back and using the heels of my shoes to slow me.

"What the hell are you doing?" Burn grabs for me but misses.

"I'm going down near the water!" I shout back. "Out in the open, so Drake can spot me."

"If there are Shredders around, they'll spot you, too."

That thought gives me chills, but Burn doesn't sound convinced. My plan's worth the risk. If Drake's being carried by my father around the perimeter of this lake, he'll see me.

I've descended about twenty feet when Burn catches up. He glances over as he passes. One side of his mouth quirks up in what could only be called a grin. "Good plan. Low risk of Shredders here, anyway. Not enough dust."

It takes a moment to process this as praise. My heart flies as we continue to scramble and slide down the rocks. When it becomes flat enough to stand, he reaches for my hand to help me up but I ignore him. I can walk over rocks.

Reaching a particularly big gap I regret not accepting help, but gather my strength and leap, landing safely on the other side. I jump down from the last big rock to what, if I'm to believe Burn, was once the pebbled bottom of this lake.

I race forward then spin. Shielding my eyes when I turn to the sun, I scan the row of trees and rocks high above us.

"Might as well get water, now that we're down here." Burn trudges forward across the pebbles, pulling water bladders out of coat pockets.

I proceed slower, searching above us for signs of Drake. When I turn back toward Burn I gasp. The water containers all filled, he's removing his clothes.

"What are you doing?" I raise my fingers to my lips, realizing I pretty much shouted.

He turns back. "Washing. Got a problem with that?"

I step forward slowly, marveling as each layer of clothing comes off his broad body until he's down to his bloodstained shirt. He pulls that off, too, and all I can do is stare as the sunlight glances off the planes and ridges of his back, his shoulders, his arms. He reaches back to test the nearly healed wound on his shoulder, then drops his shirt into the water. Crouching at the edge, his back muscles flex as he kneads the shirt, then lifts it and rings it out.

He unclips the elastic cord that holds up his oversized pants. They drop to his ankles. He doesn't have anything on underneath, and I suppose it would be hard to find underwear that would both stay up when he's normal size and not tear to shreds when he gets angry.

He kicks off his boots, steps out of his pants and crouches to rinse his clothes. My breathing grows fast and shallow, completely out of control, and I want to look away, but I can't. I've seen drawings of the male body nude, but never imagined the strength and power and beauty. It's the beauty that shocks me. The hard curve of his buttocks, the slope of his back, the ripping of his muscles as he kneads his clothes under the water. I'm mesmerized, studying the lines of back muscles, how they connect, how they flex under his smooth skin.

Finished, he twists in his crouch to toss his wet clothes back onto the pebbles. His eyes meet mine and his lip quirks. I look down, embarrassed, cheeks hot. Hearing splashing, I raise my eyes as he runs, water spraying up around him. When the lake gets deeper, he slows. Just as it reaches his upper thighs he dives, disappearing under the surface.

I almost scream. What if he's swallowed up by the water and I'm all alone?

But he breaks out, arms first, and leaps into the air with a whoop. He spins and streams of water fly from his hair and body. His smile transforms him into an entirely different person. I can't help but smile, too. How funny to learn that Burn can transform in two completely opposite directions.

"Come in." He traces his arms along the surface of the water and it sprays toward me.

I've never seen anything like this. Never imagined it.

Not only have I never seen so much water in one place, it

never occurred to me that one could enter such a pool. Stepping up to the edge, I bend and touch the surface. My fingers send ripples radiating outward. I look up and Burn is on his back in the water, his chest and head above the surface, and he's kicking and moving his arms. While I'm scared, I'm also excited and can't strip my clothes off fast enough.

Leaving on my T-shirt and underwear—they need washing anyway—I remove my shoes and tentatively stick one foot into the water. The underwater surface is pebbled, not as slippery as I expected, and I slowly move forward, taking each step with care until the water licks the tops of my knees. I don't think I've ever felt anything quite so marvelous.

"Come on!" Burn shouts. "It's easier if you get in quickly. Run."

He rises up from the water, its surface licking just below his waist, and his chest glistens like it's been glazed. Raising his arms above his head, he gestures for me to move forward, so I drop my fears and run. The water slows my progress, nearly tripping me, but I laugh, assuming I look like a small child running for the first time as the water splashes up the sides of my body.

"Dive," Burn says and puts his hands up over his head to demonstrate.

"No way." The water laps my underwear with glorious coolness.

Burn lunges over, picks me up, and I scream as he tosses me into deeper water.

I splash and flail, at first fearing I'll drown, but I quickly realize I can put my feet down. When I open my eyes, he's grinning, and then he flops back into the water. It looks so fun, so I do the same and stare up into the bright blue sky as the water rushes over my body. Sinking, I put my feet back down, but Burn is beside me in an instant.

"Lie back. I'll show you how to float."

I bend my knees until I'm in the water almost to my chin, then tip my head back and let my legs rise from the lake bottom. I twitch as Burn's hand sweeps under my shoulders, but he's smiling—such a rare sight—so I force myself to relax and his other arm brushes under my bottom and legs, barely touching, but amplifying my confidence. I'm safe.

The water laps and slides over me and I've never imagined feeling this fresh, this clean, this happy. All thoughts of danger and dust fade, diluted by the water dipping into my ears.

"Stay still. Don't worry." Burn's voice is deep and soothing and slightly muffled by water. "I'll keep you safe."

At those words, I flash back to Cal's assurances.

I snap out of my water-induced euphoria. Bending at the waist, I start to sink and I flap my arms to keep from drowning.

"Hey." Burn steadies me until my feet are down again, but I back away from him.

"What happened?" He looks genuinely concerned and maybe hurt, and then he looks away. He pushes off and propels himself backwards through the water, leaving a V-shaped wave in the water behind him.

I stand, stupefied, embarrassed at how I reacted. He was just being nice, just trying to teach me something new, and I snapped, acted like he was trying to kill me. "I'm sorry," I call after him. "It's hard for me to trust anyone."

"No kidding."

I sink down and let the water wash up to my chin, then tip my head back and remove the string holding my hair. As I rub my fingers over my head, my hair fans out, the water waking nerves on my scalp I didn't know were there. Our lives in Haven were so dependent on water, but I had no idea it could be so miraculous.

The sun warms my skin when I rise, and the water snaps it with cold when I duck back under. Stretching out, I let the water slide over me and discover it's easier to float if I move my arms, like Burn does. The real sky is so beautiful and I wonder if Management knows what it's like outside Haven, outside that wall.

My hatred for Haven grows as Burn's theories about Management's motives start to cement. The original Management team might have saved a lot of people by building Haven's dome, but we're no longer employees, we're slaves kept ignorant and scared.

I close my eyes, curl into a ball, and let myself sink under the surface, then burst out of the water.

When I open my eyes, Burn's right in front of me, staring down with fire in his eyes. My first instinct is fear—is he angry?—but then I recognize his look. It's the same look Cal had before he kissed me, but different. Burn's look is darker, deeper, more ferocious, and I see his monster within the heat of his gaze.

Turning away, I dip down into the water again. When I

come up, my hair's across my face. I stay crouched, the water almost up to my chin. It's about waist height on Burn. He steps forward, brushing the hair from my face, then cupping my jaw, and he softly guides me up from the water until I'm standing, our bodies an arm's-length apart.

The heat from his eyes lights a fire the water can't cool. Heat and water swirl between us, pulling us closer together. I long to yield to the moment, to let him draw me into his arms, to feel—but fear invades.

Fear of trusting, fear of his monster, fear of feeling too much at his touch.

My eyes tingle. I look away quickly.

How can I be around Burn—around any boy who makes me feel strong emotions—without causing him pain? Besides, after Cal's betrayal, I don't want to trust a boy ever again.

"Look at me." Burn's voice is husky. His hand traces along my jaw, his thumb brushing over my face, lighting fires along my cheek. "You can control your gift. I trust you."

Tentatively raising my glance to meet his, I nearly fall back, slammed by the intensity in his expression. His hands draw me up until I'm standing, so close that if I leaned, I'd be pressed against him. He bends toward me and the muscles below his ribs flex and ripple. His lips are cracked and dry but it's sexy, rugged, and when I see how intent his gaze is, something deep inside me clenches, hard. With so much swirling inside me, I don't dare continue looking him in the eyes. I focus instead on his lips that draw close.

We're startled by a sharp whistle.

I bend my knees, dropping down to my shoulders in the

water, fear washing out everything else I'd been feeling. Burn raises his fingers to his lips, makes a similar whistling noise, and it's answered by another from above.

He turns to me, smiling. "We've found them."

CHAPTER TWENTY-FOUR

UNGS BURNING, I SCRAMBLE OVER THE ROCKS. I'VE FOUND my brother.

"Careful," Burn says from below. "No sense getting yourself killed."

He reaches up to grab one of my feet, and I stop for a moment, leaning against the rocky cliff, panting and shading my eyes. I can no longer see Drake or my father from this angle, and I've realized a flaw in my let's-go-down-to-the-water plan. While it wasn't that hard to slide down the steep edge of the lake, getting up and out is another matter.

Can Burn jump the remaining distance? I'll bet Angry Burn could, and wonder what it would take to make him change.

He points to the right. "It slopes up more slowly over there."

I look up, searching for handholds above us, but he's right. The bank is nearly sheer here. There's no way up.

We head to the right and I slip on a large boulder.

"Easy," Burn says. "They saw us; they're not going anywhere."

Unless my father doesn't *want* us to find them. Unless the Comps catch up with them. Unless those horrible men from the fort chased us here. Unless there are Shredders attacking Drake right now, or one of those Shredder dogs.

Disasters flutter in my brain, marring the lightness I felt on first spotting them high above us on the bank.

Burn stops and studies the rocks up and to the sides. "Let's try here."

I don't see a path, but I want to get up to the top so badly—and I trust his judgment. How ironic that I trust Burn to lead me to the man who warned me never to trust anyone, then proved he was least worthy of trust.

Nerves about facing my father twist my stomach, so I try to focus on the climb and on watching where Burn puts his hands and feet on the steep slope. After a few minutes of climbing I glance down. Big mistake. If my hand or foot slipped, there'd be nothing to break my fall and, even if I managed to survive, few of my bones would. I'd be smashed. Dizziness threatens to fulfill my nightmare, but Burn's hand lands on mine as he reaches back for me.

"Almost there." He looks into my eyes and I nod, shocked at how comforted I feel.

We climb for another few minutes then he stops on a

shelf of sorts. It's not that bad. I've been on plenty of narrower window ledges inside Haven, and I'm relieved we can take a brief rest before completing our climb. I turn and slide my back down the rock to sit, just fitting on the rock ledge with my knees tucked into my chest.

"Crap," Burn says, and I look up and see what caused him to use off-policy language.

Nauseated, I rise to my feet. "Do we need to go back down?" Above us, there's almost fifteen feet of vertical cliff. The ledge we're on tapers off to nothing not far ahead. Almost at the top, we've run out of a safe route.

"Hector!" Burn yells, and a few moments later I see my father's face and shoulders emerge from the cliff's edge.

"Got yourself into a bad spot, haven't you." He grins, and I look for a loose rock to throw at his face.

"Hand her up," my father says and, before I can even think about what he means, Burn bends and grabs me below my knees.

"Keep straight," he says, lifting me, and I put my hands in front of my face and freeze every muscle as my body rises up the edge of the cliff. If I struggle, or even let my torso bend, I'll fall.

Fear races through me as my father's hands reach down. Burn thrusts me higher and my father looks directly into my eyes. "Take my hands."

All-too-familiar sparks ignite behind my eyes and I can sense his thoughts: *Trust me, Glory.*

Trust him? Is he kidding? Anger builds.

I'm not deliberately trying to hurt him, not trying to use

my curse, but it's obvious when the pain strikes. I see it in his face.

Breaking eye contact, I fight to regain my center, to squash my fear and hatred. I don't fully understand what just happened. I can't have really heard his thoughts, and in spite of Burn's misconceptions, I can't control my curse. Still, if I want to see Drake, I have to find a way to avoid killing my father—at least until I get to the top of this cliff. I need to trust him to help me.

I look back up. He's still there but his expression's grim. I raise my arms and he grabs on to my wrists. I grab his, too, and we're linked. My life is literally in my father's murderous hands.

"Got her!" he yells. Burn's hands slide to the bottom of my feet, and he gives a final thrust. I rise and imagine Burn pressing his arms straight under my feet.

My father grimaces with strain, and then he releases one wrist, grasps my upper arm, and slides back on the rock. He lets my other wrist go and I dangle for a terrifying instant, but sling my free arm over the top to grab onto the edge of a rock. It thankfully doesn't shift under my weight.

My face and chest are over the top now, and my dad pulls on my other arm as I push and wiggle until my weight safely transfers onto my belly. My still-healing ribs scream.

He reaches over to help me pull farther forward, but I swat his hand away and push down with my arms. I pull up one leg then the other. I made it.

It's only then that I wonder how Burn's going to follow. Even if he can jump that high, the angle's too sharp, the ledge too narrow. I spin around on my belly and stick my face over the edge. He's gone.

I spot him down and across from where we were, and he's searching for another way up.

"He'll make it," my father says. "Don't worry."

"Hi." Drake's voice comes from a few yards away. I scramble to my feet and see my brother leaning against the trunk of a pine tree—standing.

"What?" I race over and pull him into my arms. "How?" I push him back so I can see his face. His huge grin erases the sting and ache from every scrape and bruise on my body. "You're standing."

He nods. "Can't walk yet—not more than a step or two—but they have feeling and I can move them. Look."

He slides one of his legs away from the other. He teeters a bit, and I grab his shoulders to keep him from falling, but he's already caught his balance.

"Drake, I'm so happy." Tears threaten to choke off my words, so I close my eyes for a moment to calm myself. "I'm so glad you're okay and I'm so sorry I left you in that tunnel. I was only trying to distract the Comps and—" I stop to catch my breath. "Your legs. How long have they had feeling?"

He leans back against the trunk again. "They started to tingle almost as soon as we got out of the tunnels. Dad says it's the dust." He shakes his head, as if he doesn't believe it himself. "When I woke up the first morning, I could bend them, and after a little practice, I could stand. They're getting stronger and stronger, but get tired easily." He bends them and I help him slide down to sit.

Shaking, I sit down next to him. "I'll never leave you again. Ever. I'm so sorry."

"That's okay."

"No, it's not, Drake. It's my job to protect you and I left you all alone. I don't think I could survive if I'd never seen you again."

He hugs me. "You were trying to draw the Comps away. It was brave."

"It was impulsive. I didn't think it through."

"We're together now. Why worry about what might have happened?"

"When did you get so wise and grown-up?"

His face is full of concern, and I can't believe how our roles have reversed. I'm the one who takes care of him. I'll never let him down again.

A shadow moves. I look up to see my father standing nearby. Has he been spying the entire time? I was so excited to see Drake—Drake standing—I'd forgotten he was here. I pretend he's not. I will not let my father ruin this perfect moment. I've found my brother again. With me, he'll be safe.

Sounds emerge from the forest and I prepare to shelter Drake from whatever comes, but it's just Burn. He crashes past a branch and nods toward us.

"Reunion over?" he asks. "Let's get moving."

I spin back toward my father, but Drake's grinning in his direction and I'm too exhausted and sore to face the full reality of this situation, or think about my father's crime. For a moment, I'd rather pretend I've got a parent again. Just for a while. Just until I regain my energy.

One false move and I'll kill him.

Lying in the small cave Burn found, I grab on to the sleeve of Drake's jacket. No chance anyone will take him away while we sleep. In fact, I don't plan to sleep but I've had that falling feeling a few times, and I might not have a choice. Sleep will eventually win. Burn and my father are lying near the cave's entrance, and I'm glad to know that if Shredders show up, Drake won't be the first taken.

I stretch the aching muscles of my legs and flex my throbbing feet. We walked all day, and Dad and Burn took turns carrying Drake. I worried that the straps of the harness Burn uses for Drake might reopen his shoulder wound, but he didn't complain or show any signs that he's injured.

Drake talked nonstop for the first few hours, telling me how he and Dad had to wait at the mouth of the tunnel for a full day before they could leave safely, and how Dad snuck them past ten sleeping Shredders once they did get out. While I'm glad I'm back with Drake and glad he seems happy, I cringe, thinking about how much danger my brother faced, how I let him down, how if I'd been smart and moved us more often, how if I'd stayed away from Cal, we might now still be safe inside Haven.

But I'm no longer certain that would be preferable. Crazy—since I'm currently lying on hard, cold stone—but true.

As scary as it is Outside, especially when the wind picks up and we have to put on our masks, I've never felt more alive and free—almost happy.

I dream about my mother, all of us together again, but when I wake and I'm not in the old apartment we shared, I panic. Remembering quickly, I reach for Drake.

He's gone. I'm all alone.

I scramble to the mouth of the cave and spot Burn not too far outside, leaning against a rock. He waves, and then looks away. I'm glad I'm not alone, but it's not Burn I'm looking for. I stand and run forward. Horror seizes my chest.

My father has his hands cupped in front of Drake's face. He's feeding him dust.

"What are you doing?" I shout. "Stop!"

I race over the rocky surface, grab the shoulder of Dad's jacket, and yank as hard as I can. He drops his hands and dust falls to the ground. Drake gasps for air.

"Don't touch him!" I yell. "I should have killed you when I had the chance."

My father's face falls and he backs up a few steps.

I grab Drake by the shoulders.

"It's okay, Glory," he says. "The dust helps my legs."

"You'll get dust madness. He's trying to get you addicted."

I start to lift Drake, to get him farther away from my father, but Drake uses his legs to fight me.

"Stop it, Glory!" he yells. "Dad was helping me."

I glare at my father. "I take care of Drake. Me, not you.

Leave him alone." I narrow my eyes and lower my voice. "Murderer."

The color drains from my father's face.

"Shut up, Glory," Drake says. "If you knew the truth—"

"Quiet," my father says low and hard.

"What Drake?" I ask. "What don't I know? Please. Enlighten me." I charge toward our father and push on his shoulder. Burn steps over and puts his hand on my arm, but I shrug him off. "Leave me alone. Both of you. And leave Drake alone. I can take care of him."

Burn turns to my father. "He has had enough dust."

"I told you." I glare at my father. "I won't let you hurt him—ever again."

My father's eyes twitch. "I'd never hurt Drake."

I slam the heel of my hand into his shoulder. "How can you say that?" Tears rise in my eyes. "After what you did— how can you possibly say that? How can you possibly expect me to believe that?"

I can barely see, can barely breathe, can barely think. Fire builds behind my eyes. No one will look at me. "You killed Mom, paralyzed Drake, left me unconscious, and yet you expect forgiveness?" I punch his arm.

My father reaches toward me but drops his arm down before his fingers make contact. Smart move. If he tries to touch either of us again, I'll kill him.

"I'm sorry." My father's voice is soft. He keeps his gaze down by his feet where a pocket of dust has collected in a crevice between the boulders.

"Sorry?" I say. "You think a pathetic apology makes it

okay?" Heat sets my cheeks aflame. No one will look me in the eyes. I'm not surprised. "Are you going to claim it was an accident, too? As if that makes any difference. Murderer."

"Shut up, Glory." Drake staggers forward.

"What?" I step toward him. "Are you going to defend him again?" I grab his shoulders. "How can you possibly forgive him for what he did?"

Drake shakes his head and looks directly into my eyes. "Glory. *He* didn't kill mom. *He* didn't kill anyone. *You did.*"

CHAPTER TWENTY-FIVE

"WHY WOULD YOU SAY THAT?" I ask Drake.

No one interjects to set things straight, so I grab Drake by the shoulders. "He's been feeding you lies." Lies more toxic than too much dust. I shake my brother and his shell-like armor appears in an instant.

I drop my hands from his arms and stagger back. He almost falls, but Burn's there to prop him up. My father backs away and stands watching.

"It's true," Drake says. "Dad wasn't even home when it happened. You were angry. Yelling at mom. She collapsed and I went to help her, but when I looked back at you, pain stabbed inside me."

"No, that's not what happened."

"You blacked out and forgot." Drake holds up his armored arm. "When I felt the pain, my Deviance appeared for the first time. The pain in my chest stopped, but as I turned back to mom, a searing pain hit me low in my back. I never felt my legs again. Not until I got Outside. Not until Dad taught me to inhale dust to cure my paralysis."

I collapse like I've been struck down by a girder. Hitting the ground, I turn away from everyone and curl into a ball.

Could I have possibly? The idea tears through me like a jagged knife.

I did it. Me. I paralyzed my little brother. I killed my own mother. I'm the worst kind of monster. I suck in ragged breaths but I'm crushed, buried under tons of rocks and the weight of this accusation.

Images of that day drift back and don't help. I was angry. Very angry. In fact, I flew into a rage because—I am so ashamed—because my mother wouldn't give me permission to go to the Hub without her. I wanted to go with the older kids. With Cal. Even if she'd given me permission, I would have felt out of place with a bunch of kids about to graduate from GT.

Cal asked me to go with them, but even back then I knew he wasn't inviting me. Not like that. Not how I wanted him to. He was nearly sixteen; I was thirteen. Juliana Holder, a pretty girl his age who liked him, was going. I wasn't even that angry with my mother and certainly wasn't angry with Drake.

I was angry that I was only thirteen. Angry that I wasn't prettier. Angry that I still had three years to wait before I could date. Terrified Cal would get a bracelet with Juliana, not me.

A hand lands on my shoulder and I jump, springing back and pushing with the heels of my shoes to get away.

"Glory." It's my father. "Stop that." He takes my hand off my head and I realize I've been tugging at my hair. No wonder my scalp hurts. I bring my fist down hard on the rock beside me.

He lifts my hand and presses his lips onto the already rising bruise. "I didn't want you to know," he says. "Ever."

I pull away. "You lied."

He blinks and leans back, and I realize my inappropriate, misdirected burst of anger almost hurt him. I bury my head in my arms again and he runs a hand down my back, his fingers stroking me in the same familiar way they did when I was a child.

"You didn't mean to," he says. "You didn't know you had a gift. None of us did. If it's anyone's fault, it's mine for not watching you more closely for signs you were Chosen."

"Chosen?" I spit out the word. "Management might not have much right, but *Deviant* is a much better word than *Chosen*."

"It wasn't your fault," my father says softly and carefully, like I might not understand the words, or maybe afraid his words will detonate a bomb.

My throat closes. My father's afraid of me. Of course he is. Who wouldn't be? I'm a monster.

I've hated my father for so long and now . . . I can't even begin to deal with now.

I need to escape. I need to go . . . somewhere. Anywhere but here.

I jump to my feet and run.

Tripping over the edge of a boulder, I land hard but rise quickly and keep running. Pain shoots through my knees and shins and hands. I don't care. I deserve it. After what I did, I deserve pain. I deserve to die.

At that thought, I change direction and head for a cliff we passed late last night before reaching the cave. If I run as fast as I can and jump out, my body will smash on the rocks. If I don't die from the impact, I'll suffer horrible pain until death.

Not that it will begin to make up for killing my mother, my mother with the same dark hair as Drake, my mother who picked up our rations and made sure we stayed clean and fed, who worked at the garment recycling factory until her fingers were so cracked and raw that they bled. My mother who worked tirelessly for our family but never once complained. I had no idea how much she did to take care of us until the job fell to me.

I can't live with what I've done. I don't deserve to.

Through the trees I see the cliff.

My legs and lungs burn, my mouth tastes like metal but I'm almost there. Just another few seconds and—

Something slams into me from the side, hard, and my feet lift off the ground. It's Burn, real Burn, normal-sized Burn, and he's holding me tight in his arms as if I've been bound in steel.

"Let me go." I struggle against him with all the energy I can muster.

"So you can kill yourself?" he growls in my ear, and I realize there's no point in struggling. I'm just making it harder for him. He doesn't deserve that. And goodness knows I don't want to send him into a rage. Not that I care if he kills me, but what if he hurts my father or Drake? Besides—I let my body go slack—maybe if I calm down, he'll let go and I can continue my race toward death.

He scoops me up. I don't even fight back as he carries me, then sits down against the trunk of a large pine tree. My back leans against one of his bent knees and he swivels my legs under his other leg and straightens it to trap mine beneath his.

Burn is smart. I'll give him that.

And he's quiet right now. Good. But what's he supposed to say? *Bummer that you killed your mom. Bummer you ruined your brother's life. Bummer that your dad almost gave his life for your crimes.*

As we sit in silence, my palms sting and I realize they're raw from scrambling over sharp rocks. Blood stains the knees of my pants, too. Relishing the pain, I let it wash through me, and I look up. A light breeze blows through the boughs of the trees, changing the shadows, filtering the glare of the bright sky and releasing the occasional dried needle to flutter toward the ground.

I want to be one of those needles. I want to float away into nothingness. I want to be trampled into the ground. I want to be finished.

The world around me blurs. I blink and tears stream down my face. I can't remember the last time that happened. It feels strange, foreign, something that happens to other people's faces—not mine.

My thumb finds my ring, but instead of offering comfort, it burns. Who am I to seek comfort, especially from my mother? The ring sticks on the way off and I relish the pinch. As soon as it's free, I fling the ring as far as I can, not watching it land.

"You done feeling sorry for yourself?" The bass of Burn's voice vibrates my ribs and I don't answer—too numb to think, never mind speak. "Now you know. Time to move on."

I pull away from him as best I can with my legs trapped. "You knew?"

"Hector told us when we found him."

"*You* found him?"

"Not just me. But, yes."

"And since then, you've been watching me, watching Drake?"

"Again, not just me. The Freedom Army looks for people in danger. Gets them out if needed. Protects them when we can. As soon as we found Hector and heard what happened, we got Drake's records taken out of the HR database."

I suck in a sharp breath. That makes so much more sense than all the theories I had. Of course it wasn't just luck or an accident that Drake dropped off Management's radar screen. Suddenly, I need to know everything about the day my dad was expunged.

"What happened to my dad? How did you save him?" He took the blame for my horrible crime, and guilt engulfs my every pore, my every cell. At this moment, all that matters is my knowing what happened. I need to know every detail of how my father suffered for me. I need to feel the full weight of my crimes.

I draw a ragged breath through my nose.

"You should ask your dad," Burn says.

"I want *you* to tell me." I turn to him and look directly into his eyes. "I can't bear the thought of asking him." I raise my hands up to cover my face. "What I did . . ."

"I can tell you some of it." His hand runs softly down my back. "But I don't know everything."

I look up to him expectantly. "Please." I can't believe I'm begging Burn, begging anyone for anything. But I've never felt quite so desperate, so vulnerable, so pathetic.

Burn bends his arms, puts his hands behind his head, and stares up. "I was only thirteen or fourteen, but because of my size and strength, I was already on an Extraction Team."

"Extraction Team?"

"For the Freedom Army. They're based in the Settlement we're headed for. We're who saved you and Drake."

I nod. This army must be the people Management calls terrorists. "Go on."

"Your dad was lucky. We didn't know there was an expunging that day. My team was headed toward Haven on a routine mission to identify and make contact with the Chosen. It was supposed to be my first time inside the dome, but we never got there."

"You didn't?"

He shakes his head and drops his arms down. "Our team leader was monitoring the Haven TV broadcast, and we saw the expunging begin. Usually the Comps just let the Shredders get down to business, but with your dad, it was clear they weren't leaving anything up to chance. They made sure the Shredders would get him."

A pinching pain rises inside me, closing in on my throat and pressing hard on my temples. I want to cover my ears but I don't. "How?"

"They tossed him outside without shoes or a shirt. He'd been whipped and was bleeding badly. I think they knew his blood would draw the Shredders. They were right. Bastards were on him in seconds, inflicting more wounds and messing with the ones already there."

Blood rushing in my ears, my breaths coming too quickly, I struggle to hear him.

"Your dad's strong. The Shredders would've recruited him if we hadn't arrived when we did."

"Recruited? I don't understand."

"The torture isn't just sadism."

I shudder. "It's not?"

"The Deviants they capture, the strongest ones, the ones who survive the torture—"

"Become Shredders." I finish his sentence. Every cell inside me hurts. My body feels weighed down by a thousand stones. I'm not sure I can take any more, but I need to know everything that happened. "How did you save him? Tell me more. Tell me everything."

He draws a long breath. "There were only five of us that day. I was ordered to stay back, to stick to the entrance of the tunnel, but when I saw what those monsters were doing . . ." His voice trails off and he looks away. He forms fists.

"Don't feel bad," I say softly. "You were too young to help."

He looks straight at me and there's pain in his eyes. "Oh,

I helped. Believe me, I helped. But I killed one of our men in the process and I dislocated your dad's shoulder."

"Oh." I don't know what to say.

"It was the first time I changed. The day I discovered what I am—a monster."

"You're not a monster." Although that's exactly how I've been thinking of him since I first saw him change, maybe even before. I vow to stop thinking of him that way. It's not fair.

"Neither are you."

I take a deep breath. I need to absorb all I've heard, to sort out my feelings. It's not easy when I want to crush them, too. But I keep returning to the bottom line: I killed my mother and I paralyzed my brother, which led to my father's torture and near death.

As bad as Burn might feel about hurting people that day, or cracking my ribs, he saved my father's life and rescued me. It's not the same thing.

I've tried to be a good person, to do the right thing, to protect my brother, but I am not a good person. I never do the right thing and I constantly put everyone I love in danger.

Hanging my head I force out my emotions, let numbness permeate, dull everything. Burn can't trap me under his leg forever. When he finally lets go, I'll disappear. Being around me is toxic, dangerous, fatal.

"Hey," Burn says.

I don't respond or even open my eyes. I'm done talking.

"We need to go. Now." My father's voice snaps my eyes open.

Burn rises, pulling me with him, and I'm a limp rag in his arms. "What's up?" he asks my dad.

"Shredders," Dad says. "We spotted them in the distance."

"Where's Drake?" My rapidly beating heart pushes through the numbness. Did he leave my brother alone to be tortured by Shredders?

"I'm going back to him now," my father says, then disappears.

"Where did he go?" I search all around us. Does he run even faster than Gage? He can't have just vanished. Did I imagine him being here?

"I'll explain later." Burn swings me up onto his back. "Hold on."

We run. Or rather, *he* runs and I keep my head down, my face buried in his thick neck to avoid scratches from the pine boughs. I should let go, let myself drop to the ground, let the Shredders find me and do what they will, but that plan won't work.

If I drop down, Burn will stop.

As much as Burn likes to think he's a monster, he'll try to save me. I'd put him in danger, again.

CHAPTER TWENTY-SIX

WITHIN MOMENTS WE CATCH UP WITH DAD AND DRAKE. Burn sets me down and takes my brother. But we haven't run another hundred feet before a Shredder steps from behind a tree. His shirt, fabricated from human finger bones, rattles as it moves over his maroon-skinned chest. Fingernails stretch out like talons and his eyes shift rapidly, like he can't control them.

"You're all together now." The Shredder's voice is so loud and grating it scrapes my ears. "How handy."

We turn but there are two Shredders behind us.

"I'll distract them," my dad tells Burn. "You take the kids to the Settlement."

Burn nods and grabs my arm. Before we can move, my father disappears. He reappears behind the first Shredder and brings a rock down on the monster's skull. The Shredder roars in anger and pain, the rock lodged in his skull, a bizarre hat to match his horrific bone-shirt—yet he's not dead.

The other two rush forward. My dad disappears, then reappears between us and the other Shredders. He swings a huge sword-like chunk of metal, and it slices into the leg of one of the Shredders with a thud.

"This way." Burn grabs me around the waist. He bounds forward, running as fast as he can, but even with his strength and speed, holding Drake on his back and me on his side, he's not fast enough. They'll catch us—after they kill my father.

"Stop." I push against his body. "Burn. Stop."

He glares but lets me go, and I drop to the ground.

"I can't leave him behind. I can't let my father sacrifice himself to save me. Not again. I need to help." I back away.

"No!" Drake yells. "Dad can save himself."

The Shredder with the rock-hat grabs my father's arm and the other two look back at us, as if deciding whether to go for the victim in hand or the three in the bush.

"Why doesn't he teleport?" Drake asks, and I realize teleportation must be my father's Deviance.

"He can't," Burn says. "Not when someone's touching him."

I don't wait for Burn or Drake to say more. I race toward my father, but so do the other two Shredders. By the time I get there, all three are busy slicing and jabbing my father with their knives and sharpened fingernails. I'm about ten feet away and trying to figure out a plan, when my father looks up. He shakes his head. I stop.

One of the Shredders turns to see what my father is looking at. Then the Shredder grins, his teeth brown, his lips cracked and nearly black. He saunters toward me, casually, as if there's no hurry, no question in his mind that he has me trapped and will eat me for dinner.

It's hard to tell what's skin and what's clothing—everything's stained dark with blood. But he must be wearing a shirt, because he's got shards of metal sticking out across his shoulders and down his arms like studs. They can't be part of him. They can't.

They are.

He stops several feet away and looks me over. "Aren't you cute." His voice is like razors. "Can't wait to see if you're worthy. We could use you for breeding."

The Shredder with talon-like fingernails slashes them down my father's cheek, and he cries out in pain. Anger builds, diluting my fear. These monsters are hurting my father. My father who's already done so much more for me than I ever imagined.

Look up, I think as I keep my eyes trained on the Shredder, but his eyes remain hungrily on my chest, not my face.

"Hey!" I yell. He finally looks up.

Big mistake.

My eyes latch on to his and I focus, drawing out every ounce of hate and anger I can find, letting it build and flow. I focus on his brain. I twist. I squeeze.

The Shredder's hands rise to his head and he wails in agony. The sound scrapes through my mind and nearly makes me lose focus, but the Shredder can't look away. I've never targeted a brain before, but it's like I can sense the monster's thought patterns, feel the red and black sparks of malice in his mind. It helps build my power. It's like I'm using the Shredder's own mind, his own hatred and rage, as fuel for my weapon.

His skull bursts.

I stagger back as pieces of bone and brain fly through the air.

My chest heaves as I drag air into my lungs. The world warps and fades. I'm going to pass out. I can't let that happen. Two Shredders still have my father, and I don't know if Burn got my brother to safety. I can't pass out now. . . . I can't.

My eyes snap open. Dad's shaking my shoulder. His lips smile but there's concern in his eyes.

"What happened?" I ask, but I remember more this time—everything that happened until I blacked out. At least I think I do. "Did I make a Shredder's head explode?" My voice is hoarse; the words hurt.

My father nods.

I try to move. My head pounds. "Drake?" I call, then relief floods through me. Sitting nearby he waves, a shaky smile on his lips.

But I don't see Burn. "Where's Burn? What happened to the Shredders? Did they kill him?"

"No," my father says. "Can you stand? It's unusual to see Shredders around here—there's not enough dust to live off. But we should leave in case their pack's near."

With Dad's help, I stand and look up into his eyes. When he doesn't look away, my heart fills with guilt, regret, sadness.

I look down. "I'm so, so, so sorry."

"Sorry?" he runs his hands over my shoulders. "You saved my life."

I shake my head. No matter what he says to console me, it can't erase what I've done, or the sacrifice he made.

"Time to head out," he says. "We might get to the Settlement before sunrise." The sun is setting, casting a yellow glint on the rocky ground.

"I won't leave Burn behind."

"He's fine." Hands on my shoulders, my father pulls me forward, and I realize he's trying to keep me from looking behind me. I slip out of his grasp and dash back.

The ground is strewn with body parts and, horrified, I search for evidence of Burn, but all the chunks are dark and dry. All Shredder. At least I hope so.

I turn back to my dad. "Did he—?"

My father's jaw is tense and he nods. "The Shredders charged toward you when you fell, but before they reached you, Burn's gift kicked in. He tore them apart."

My heart slams against my ribs. My head throbs. "Where is he?" He swore he'd never change again. He must feel horrible.

Dad shakes his head. "He ran off. But he'll be fine. He'll find us."

"Let's go," Drake says.

I turn toward him. He's risen to his feet on his own and

he takes a few deliberate steps toward us. My heart lifts. He's walking stronger every time I see him.

"Get on," Dad says to Drake. To my amazement, my brother jumps slightly to get into place on my father's back.

We walk quickly and silently as the light fades and darkness falls. The moon's bright, but I can't see too far in any one direction as the forests have become more plentiful and dense.

I have so many questions for my father, so many ways I want to say sorry for everything I've done, but his silence is soothing, soaked in forgiveness.

Now, if only I can find a way to forgive myself.

CHAPTER TWENTY-SEVEN

BY THE TIME MORNING BRIGHTENS THE SKY, I'M OVERFLOWING with worry and dare not look directly at anyone. We haven't seen Burn. Yes, he took out those Shredders—*took out* is an understatement—but what if he was found by others?

Horrible thoughts torment me. He might have found a stash of dust and succumbed to dust madness. The combination of Burn as both monster *and* Shredder is too terrifying to imagine. But even more terrifying is imagining him alone and hurt, either physically or emotionally. He swore he'd never change into his beast again.

Drake chattered for a while last night as we walked, asking questions about the Settlement and the Freedom Army and digging for more details about life BTD, but I wasn't really listening, and only the occasional word penetrated the murk in my mind. I don't know what to expect when we reach the Settlement.

For the past two hours, Drake has been quiet, resting his head on my father's shoulder. I keep thinking he's asleep, but his arms remain clasped around Dad's neck. He's even using his legs to grip and help distribute his weight. Dad's steps are growing heavier and I should offer to carry Drake, but my body and head feel like I was in a physical, not mental, fight with that Shredder.

Plus, I'm too depressed to form the words to offer.

We step out of the shelter of trees. Across a field, the ground rises sharply.

Just days ago, mountains and rocks were nothing but concepts, things I'd read about but never seen, and I tip my head back to look up to the top. Drake slides down from my father's back and takes a few stiff steps.

"We'll rest here for a few minutes," my father tells him. "Stay close,"

Drake winds around us in circles, practicing, and his gait improves with each step. My father has Drake in sight so I stare at the rocks, hard like my mood. A black vein traces up and over a small hump in the granite, as if the rock is expelling the darkness within.

"You okay?" my father asks. I turn without thinking.

He smiles tentatively, testing me, like he's worried I'll attack. Given the circumstances, I understand his apprehension, but right now I couldn't muster the energy or emotions to kill a rat.

"You did a good job," he says.

"Killing that Shredder?"

"Keeping Drake safe. Taking care of him, of yourself. You

were so young." His voice cracks. "I couldn't be more proud."

"Proud? I—" The sentence won't come. He knows all the horrible things I did.

"Yes." His voice is firm. "Proud."

Drake stops and points up. "Are we really climbing up there?"

"The Settlement is over this ridge, down in the valley below. Dust rarely blows up that high. Most of the settlers don't even carry masks." He grins at me as if I'm supposed to start jumping up and down with glee.

I turn away but he continues. "There's a lake down in the valley with plenty of clean water, and farms and trees, and anyone who wants one can build a home."

It does sound idyllic, like a story set in the world BTD, but I don't feel happiness or even excitement. It's like I can't feel anything, like everything I've done has erased my ability to feel. Perhaps that's for the best. When I feel, people die.

A sudden breeze blows past, and my father extends his arms to wrap them around Drake and me in protection. Every muscle inside me tenses.

"Glory?" a man's voice says, and I duck out from under my father's arms.

"Gage!" I rush forward and embrace him, and for a split second I forget my despair. He looks stronger now, and while his clothes are still torn and bloodstained, I don't see any evidence that his wounds are still bleeding.

"Where's Burn?" he asks.

"Gone." My despair returns. "We haven't seen him since yesterday afternoon." My teeth worry my lip.

"I've seen him since then," Gage says.

"Really?"

"How else do you think I found my way here?" He turns to my dad. "You must be Hector. I'm Gage." He grins. "And I bet you're Drake. I've got a son about your age."

My insides pinch as I realize how much Gage left behind in Haven. I'm ashamed I didn't press harder and find out if he had a family. Whoever betrayed Gage, betrayed them, too. Dad looks at me for an explanation, but I focus back on the rocks.

"They know you up there, right?" Gage asks Dad. "Because they didn't seem all that friendly when I ran up to take a look."

"Who are you?" My father's voice is tight, deep and laced with suspicion, and I recognize the man who taught me not to trust.

"Gage Trapp." He extends his hand to shake, but my father doesn't take it. "I was expunged from Haven three days ago. Tried to outrun the Shredders and Comps—I'm fast—but they slowed me down with chains and concrete blocks. Shredders caught me, but then I ran into Burn and Glory." He steps over and tips my chin up with the crook of a finger. "You kids saved my life."

I resist squirming. I didn't do anything to save him, no matter what he says, and even if I had, it wouldn't make me less of a murderer.

"What makes you think they aren't friendly up there?" my father asks, his voice still suspicious.

"Those." Gage points up.

My curiosity gets the better of me and I look to where he's pointing. Along the top of the ridge, I can just make out what looks like wooden towers.

"They've got guns," Gage says.

My dad nods. "They're defending the Settlement against Shredders."

"Get many up there?" Gage asks.

"None," Dad says. "But we can't be too careful. We came across some less than thirty miles back." He reaches for Drake. "Let's get going."

"I want to walk," Drake says.

Dad narrows his eyes. "Okay. For the first while. It gets steep."

Drake starts off quickly, and his happiness almost penetrates my blackness.

"Come on," he calls back to me. "Stop dawdling."

I run to catch up, leaving Gage and Dad talking behind us.

Drake and I walk in silence as the ground starts to rise. He stumbles, and I reach for him. "Let me carry you."

He shakes his head and continues. "It wasn't your fault, you know. You didn't know you could do that. How could you have known?"

I tense at his words but trudge along, keeping him in my peripheral vision, ready to lunge for him if he falters. "Why didn't you tell me the truth?"

He steps over a rock. "Would it have helped if you knew?"

I turn back. Gage and Dad are gaining on us, and I

don't want either of them invading this conversation. I pick up my pace. "It would have changed *everything* if I'd known."

"If you'd felt bad, or turned yourself in, you might not have done such a great job keeping me hidden."

I bite my lip. For the past three years, I thought I was protecting Drake but he was protecting me, too.

"You were only ten," I say. "How could you . . ." I'm not sure what I want to ask.

Drake ducks to avoid a tree branch. "I was old enough to keep a secret. Dad and I agreed—"

"You *agreed*?" Shame pinches its way up my throat and grabs at the insides of my ears. "You and dad made *plans* to keep this from me?"

His ankle wobbles. I step closer. He doesn't resist as I duck and pull his arm over my shoulder, to take some of his weight and guard against his falling.

"Dad told me never to tell you," he says. "He told me to stay hidden as long as I could."

"He told *me* to tell everyone you were dead. To hide you." I help him over a fallen log. "I still don't remember what happened. . . ."

Drake squeezes my shoulder. "As soon as it happened, you passed out, cold. I was terrified."

"Because I almost killed you."

"Because Mom was dead. Because I thought *you* were dead."

"And Dad?"

"You were unconscious when he got home. The best

we could figure was that your Deviance triggered mine. The danger brought out my armor and protected my vital organs."

"But your legs."

"My armor doesn't extend low enough, or didn't come up fast enough." He shakes his head. "I'm not sure."

Footsteps approach. Dad and Gage have caught up.

"Get on my back," Dad says to Drake and he nods, clearly tired.

"I need to stretch my legs," Gage says. "Now that I know how great it feels to have open space, I can't get enough." He races off in a flash.

I stare at my dad as he gets Drake settled on his back. There are still so many questions, so much new information to process, and so many things I don't understand. "You can teleport?" I ask him.

He nods. "But I can't carry anyone with me." He grins. "Otherwise we'd be at the Settlement by now."

"Why didn't you teleport out of the dome—"

"Where to? I didn't know there was life Outside."

"But once you were out . . . Burn told me how they found you. If you can teleport, then why didn't you do it to get away from the Shredders?" *And why did you take the blame for what I did?*

"I didn't even know I was a Deviant then. My twin sister was, so I always wondered about you kids."

I stop. "We have an aunt?"

"Really?" Drake says, excited.

"Had." Dad looks down. "She was expunged when we

were teenagers. Once I realized there was life out here, I hoped I'd find her. . . ." He shakes his head.

I walk in silence, trying to push through all my questions to ones I can voice, ones that won't scrape coming out, ones whose answers I can bear. My father lost more than I imagined. His kids, his wife, his sister.

"I want to walk again," Drake says.

My dad shakes his head, then says, "My gift didn't manifest until I was exposed to the dust."

"Really?" I suck in a breath, considering the implications.

"Best I can figure. I've met others at the Settlement whose gifts weren't fully revealed until they were exposed to the dust."

"Does that mean others inside Haven might discover they're Deviant if they got out and breathed dust?"

He shakes his head. "I'm not certain, but I think so."

My mind spins. "I guess it'd be a risky thing to test."

"There's the rub. No one knows how much dust is too much. Even for us Chosen. If we take too much—" He stops himself.

"We become Shredders," I finish.

His head snaps toward me and it's clear he didn't know I knew this. He nods, a grim look on his face.

"Is everyone at the Settlement a Deviant?"

"No. And we don't call it Deviant. We call it Chosen."

"Chosen for what?"

"Chosen to adapt to the dust, I guess, to survive." He pauses for a moment as if considering what he just said. "But some at the Settlement can't tolerate any dust without choking. A lot of people traveled up here from the South. They survived for generations in bomb shelters and mines—anywhere they could find—but when they came out from hiding, the dust was so thick it made what little soil was left impossible to farm. Most water supplies had dried up. They came north."

Burn told the people at the fort that we'd traveled up from the South. Now I understand why, but I don't know if Burn told my father about how we were captured and taken to the fort. I certainly don't want to, so I keep my mouth shut.

We're nearing the top of the ridge when Gage runs back to join us. "The air is so fresh here. Almost no dust. Amazing."

Dad nods and I decide to stop asking questions. For now.

We enter a clearing and Dad climbs a lone tree at its edge. Near the top, he unclips a cord that's wrapped over a branch. He unfurls a bright red flag then waves it in a pattern—two small swoops to the right, a giant figure eight starting down to the left, then three circles above his head. A moment later, I spot flags waving in similar intricate patterns from the two guard towers. Dad climbs down and we continue up the hill to its crest.

When I reach the top, my breath catches. Stretching below us are thousands of buildings, all much smaller than the high rises in Haven, but even from a distance they instantly look more like homes than anything I've known. Farther ahead there's a gleaming lake surrounded by green. Green brighter than the skin of the cucumber Cal fed me. Greener than the needles of the pine trees we've walked through. And there are fields of soft gold, too. It's so beautiful.

"What do you think?" my father asks.

"Spectacular!" Drake says and grins.

"Holy moly." Gage runs forward.

Joy spreads inside me, trying to push out the blackness, and I think I might let it. Drake's always been a positive guy, but looking at him now, it's like I've never seen him smile before. The entire world seems brighter. Even though I know I don't deserve the happiness this place promises, at least I've accomplished my goal. Drake is safe.

We continue to walk down a well-worn path that zigzags in long, sweeping passes. Soon both sides are lined with small buildings. Like the uppermost parts of Haven, many of these dwellings are constructed from materials clearly salvaged from ruins, but some are made of wooden planks that look new. Fresh wooden planks are something I never saw in Haven, although I now realize there might be many things Management had access to that I never witnessed.

Ahead, a woman steps out of a doorway and shakes a small rug. "Good morning," she says as we pass. Her smile's broad and genuine, but her eyes are the strangest color I've ever seen—bronze, and they sparkle so much it's like they're faceted. Whether she can do anything beyond seeing with those eyes, her appearance alone would brand her a Deviant. I hope she never lived inside Haven.

After we round the next bend in the road, a group of about ten men and women appear. They're walking with purpose and authority toward us. At the group's apex is a man who's well over six feet tall. While his height makes him seem slight, his figure's imposing and his hair's closely cropped and coppery. His tightly fitting suit is made of the heaviest material I've seen. It looks thick and strong like the Comps' armor, but it flexes more easily, almost like leather but it can't be—leather is way too rare to make into such large garments.

The two men flanking him are similarly dressed and panic skitters in my chest. Their approach is too much like Comps marching toward us, or those men at the fort, but Dad keeps going so I don't let fear stop me either.

Burn steps out from the back of the pack.

My heart skips and a smile bursts onto my face. Waving, I start toward him but he immediately turns away.

The air rushes from my lungs like I've been punched. I know he saw me.

Drake tugs my arm, pulls me forward, and the tall red-haired man steps up to us. He shakes my father's hands and they lean in for a quick, backslapping embrace. Burn holds back, not even looking in my direction.

"Welcome to the Settlement," the man says. "I'm Rolph. Commander of the Freedom Army."

"Army commander," Gage says, with caution in his voice. "Do you welcome all guests like this, or are we special?"

Rolph turns toward Gage. "Not sure about you, yet." One corner of his mouth twitches up. "But you"—he turns directly toward me—"you might prove very special indeed."

CHAPTER TWENTY-EIGHT

THERE'S NO MORE MENTION OF MY BEING SPECIAL, AND I DON'T bother to tell the commander how very wrong he is—unless he deems murderers special.

The commander takes Dad forward to walk with him, and every few minutes my father glances over his shoulder, like he expects Drake and me to vanish. Burn still hasn't said hello.

The hair at the back of my neck remains on alert, as if it's expecting Comps or Shredders or some unknown danger to leap out at any moment, but nothing scary happens and I have to admit that the atmosphere here is more welcoming than hostile. As we pass, people stare, but we also get nods and smiles. As we descend farther into the Settlement, my neck hairs stand down, the tightly bound muscles in my shoulders unfurl.

Near the bottom of the hill, where the land flattens and

the town seems to spread out forever, Drake, Gage, and I are ushered into a building that's made of stones piled up on each other. The building has windows—with real glass!—and I can't resist walking over to a window and running my fingers over its surface. So smooth, so hard, yet virtually clear. A few bubbles are scattered inside the glass, and as I move my head to the side, I notice that in some places the glass bends slightly from within, distorting the stones of the building across the street.

The room appears to be a restaurant, but not like the ones in Haven. Here you can sit down to eat and drink. Although I've yet to see any food, the mere smell makes my stomach cramp and scream to be filled.

"Hungry?" my father asks. He puts his hand lightly on my shoulder and, for some reason, his tiny gesture sparks tears at the back of my eyes.

He should hate me. He must hate me. How could he not hate me? And yet I can't find evidence of hate in his words or actions.

Not waiting for me to answer, Dad guides us over to a long bench that looks like it was made from half a trunk of one of the pine trees. After we sit, a man, with a round face and even rounder belly, sets a large black pot at the other end of the table. Steam, carrying the most delicious smell that's ever hit my nose, rises from the pot and my stomach twists and growls.

The man returns with a stack of bowls. My eyes almost leap out of my head as he starts to ladle liquid, with big chunks of white and green and orange, out of the pot.

"What is it?" Drake asks.

The man laughs as he passes the bowl to the woman at the far end of the other side of the table. "Soup. Chicken and vegetables."

"Chicken?" I've heard the word but can't remember where.

The man makes a noise that sounds like *tut-tut* and then passes a bowl to my side of the table. My eyes widen, realizing that everyone's passing the bowls down. The first bowl will end up in front of Drake, and the second bowl will be mine.

My father, sitting next to Drake, turns to us. "A chicken is a small bird. Its flesh is good to eat and it lays eggs that are tasty, too, and a good source of protein."

"But," I say, "there are no living things Outside except Shredders and rats." I smile at my mistake. I know better now, yet can't stop reciting what I've always been told.

"Oh, you poor kids," the man serving the soup says.

The man next to me pushes the bowl of soup in front of me. My head snaps back at the scent, then my nose is drawn down to the liquid. I could satisfy my cravings by merely inhaling the scent from this glorious and mysterious concoction.

My father picks up his spoon and dips it into the liquid in his bowl. He blows on the broth to cool it, and then puts it into his mouth. It's not my first broth, but I've never seen soup filled with so many marvelous things and I'm glad for Dad's demonstration, letting us know it's okay to eat.

I dip my spoon in and stir, awed at the bowl's contents.

There are chunks of what I now recognize as meat, and I lift a spoonful with one of the orange-colored chunks. I look up.

"Carrot," my dad says without me having to ask, and I try to reconcile this bright disk with the dried gray cubes I've had in my rations.

I slip the spoon into my mouth and the heat of the broth instantly warms my insides, as if it has flowed more places than just down my throat. I bite down on the carrot. The fresh, sweet flavor jumps on my taste buds. Trying another bite, I discover that chicken tastes a lot like rat—except better—and it's tender, easier to chew.

"Eat up," says the man with the pot. "There's lots more where that came from."

I continue to spoon the food into my mouth, savoring every taste, and I wonder if there will ever again be a time in my life when I'm this happy.

"Drake, you can sleep over here." Dad points to a mattress against the wall and close to what he's already told us is a stove that's used not only for cooking, but also to heat the cottage during winter months. "And Glory, I rigged a curtain for you here so you can have some privacy from us boys." He pulls back a sheet of blue fabric hung on the other side of the room, to reveal another mattress, raised up off the ground on a legged platform and covered by a clean lavender blanket.

Without even thinking, I dash toward it and run my hand over the blanket's soft nap. "It's beautiful." My father's beaming, and a rush of memories wash over me. Memories from before our lives fell apart.

Before I ruined our lives.

For my eighth birthday, Mom gave me a new blanket made from scraps she'd salvaged in the factory. It wasn't as soft as this one, but at the time it was the most luxurious thing I'd ever seen, never mind owned. The Health & Safety people used it to wrap Mom when they took her body away.

I sink to the small rug in front of my bed and bury my face in the edge of the blanket.

My father sits on the mattress and pulls me up from the floor and into his lap. I resist but his hug transfers warmth and comfort—comfort I don't deserve but accept.

"Why did you do it?" I ask, my voice shaking. "Why did you sacrifice yourself for me?"

He squeezes me more tightly. "You're my daughter. I would do it again in a heartbeat."

"I'm so sorry." Pain constricts my throat and pinches my temples. "I know it's not enough just to say it, but I'm so, so, so sorry."

"Oh, Glory." He hooks his finger under my chin, trying to look into my eyes, but I won't let that happen, not when I'm feeling so much my eyes sting.

"This is the last time I want to hear you apologize," he says. "It wasn't your fault. I won't hear another word about it." His words are stern, but his tone isn't and I press my cheek into his shoulder.

Drake crosses the room. My dad rises, setting me down, and the three of us embrace.

"I'm so happy our family's together again," Drake says.

A lump clogs my throat. "But Mom—"

"Nothing," my father says. "No one can tear our family apart. Not again."

There's a knock and Dad lets us go. He opens the wooden door a crack, enough so I can see who it is. The commander nods at my father, who shakes his head sharply then steps outside, closing the door behind him.

"Do you think everything's all right?" Drake asks but I've run out of reassurances.

A few minutes later, my father returns and tells us that he has to leave for a meeting. He suggests we get settled and take a nap. The second that Dad leaves, Drake crosses to his mattress, plops down on his belly, and falls asleep on top of his blanket. I drape mine over his sleeping body, smiling at his splayed legs as he lies as peacefully as a baby.

I'm tired, too, but my mind is moving so quickly I doubt I could sleep. I don't want to leave Drake alone, but this place seems safe and I'm curious about the Settlement.

When I open the door, I'm temporarily blinded by sunlight and raise my hand to shield my eyes. Burn's standing about twenty feet away, leaning against the wall of another house and staring at me. Heat traces through my body and I'm not sure if it's anger, or surprise, or something else entirely.

He crosses over. Once he's nearer, his body shades mine from the sun, but I keep my eyes trained on his chest. He's taken off his signature long coat and several layers of clothing, and even though his T-shirt's several sizes too big, it can't hide the definition of his muscular shape. Cal seems like a distant memory. A distant *bad* memory, and I let myself imagine a life here at the Settlement. A life with my father and brother. A life with safety and security. A life with Burn.

"Hector will be gone awhile," he says. "Want me to show you around?"

"Yes, please." This is exactly what I want and I'm surprised that I don't want to be left alone to explore. Perhaps I have changed over these past days, become someone different—a person who accepts help and trusts others. Here I almost believe it's possible to do that and survive.

He looks down. "You aren't afraid?"

"Of what?"

"Of me. What I did to those Shredders."

"No." *Maybe a bit.* "Is that why you ignored me before? Because you thought I'd be afraid?"

He stares at the ground.

"Burn, you saved my life, saved my family."

His head snaps up, but he quickly looks away to face the road. "What do you want to see first?"

"Where are the chickens?"

"The chickens?" He looks at me like I'm nuts, but then he nods. "I forget so few people in Haven see the agricultural factories."

A grin spreads on my face. "And we don't have chickens."

"Yes, you do. But only Management gets to eat them, and they segregate the farm workers assigned to the chicken coops."

That might explain a few unexplained disappearances.

"Do people who recover in the Hospital go to work in the coops?" Whatever coops are.

"No," Burn says sharply. "One of the main goals of the army is keeping Haven employees out of that Hospital."

"Do you know what happens in there?"

"We have our suspicions."

"Jayma's brother died in there." I touch his arm. "What do you think happened to him?"

"You don't want to know." His expression turns grim. My hand drops from his arm.

"I *do* want to know."

"It's classified." He turns to face down the street, and I resolve to keep asking until I have answers. But right now I'd rather focus on happy things, on the Settlement, and forget Haven and the Hospital exist.

Burn continues to answer my questions as he shows me around the Settlement, and I'm shocked to discover there are animals beyond chickens at the farms. Animals I thought were extinct—cows and pigs and goats.

He explains how, when the dust fell, some people managed to protect not only themselves but their animals, and have been carefully breeding them since. I ask more about the Shredder wolf we ran into, but Burn doesn't really have many answers, except that humans and animals react to the dust in a similar way. A little is okay; too much is bad—causing either death or the madness of addiction.

When we reach the water's edge, he jumps onto a large rock and reaches down to help me climb up to join him. From there, we sit and watch as the sun starts to set.

"What do you think?" he asks, his voice low.

"It's wonderful."

"Not exactly paradise but we get by."

I don't know what paradise means, but it seems to me as if *getting by* here would be easy. Once again, I dream of the future. "What will I do here?" I ask. "Am I too old for GT? Are there training centers? When will I be assigned my work placement?"

He laughs. "You just got here. Why worry about that?"

"Just wondering." I want to flesh out my dreams of a new life. I want to fall asleep tonight imagining how it will be. Plus, I don't think I can take any unexpected disappointments. If life here will be even close to as tough as it was in Haven, I want to know now.

"You can do whatever you like," Burn says. "What do you want to do?"

I turn to him, confused. "What do you mean by 'whatever I like'?"

"You can look after chickens, help in the fields, work in one of the factories, or the mill. The hospital is always looking for smart people willing to train as doctors."

I suck in a sharp breath. "There's a hospital?"

"Yes—but here they actually save people's lives."

I'd like to look into his eyes to figure out what he's thinking, but emotions rise in my chest. Although they're all warm and happy emotions, I don't want to risk hurting anyone—ever again.

"What do you do here?" I ask, and then realize I already know the answer. "You're in the army, right? Will you be gone often?" I wish Burn didn't have such a dangerous job, and sadness seeps into my heart. I push it away.

He leans back. "I'm not sure anymore."

"Why?"

"It's hard for a wanted kidnapper to keep a low profile."

I look away and drop my head down. Someone else whose life I've ruined.

"You okay?" Burn asks and even though I'm filled with emotion, I risk turning toward him. His eyebrows have drawn closer together.

"I'm fine." I shake my head and smile.

"Good," he says and, although I'm looking right into his eyes, he's not showing any signs of physical pain.

Filled with happiness, I reach up to cup his cheek. His breath hitches. Heat grows in his eyes and his breathing accelerates like he's been running. Worry flashes inside me but I know I haven't captured his lungs; that's not what's heightened his breathing. I know I'm not hurting him, not like that. There's no telltale stinging behind my eyes, and while I'm aware of Burn—very aware—I'm not locked on to anything inside him, not with my curse.

Hope floods. Maybe I *can* control my curse. Or maybe good emotions don't bring it on. I've never been certain. Maybe it's not crazy for me to hope that one day I'll find love.

Stretching, I lift my lips toward Burn's. He tenses but I trace my lips over the rough surface of his, nibbling along them with small kisses, coaxing his into action. His large hands trace up the sides of my body, like he's afraid to hurt me, or lose control, and yet his gentle touch ignites trails of pleasure and joy.

My fingers drift over his T-shirt and he's so warm, so hard, and my body sparks inside and grows lighter like I've returned to the lake and I'm floating, drifting free as his hands slide tentatively, carefully, tenderly.

I lean closer, pulling him toward me, my hands on his broad back. I need to show him how much I want this, that I'm ready, that I want to be kissed—really kissed. I draw back to look into his eyes. He doesn't need to be afraid. I won't hurt him.

The instant our eyes meet, his hand lifts and wraps around the back of my head, then his lips capture mine in a strong kiss. He tastes salty and hot and I can't believe I thought kissing Cal felt good. This is so much better. Sensations ignite that I can barely describe, and although Cal is technically older, it's like Cal is a boy and Burn is a man.

His lips grow demanding, his touch bold, tracing over my back, my hips, my legs, pulling me against him. His back muscles flex under my touch, almost like they're expanding.

My eyes snap open. He *is* expanding. His eyes are still full of the heat I saw earlier but they've darkened. The tenderness is gone—completely gone. He lunges and presses me back against the surface of the rock.

I try to shout, but my mouth's covered by a kiss so aggressive it's as if he's trying to steal my air, trying to inhale me, consume me. Pinned between the cold stone and the heat emanating from Burn, my body implodes with fear.

I struggle and push, but he presses against me with too

much force. I grab his head in my hands and push back, hoping he'll look at me, recognize me, realize what he's doing. He lifts his head but his expression fills me with terror.

In it, I see nothing of Burn. His eyes have darkened, his skin has thickened and his expression has turned his features grotesque, like the gargoyles hanging from the lower parts of some of the oldest surviving buildings in Haven. It's like Burn's not there at all. He's been replaced, taken over by a monster. A monster that kills.

But I've caught his gaze. My curse comes to the rescue and I focus hard on his eyes, keeping him trapped. His blood races quickly through his veins, like it's running from fire, and I take hold of the closest organ—his brain—and tighten.

Roaring, he pushes back from me but doesn't let go, and anger joins his animalistic expression, twisting his once handsome features. Fires rage in his eyes, but in spite of his physical strength, the one thing he can't do is break eye contact. I've got him.

I don't want to kill him. But if I don't, he might hurt or kill me.

Dizziness takes hold and my focus fades. If I pass out while he's this monster, he'll rape me, kill me. My mind floods with anger almost like it's coming directly from Burn. I can't let anger win. I'm losing control.

Don't hurt me, I think. *Burn, it's me, Glory. You don't want to hurt me. I don't want to hurt you.*

His face contorts and twists, and I imagine a moment of lucidity in his eyes, a moment of recognition. I pray that I'm right.

Taking the risk, I release his gaze and he leaps off the rock and races into the twilight.

Drawing my knees into my chest, I rock, trying to stay conscious, trying to reconcile what just happened, trying to sort through the roller coaster of sensations inside my body. Burn's transformation isn't just about getting bigger and stronger—he turns into an actual monster. The Burn I know wasn't there.

I was crazy to think he could ever be mine.

I've always assumed my curse would keep me from finding love, but in this case *my* Deviance isn't the problem—Burn's is. He becomes far too dangerous.

CHAPTER TWENTY-NINE

THE NEXT MORNING I WAKE TIRED AND BRUISED, BUT I HEAR Dad and Drake talking on the other side of my curtain. Realizing I'm finally safe from the Comps and Shredders, realizing our family is together, soothes my physical pain. Too bad it can't wipe my memory. This time, I wish my curse *had* triggered a memory-zapping blackout.

Will Burn remember what happened? One way or the other, I'm not sure how I'll face him, but I need to move past it. I'm safe, I've got my family—I can live without Burn. I have to.

Drake and I spend the morning touring the Settlement with Dad and talking about whether I'll continue with training—they call it *school* here—and what I might like to do with my life. Overwhelmed by choices, I don't want to rush it. All I know is I want to do something safe, something where I'm helping others, and something where I can be home every evening to see Dad and Drake.

By midafternoon, a man delivers a handwritten message. Dad doesn't look happy.

"What is it?" I ask.

"Nothing you kids need to worry about." He reaches for his jacket.

"Are you going out?" Drake asks. "My legs could use a stretch."

Dad nods. "You and Glory should walk down to the lake."

"I want to go with you." Drake sounds much younger than thirteen.

Dad shakes his head. "I'm going to the pub. For a grown-up meeting."

"What's the pub?" Drake asks. "I want to go to the pub."

I put my hand on Drake's shoulder. "Dad obviously doesn't want us around."

Dad's expression softens. Then he sighs. "I guess it won't do any harm. You guys can wait while I have my meeting, then we'll all head down to the lake. How does that sound?"

"Sounds great." Drake leaps up and hugs Dad, and I can't remember when I've felt this happy. My insides are glowing.

The pub is similar to the place where we ate yesterday, but in addition to the chairs and tables, it has a long wooden counter at one side. Talk and laughter fill the air, and I can't wipe the grin from my face—why would I want to? Then I see Rolph, the army commander. My grin vanishes.

The tall man rises from behind his table and stares at me as if he wants something. For an instant I'm scared he thinks I'm special in the same way that General Phadon did, but I brush that frightening theory aside. My father ushers Drake and me to the table at the opposite side of the room and orders us glasses of something called milk. Then he joins Rolph.

Our milk arrives, carried by a smiling woman wearing a striped apron. Milk's a thick, white liquid that doesn't smell like much, but I can't gather the courage to take a sip—especially once she tells us it came out of a cow. Drake, on the other hand, drains his mug, then leans back in his chair and falls asleep.

Talking to Rolph, my father shakes his head a lot, but my view is of the back of his head and I can't hear a thing over the noise. I double-check that Drake isn't likely to fall off his chair, and then walk slowly toward Dad and Rolph, keeping my back to the stone wall and trying not to be noticed. I stop about five feet away.

"Leave her alone." My father slams his fist on the table between them. "You will not use her. I won't allow it." His voice is deep and forceful, and although I have no idea what he's protecting me from, my heart warms before guilt rises to squeeze it out. My father has already saved me enough for ten lifetimes.

"Don't you see," Rolph says. "She's the only one who can do this. Given what happened, she's uniquely positioned. Furthermore, her gift is well controlled and difficult to detect."

"It's too dangerous," Dad says.

"We need her. Because of her, Burn can't go inside anymore, and he was one of our best Extractors."

I step forward. "What do you need?" Nerves skate through my body, igniting excitement and fear, but I tamp them down. "How can I help?"

My father stands, and his chair shoots back, clattering to the floor. "No." He leans on the table, positioning his body between me and Rolph.

"Dad." I put my hand on his arm. "At least let me hear what he has to say."

My father scowls but picks up his chair and sits down. I glance across the room to make sure Drake is still okay, then take the chair at the end of the table between them. I turn to Rolph. "You have something to ask me?"

"How would you like to be a soldier in the Freedom Army?"

"A soldier?" I swallow, hard. "I'm not strong or fast."

"You have other ways to be valuable." The intensity in his eyes scares me, so I look down to study the grain in the wooden table.

If he asks me to kill for him, I won't do it. "What is the army doing?" I ask. "Moving Deviants out one by one?"

Rolph leans back. "There's more to it than that."

"What?"

"Our mission is to overthrow Management. Free the so-called employees."

"How?"

He shakes his head. "The less you know the better. No time to put you through Torture Resistance Training."

I shudder. "But you said I'd be valuable?"

"Management thinks you were kidnapped," he says. "If we

can get you back inside, you have a valid employee number and can live without hiding. You can work for us from the inside."

"A spy?" I draw in a long breath through my nose and blow it out slowly through slightly parted lips. "They must know by now that I wasn't kidnapped. The Comps saw me Outside."

"You weren't identified. Our scouts have confirmed that Management is still broadcasting your photo and Burn's. They're still looking for you both." He shakes his head and the right side of his mouth crooks up. "That boyfriend of yours is persistent and must be well connected. Another reason you're valuable."

My eyes narrow. Turning us in wasn't enough; he's making sure Management doesn't give up searching. Cal's betrayal keeps expanding. "Are they looking for Drake, too?"

"Just you."

I press my back into the chair's rungs. That doesn't make sense. If the Comps came to get Drake that night, wouldn't they be looking for him, more than me?

"Glory, don't do this," Dad says. "You've already been through so much and you're still a kid. No way am I letting you do this."

I offer my dad a slight smile. That he can care about me, after what I've done . . .

"What would I have to do?" I ask softly. My father shoots me a look but I take his hand and squeeze. "I just want to understand."

"We can discuss the details," Rolph says, "but your boyfriend's place on the Junior Ethics Committee is a boon."

I lean back. "He's not my boyfriend."

Rolph straightens. "Burn said he was."

I wince, unsure why this hurts but it does. "We *were* dating before I left but"—*but what?*—"I'm not sure we would be if I went back."

"If we do this, you should maintain your dating license. Change nothing in your life. Nothing that would arouse suspicion. Plus, it would be advantageous to our cause to have an FA soldier with connections to Management."

"I don't have connections."

"Your friend."

I look down.

"Glory," he says. "Service in the FA is voluntary. But you'd be our first chance to have someone working on the inside. And if your Jecs boyfriend trusts you, maybe we can learn who the Comps are targeting before he or she get expunged or moved into the Hospital." He puts a hand on my shoulder. "You could save so many people."

"No!" Drake shouts. I didn't notice he'd come over. He pushes Rolph's hand off me. "She's not going back to Haven. Ever."

"I agree," Dad says. "It's too dangerous."

I look back and forth between my brother and father. My mood sinks. I knew the idea of us living here as a family was too good to be true. Too good for someone who murdered her mother and paralyzed her brother.

But the thought of leaving is too much to bear.

Drake grabs my arm and tugs me forward. Grabbing my face in both hands, he forces me to look directly into his eyes.

"You can't do it," he says fiercely. "You promised. You promised you'd never leave me again."

I run from the pub. Without a clear idea of where I'm headed, I tear through the streets and emotions spark the back of my eyes. I keep my gaze down.

Fleeing the crowds I head toward the lake, and when I get there I bend over panting, waiting for my breathing to slow. The hair on the back of my neck rises and I straighten and spin.

Burn. He's about twenty feet away, his legs spread wide, arms crossed over his chest.

I stomp toward him. "Stop following me. Leave me alone."

He adjusts his stance but doesn't move, and when I reach him I push hard on one of his shoulders. But my strongest force doesn't make him waver, so I punch him in the arm that was injured. In a flash he reaches up and grabs my wrist before I can do it a second time.

I look up into his eyes but he's wearing his dark glasses.

"Coward!" I shout. "Take those off."

Still holding my my wrist, he pulls off his glasses with his other hand, then stares right into my eyes, bending down over me. "How's that?" he asks. "That close enough for you to kill me? Is that what you want?"

I look away but he ducks around to find my gaze again. "Come on, Glory. Hurt me. That's what I did to you yesterday, isn't it?"

I don't say a word.

"Isn't it?" His voice is a growl.

"Yes," I practically spit. "Is that what you want to hear? You hurt me. You scared me."

He drops my wrist and backs away a few steps. "We can never do that again."

"Do what?" I ask, but I know the answer before the two small words are out of my mouth.

"Kiss." He looks up. His neck and cheeks turn red. "I can't do that. At least not with you."

"Not with me?" My insides squeeze like I'm being crushed. "What do you mean?"

"I thought only rage brought it out. I've never changed, never turned into a monster . . . Not around someone I like." Backing away, his calves hit a rock. He loses his balance, drops onto the rock, and buries his head in his hands. "What did I do to you?"

I sit down beside him, wanting to touch him but knowing I can't. "If anyone knows what it's like to hurt someone, without knowing or remembering, it's me."

He stays still and silent for a long time, so I break the silence. "They've asked me to join the Freedom Army."

"I know. Rolph asked me whether I thought you could handle it."

I suck in a sharp breath. "What did you say?"

"I told them you could handle anything."

"I'm not sure I can handle facing Cal."

His head snaps up and I wish I could kick myself. "Because I want to kill him," I add so he doesn't get jealous. He doesn't need to know how Rolph's also asked me to maintain my dating license and pretend nothing's changed.

"Why would you want to kill Cal?"

"For what he did to Drake and me. He set the Comps after us."

Burn leans back and stares up at the sky. He shifts his weight and the sunlight accentuates the muscles in his lower arms. "I don't think that's what happened."

"Of course it is. Cal knew about Drake. He's in the Jecs. He led the Comps right to us. You saw that."

Burn pushes off the rock and crosses his arms over his chest. "They weren't looking for Drake that night. They were looking for me."

My head snaps back and I gasp. I rerun the horrible events—every word Cal said, everything I heard in the tunnel. There was no mention of my brother. Ever.

If Burn's right, then Cal didn't betray me.

The implications add heavy stones to the guilt I already carry. I need to do something to cast them off, something to make up for everything I've done.

"Is it true that you can't go back into Haven?" I ask.

He looks down. "I only have to stay away from the Comps and their cameras. That's all."

"You can't risk it. They'll catch you. You can't go back inside the dome."

He grunts.

"What will it be like, if I join the army?"

He leans back. "I don't know. It'll be different for you. The rest of us hide. Sneak in and out of Haven through the tunnels. Stay in the shadows. You'll be there as an employee."

"Will that make it easier?"

He turns and looks me in the eyes. "Easier *and* harder."

I chew on my lower lip and think through what he means. As long as they believe I was kidnapped, I'll be able to move around freely, live legitimately, claim my rations—but I won't be able to come and go like Burn did. "How often will I be able to come to the Settlement and visit my family?" *And see you.*

"You won't be able to leave Haven."

My chest tightens. Now that he says it, it seems obvious. Soon after I return, I'll get my work placement. If I don't show up for a few days, Management will instantly know something's wrong and I'll blow my cover. Emotions spark the back of my eyes and I look away as the reality stabs through me. If I do this, I'll be separated from my family. I won't see Drake grow into a man. I won't be able to make up to my father. Not that I can ever make up for what I've done.

But there it is.

Joining the army is my chance to make things right. To do the right thing. To save other people in danger.

I turn back to Burn. "Do you think I should do it?"

"You have to decide."

"But what do *you* think?"

He pauses for a moment, then turns to look out at the lake. "If they catch you, they won't take a chance on an expunging. They'll kill you."

Burn leaves me alone to think, and I sit for hours staring out at the lake, watching the sun's reflection slide across on its surface, changing the water's color until it turns a deep blue and the moonlight strikes. Goosebumps rise on my arms and I rub them, then lie back on the rock, still holding warmth from the sun. How can I leave here? How can I go back into Haven now that I've seen Outside?

And as fabulous as I am at keeping secrets, how can I not tell Jayma what I've seen—and Cal. I'll have to keep so many secrets from Cal. Lie to him. Try to get him to trust me with his secrets, while shielding so many of my own.

I turn to my side and tuck my knees to my chest. After being so sure Cal betrayed me, what Burn suggested makes sense. There was no mention of Drake that night, no mention of him when we overheard the Comps in the tunnels. It wasn't Cal who drew the Comps our way that night; it was Burn.

Burn drew the Comps to our building, and I drew them to our room. If I'd listened to Cal and let them question me in the hall, they might not have come to our room—at least not before I had a chance to hide Drake.

I have no idea how many Deviants are hiding in Haven, how many people are hiding injuries or illnesses like Drake's, how many innocent people are suffering or in danger of being expunged. Staying here would be selfish. I don't think I could live with myself, knowing I'd turned my back on so many.

As much as I've considered my Deviance a curse, I see now it might be a gift—and I'm lucky. Lucky my eyes don't glow, my skin doesn't change, that I don't have sharp teeth on my knuckles, or gills on my neck. Lucky I can hide what makes me special—one of the Chosen.

And with practice, I'll grow better at controlling my gift. Just look at how much I learned on my own, even though I barely knew what was going on. And since I was exposed to the dust, my control has improved. I'm keeping my memories now and didn't even black out the last time. Maybe Burn can learn to control his beast, too. Not that I'll be around to find out.

"Glory!" My father's voice calls out. "Where are you? Glory!" He sounds terrified.

I stand on the rock and wave.

Instantly I'm warm. My father loves me. He cares. I'm safe.

But I can't be selfish when so many others aren't. I can't stay.

CHAPTER THIRTY

"I'LL TAKE HER." BURN STEPS FORWARD AND ROLPH GLARES. IT'S clear our commander doesn't take well to being interrupted. I've only had three days of briefings, but I've figured out that soldiers at our rank shouldn't speak to Rolph unless spoken to. In some ways this army isn't that different from Haven's Management. I don't point that out.

"No," Rolph says. "Delta team will take her in."

"Sir." Burn widens his stance and his chest. "Management thinks I kidnapped her. If Delta is detected, they'll blow her cover. If they find me with her, it supports her story."

"But they'll arrest you," I say quietly. Rolph looks toward me, a scolding look in his eye, but Burn doesn't turn. I'm not even sure that he heard.

The reality of my decision once again floods me with fear. I might die even before I reach Haven. Not to mention the risks I'll be taking once I'm inside.

I order the fear to back down.

"In addition," Burn continues, "With only two of us, we'll have a better chance. I'm used to working on my own. You know how many times I've made it in and out of Haven unde-tected—Sir." He adds the "Sir" at the end like an afterthought.

Rolph narrows his eyes. "She's a valuable asset. If you fail in this task—"

"I won't, Sir."

"You'd better not."

And with that, my fate is decided. No turning back. I'm leaving.

I stash water inside my small pack, along with the food that I've packed for the trip. Giving up fresh and varied food is another downside of my choice—it's back to gruel, limp gray vegetables, and rat meat—but that concern is petty and unimportant compared to what I might accomplish.

My father draws back the curtain in front of my bed, sits down, and pulls me down beside him.

"You don't have to do this."

"I want to."

"But you do know that you don't *have* to, right?"

I nod. "Rolph gave me the choice. He made it clear that this was voluntary." While briefing me on my mission, he gave me several opportunities to change my mind.

"It's not pressure from Rolph I'm worried about."

I look at him quizzically.

"I know why you're doing this." He takes my hand in his. "And you're wrong. You don't need to."

I shake my head. "I don't know what you mean."

"Yes you do, Glory. You're doing this out of guilt. For what happened to your mother. For what happened to your brother, to me." He grips my hand tighter. "Our family is much better off Outside. And your mother would hate to know that you're putting yourself at risk to punish yourself for hurting her."

I pull my hand back. "That's not what I'm doing." But he's right—at least partly—although 'hurting' is such an understatement. "Dad, think of how many people I might be able to save. The good I can do. I think it's what Mom would want me to do."

He twists his lips but doesn't disagree. "And Cal?" Worry floods his eyes. "What if he finds out what you are? What you're doing?"

Emotions threaten to spark my gift, but I regain control and look directly into Dad's eyes. "Don't worry. I know better than to trust him with the whole truth. But he trusts me. I can use him to get information from the Jecs—and to pass myself off as a Normal. If I'm friends with a Jecs, no one will suspect." And if I follow Rolph's order not to make any suspicious changes, we'll be more than friends. We'll be dating.

"Don't go." Drake strides over from the other side of the room. "If you go, who's going to take care of me?"

I stand and pull him into a hug. "Dad will take care of you and"—I pull back and smile—"you're old enough to take care of yourself."

"That's not the point."

"I need to do this, Drake. I *want* to. Don't worry. I'll see you again soon." But I have no idea when, and that question stabs me. I smile and fake-punch him in the arm. "Plus, if I don't go back to Haven, who's going to watch out for Jayma?"

At her name, longing flashes in Drake's eyes, and I hug him again. "I might not even get as far as Haven. If we aren't one hundred percent certain they still think I'm kidnapped, I'll come straight back with Burn."

"No," Drake says. "If they've figured out you weren't kidnapped, they'll—"

"That won't happen." I cut him off and pick up my pack. The sky outside our window is pink with morning light.

Burn will be here any moment.

CHAPTER THIRTY-ONE

BURN WASN'T KIDDING WHEN HE BOASTED TO ROLPH THAT HE could get me safely to Haven. We moved swiftly, me clinging to his back when he sensed Shredders around and had to run more quickly than my shorter legs can move. We reached the mouth of the tunnels just after dark last night, in less than half the time it took us to get from here to the Settlement.

We followed different tunnels this time—not that I can tell in the dark. Twice, we've come close to encountering Comps, but Burn heard them coming, long before their heavy steps were audible to me, and we hid while they passed.

In our cramped hiding spaces, Burn was careful not to touch me but I felt the constant electric pull between us, thrilling and dangerous and sad. A reminder of what can't be. Now we've reached our destination, nerves buzz inside me and my knees shake. Even though I don't feel my curse coming on, I don't dare look Burn in the eye.

He's led me to a ladder under an alley in the factory district at the far northeast corner of Haven. If I go up now, in the middle of the night shift, it's unlikely that anyone will see me coming out from the metal cover that Burn calls a manhole. He's already moved it to the side. The plan is for me to lie on the road, pretending to be asleep or unconscious until somebody finds me. Once I'm found, I'll claim I was knocked out and dumped there.

"Ready?" he asks.

"As ready as I'll ever be."

He hands me my pack, after making sure it has no traces of dust or food from the Settlement. "And your cover story?"

"I know it by rote." On our journey, he made me recite it over and over until he was satisfied I could deliver it without hesitation and without sounding rehearsed.

"So, I guess this is good-bye." I reach toward him.

He steps back. "Yup."

My heart pinches. Other than when I was riding on his back, we haven't laid a hand on each other since that night on the rock, and I ache for his touch.

I'm hoping he'll be the Extractor I'm paired with—the one who'll smuggle the Deviants I contact out of Haven. But when I told Rolph that one of my conditions of going undercover was working with Burn, he made it clear that wasn't a demand I could make.

My first mission is to reintegrate into my life in Haven and to regain Cal's trust. After all that's happened, my being Cal's girlfriend seems strange, like the girl who wore that bracelet was another person.

I'm to await further instructions before attempting to identify or contact any Deviants. Working undercover against Management will be dangerous, but right now I'm more nervous about facing Cal than facing the Comps.

Burn's hand rises, and drawing a ragged breath I close my eyes, tip my face up to meet his caress, maybe his kiss. One small kiss won't bring out his beast, and even if it might, it feels worth the risk.

His thumb traces down my cheek and my lips twitch and tingle, but instead of kissing me, he slides his thumb over my forehead.

"That's better," he says gruffly.

I open my eyes. "What?"

"If they're going to believe you've been held hostage in a factory's storage bin, you need to look dirty. If there's some soot on the road up there, grind some into your clothes before you fall asleep."

"Good idea." I nod. "Thanks for getting me here safely."

His jaw twitches and I want to reach up to quiet the tense muscles, trace my lips over the stubble growing on his upper lip—but I don't. Time to let go of foolish fantasies. Not only are we both soldiers, there's no sense in pretending we could ever fall in love.

Not only will we be separated physically—him unable to enter the city I live in, me unable to leave it—we both know the real dangers of us being together. If Burn or I lose control of our emotions, one or both of us will die.

"Thanks for bringing me here. For everything."

He looks down.

Unable to resist, I squeeze his lower arm before turning to climb.

I'm not two rungs up when he takes my hand off the ladder, spins me, and pulls me into an embrace. My body's dwarfed inside his arms, my feet well off the ground, and I bury my face in his neck to memorize his scent.

"Keep safe," he says. "Don't take chances."

"I won't."

"Promise."

"I promise."

He helps me back onto the ladder and I climb.

"And Glory," he calls after me. "Keep your guard up with Cal."

Nerves scramble inside me as he reminds me that from this moment forward I'm going to have to pretend to love Cal again, pretend he's the one that I want. Trying to think of something reassuring to say, I turn down to look at Burn one last time—but he's gone.

I continue my ascent into the place I used to equate with safety. Not that my life ever felt safe, but I did once believe that my life inside Haven was the only way to stay safe, the only way to survive. Haven Equals Safety.

Ha.

Haven equals nothing but danger.

CHAPTER THIRTY-TWO

THE SUN TURNED ON AT LEAST FIFTEEN MINUTES AGO, AND I watch through squinted eyes as the dark alley brightens and shadows grow on the wall across from me. For Burn's plan to work, it's better if I appear unconscious, or at least asleep, when I'm found. The surface beneath me is hard and my body's aching to move. But I can't.

Burn was certain that a Comp patrol would pass before the sun came on, and now I'm afraid that one of the factory workers will find me instead. Nerves stir in my stomach. Being found by the Comps terrifies me, but they're more likely to believe my story if they find me themselves.

Heavy footsteps sound at the far end of the alley. I force my eyes all the way shut and will my body to relax. My heart's racing but I hope no one can tell by looking.

"Hey." A voice booms. "What are you doing there?"

I don't move.

"Shift one doesn't start for an hour. Access to this alley is restricted except during shift change."

My muscles threaten to twitch, but I stay still as heavy boots stomp toward me. More than one Comp from the sound of it.

"Get up." One of them nudges me with his boot and I roll to the side.

A hand slaps my face and I open my eyes, squinting against the light of a torch the Comp's shining into my eyes.

"Where am I?" I mumble, grateful my voice sounds hoarse. No wonder. I can't remember the last time I drank.

"What are you doing here?" the Comp asks. "What's your employee number?"

"It's her," another Comp says and moves into view above me. "It's the girl who was kidnapped."

I rise up onto one elbow, the pavement scraping my skin. I look around, confused.

The first Comp grabs me under the arms and lifts me to my feet. His armored gloves pinch my skin. "How did you get here?"

I shake my head and look around in wonder. Then I smile, reach for the Comp and hug him. "I'm free. He let me go. Thank Haven." I let myself collapse in his arms. "Haven Equals Safety."

The other Comp grabs me and pushes me back against the wall. "Who held you? Where? What did he say? Why were you gone for so long?"

Eyes wide, it's not hard to appear frightened, and I shake my head without saying a word.

The two Comps leave me for a moment and talk quietly to each other. I struggle to hear.

"We need to take her to Headquarters," one says.

"No one can see her," says the other. "Gag her. Cover her face."

I press against the wall of my small cell in the Compliance Detention Center. Coming back was a mistake. I've been interrogated for hours and they still don't believe me.

When I was brought into the building, they took all my things, including my clothes. They gave those back after spraying me with a forceful dust decontamination hose, not listening when I insisted I'd never been Outside. Then they led me into a small room, with very bright lights and cameras in all eight corners, pointing straight at the chair they sat me on. For hours, voices from outside the room bombarded me with the same questions over and over, until my voice was raw and my eyes stung from the brightness and my inability to hold back my fear.

Who took me? Where was I held? Am I a Deviant? Do I know any Deviants? How long have I known I was Deviant? Did my captors hurt me? Why did they take me? Why was I gone for so long? Why did they let me go?

And I repeat the same answers. A Deviant terrorist kidnapped me. He held me in a small box. I was blindfolded the whole time. I don't know where I was. I am not a Deviant. I have never been a Deviant. I assume the man who took me was a Deviant. I did not witness his specific Deviance but he was strong. He tried to convert me. He wanted me to turn against Haven, to become a terrorist, but I refused. He finally gave up and dumped me in the alley where I was found.

Over and over the same lies.

By the twentieth time I actually believe them. By the thirtieth, the lies seem more real than Burn or my father, more credible than the Settlement or seeing my brother walk.

A shadow passes in front of a small slot in the wooden door of my cell. The lock turns.

I tense.

"Hello, Glory."

It's Mr. Belando. The Junior VP of Compliance I met with Cal.

I don't answer.

"I hope you haven't been hurt."

I don't move. If they've sent him, I'm in more trouble than I thought. They don't believe me. I'll be terminated—expunged if I'm lucky.

He sets down a chair, then closes the door behind him and sits directly opposite me.

"You've suffered a horrible ordeal," he says. "You must have been terrified."

I stay silent.

"Cal wants to see you."

I snap my head up.

He smiles. "He's been promoted, you know."

My teeth worry my lip.

"In recognition for the role he played in tracking your kidnapper into the tunnels, he was given the opportunity to participate in the Entrance Trials. He succeeded. First in his group. He starts Compliance Officer Training next week."

My stomach flips but I hide my reaction. Cal will be a Comp. It's what he hoped for when he joined the Jecs, yet I can't feel happy. He'll be an enforcer for an organization I've vowed to overturn. Assuming I live long enough, once Cal's a Comp I'll be dating the enemy.

Mr. Belando crosses his legs and leans back. "Do you trust me?"

I nod.

"Good," he says. "Because I have a proposition. A deal that will only hold if we fully trust each other."

I rub my finger where my mother's ring used to be and my heart rate slows.

"You will enter Compliance Officer Training, too."

He's not serious. It's a trick. He knows the truth about my alleged kidnapping and is trying to gain a confession.

"You'll be a valuable asset for the Compliance Department and, more importantly, a valuable asset for me."

It must be a trick but I'm not sure what kind. "How could I be valuable?"

He smiles, broadly. "So you *can* still speak."

I narrow my eyes.

"When you were held hostage, you gained insight into the terrorists' organization, their methods, their motives." He uncrosses his legs and leans toward me. "Yes?"

It doesn't take much to fake a shiver. "They're crazy and dangerous."

"Of course they are." He tugs his chair forward and its legs scrape the floor. "That's what you can contribute to the Comps: Deviant Intelligence. No one else has had the exposure to them that you have. You'll work undercover. Seek out traitors. And if you can draw the terrorists' attention again, you will convince them you've changed your mind, that you support their cause. You will infiltrate their organization, learn their secrets, work against them from the inside."

"Why me?"

"I've checked your performance evaluations, your family history. And I've seen enough here today to be sure you're no Deviant." My stomach clenches as he pauses.

He shifts in his chair and glares at me. "Your Deviant father killed your mother and brother. You have more reason than most to hate them."

"I do hate them."

"Of course you do."

I draw a deep breath. The danger in my life just expanded. I'm already working undercover for the Freedom Army.

Besides, I don't trust what Mr. Belando's said. My being a Comp doesn't make sense. I'd never get in.

"But I'm not strong enough. I'll never get past the Entrance Trials." Every trial at least one candidate dies, and more die during training.

His back stiffens. "I'm the Junior VP of the Compliance Department. If I want you accepted to the training program, you'll be accepted, no matter what that arrogant—" His waxy lips tighten and press together, then he slides a palm over his already perfectly coifed hair. "You let me worry about that."

"But the Entrance Trials, the selection process . . ." If I keep prodding, he might reveal more.

His jaw twitches. "The Compliance Officers are merely the muscle for my department. I'm in charge, not that power-hungry Recruiting Captain." A vein protrudes, tracing a diagonal line on his forehead. "If I want you in the training program, you're in. If I want you to graduate, you'll graduate."

"Yes, Sir." I'm not sure what else to say.

"So, are you with me?" His voice brightens. "Do you want to help take the Deviant terrorists down?"

I raise my chin and straighten my shoulders. "I'd do anything to make them pay for what they did to me." Already, lying has become easy.

He stands. "Good, very good."

Bile rises in my throat but I smile like this is the most thrilling news ever. I have no idea what he really knows, or wants from me. "May I ask a question?"

"Yes?"

"You said I'd be a valuable asset for you specifically, not just the Comps. What did you mean?"

Looking pleased at my question, he touches my shoulder, his hand heavy and warm. "All in good time."

"But I don't know what I'm agreeing to."

Mr. Belando stares down at me, his eyes flickering. "I need someone in the enforcement branch to be my eyes and ears. Someone I chose for the Comp training program. Someone who doesn't owe anything to the selection committee."

He walks around me in a tight circle. "I've been looking

for someone, someone with a certain spark, and after watching your interrogation, I've found her. You're tougher than you look. And I know I can trust you."

"Why?" As soon as I ask, I wish I hadn't.

His eyes narrow. "It's very simple. If you make one false move, I'll produce evidence that you were turned by your kidnappers and that you're working for the terrorists." He smiles. "And as extra insurance, know that I'll have your boyfriend killed, too."

My stomach twists and flips. I'm still not positive that Cal didn't betray me, but I don't like to hear him threatened. I need him to pick someone else. I can't do this.

"If this is a deal, what's in it for me?"

His smile darkens. "I knew you were bright. You'll be perfect."

"You didn't answer my question."

"Agree, and you get to live." His smile sends shivers down my spine.

"I don't understand."

"Now that you've heard the assignment, you have two choices. Accept, or I'll have you killed."

My chest caves in and I don't try to hide my fear. I keep my eyes cast down. "I look forward to working for you, Sir."

"Please," he says. "No need for formality. Call me Mr. Belando."

CHAPTER THIRTY-THREE

A FEW HOURS LATER, TWO COMPS ESCORT ME TO THE BACK exit of the building, holding my arms firmly, as if I pose imminent mortal danger. *Little do they know.*

One of them opens the door, they shove me into a narrow alley and I stumble to my knees. The instant the door clicks behind me, Cal appears and pulls me off the ground and into his arms.

"Are you hurt? I was terrified I'd never see you again." He hugs me tightly and I have to admit that the warmth and strength of his arms provide comfort.

But coming to my senses, I tense. "How did you know I'd be here?" This is all an elaborate trick. I can't let my guard down.

"Mr. Belando told me when and where you'd be released." He hugs me again but I push back from his chest.

"Don't."

"You *are* hurt." He loosens his grip and I back away.

"I'm fine." I rub my hands up and down my arms then cross them over my chest, mostly to keep Cal from hugging me again. My body and mind aren't in sync. My body still thinks Cal betrayed me, but my mind has to pretend that everything's the same between us.

"Did Mr. Belando talk to you?" Cal's eyes broadcast worry. "He told me he would get you released—"

"He did." I fight to stay calm, to keep my emotions in check, to remember my mission. I can do this. I can pretend I'm Cal's girlfriend. I can pretend the Deviants are my enemy. I can pretend to be a Normal. At that part, I'm already expert.

"What did he say?" Cal looks at me expectantly, so much hope in his eyes.

"I got my work placement. Compliance Officer Training." The words are strange on my tongue, like the food and drink I first tasted at the Settlement. But unlike those things, the words taste foul.

"I'm in COT, too!" Cal reaches for me again, so I drop my arms and let him hug me.

"Now we won't have any secrets between us," he says. "And once we're both Comps, we can hunt down Deviants together."

"Yes." I smile. *No secrets.*

"Let's get you home." Cal slides his hands down my arms to my tense fingers. "We can talk more there."

Walking home in near silence, everything left unsaid bubbles inside me, threatening to burst out. Burn seemed sure the Comps were after *him* that night—not Drake—but I need to be certain. If I'm going to trust Cal at all, I need to know the truth. He hasn't asked about Drake and that slices into my heart, amplifying my distrust. Perhaps I'm not the only one undercover and acting right now.

On a window ledge, fifteen stories above the ground, I stop. When my hand slips from his, Cal flattens his back against the building's wall and sidesteps back, until our shoulders touch.

"Why did you stop here?" he asks. "It's dangerous."

I clear my throat. "Why didn't you warn me they were coming? You promised you would, but you didn't."

He looks at me with confusion in his eyes, and it's like stifling explosions to keep my emotions in check.

"You haven't even asked me what happened to him," I say softly.

He tips his head to the side. "To the terrorist who kidnapped you?"

"No. My brother."

Cal looks down. "When the Comps didn't find him with you in that alley, I assumed the terrorist killed him, or that he'd been admitted to the Hospital." He whispers the last word. "I didn't want to bring it up and make you feel sad. I knew you'd never leave Drake behind if you had a choice."

"Of course I wouldn't." My throat tightens, but one flick of my thumb along my bare finger and I'm ready to look up and into Cal's eyes. "Why didn't you warn me the Comps were coming for Drake? You said you wouldn't turn him in. He meant everything to me." I'm talking about Drake in the past tense, like he's dead. But this is my life now, and I have to get used to it—lies and more lies.

Realization bursts onto Cal's face, then he shakes his head and turns toward me, as much as he can on the narrow ledge. "They weren't coming for *him*, Glory. The Comps were searching for that terrorist. He'd been spotted around the building. If I'd known someone so dangerous was near our floor, I would have warned you to be careful."

His fingers find mine and intertwine. I don't pull away. "I'm sorry," he says. "I should have protected you." My heart rate increases. Confusion spreads and expands until my brain seems too big for my skull.

I look into Cal's eyes and his expression is filled with anguish and caring. Even after all that's happened, looking into Cal's eyes makes me feel safe. It's hard to toss aside feelings I've had since I was a kid. He might be wrong about Deviants, but I still feel that deep down he's a good person, and I hate that I have to deceive him.

He was my first real crush. Until I met Burn, I felt sure I loved Cal. But after I thought he betrayed me, and given how I feel around Burn . . . I'm no longer certain I know what love means, never mind how it feels. All that aside, being so far away from my dad and Drake, having to pretend they're both dead, Cal is the closest thing I have to family.

"Can you forgive me?" he asks. "I love you so much and I'll never let anything bad happen to you ever again."

He raises my fingers and, as his warm lips press against my knuckles, I look into his eyes. My confusion evaporates.

Cal didn't betray me.

He wasn't the reason Drake was nearly found.

I can trust him—as long as he doesn't learn that I'm a Deviant.

My pretending to be his girlfriend won't be as difficult as I'd imagined. At least not in the *way* I imagined. I'm still not sure I can kiss him.

"Let's go." I nod along the ledge. And still holding my hand, he continues sidestepping toward the next bridge. A shadow passes overhead, bringing Burn to mind and reinforcing my strength.

The road ahead clarifies. My questions and doubts disappear.

I can do this. I can be a secret agent for the Freedom Army and help Deviants escape Haven. I can be Mr. Belando's eyes and ears in the Comps. I can handle being Cal's girlfriend, at least until he starts to want more.

There's no need to choose between Cal and Burn—I can never have either. A girl whose emotions kill isn't meant to have love.

But in spite of that, I smile. I'm the luckiest girl alive. Somewhere out there I have a brother and father who love me. I can't be near them, but Jayma, Scout, and Cal will be my family inside Haven.

And even though I can never really be with either, I have two boys—Burn and Cal—who care about me, who want to protect me, who will do all they can to keep me safe, and I care enough about both to do all I can to protect them, too.

I'm not alone.

I may not trust much, but I trust that.